BITE ME,
Your
GRACE

BROOKLYN ANN

sourcebooks
casablanca

Published by Sourcebooks Casablanca, an imprint of Sourcebooks, Inc.
P.O. Box 4410, Naperville, Illinois 60567-4410
(630) 961-3900
FAX: (630) 961-2168
www.sourcebooks.com

Printed and bound in Canada
WC 10 9 8 7 6 5 4 3 2 1

Dedicated to my mother, Karen Ann
6-11-62 ~ 2-14-09
You were the first person to believe in me.
Every day I strive to make you proud.
And to Damian.
Thank you for never giving up on me.

One

"RUINED." ANGELICA WINTHROP TASTED THE WORD on her tongue and found it to be delicious. "*Ruined*," she whispered once more and allowed a smile to creep to her lips despite her choking bitterness. "Placed on the shelf; rendered unmarriageable for the rest of one's days."

Her smile faded and the stony lump in her throat returned as she looked at the remains of her favorite book in the fireplace. All that was left were a corner of the cover and a few charred pages that would crumble at a touch. This time her mother had gone too far. She'd come into Angelica's room, snatched the book from her grasp, taken one look at the title, and emitted a strangled gasp of outrage.

"I cannot have you reading such trash," Margaret Winthrop had said when she threw *A Vindication of the Rights of Woman* by Mary Wollstonecraft into the fireplace.

"How can you call it trash?" Angelica had demanded,

fighting back tears. "It's a logical treatise on the subject of our sex being capable of rational thought. As a woman, how can you not be aware of that?"

Margaret snorted indelicately. "The author bore an illegitimate child then married an *anarchist!* I'll not have that book in my house." Her face was nearly as red as her curls. "It is bad enough that you are a veritable bluestocking. But if anyone knew you were a radical, your reputation would be blackened beyond redemption, with all hope of an advantageous marriage turned to refuse."

The sight of the book being burned thrust like a rapier through Angelica's heart. Her mother might as well have ripped away her spirit and cast it into the flames.

"Maybe I want my reputation to be ruined, Mother," Angelica had said, unable to hold back her ire… or her elation with the concept, once uttered. "Maybe I don't want to be a broodmare for some inane boor while he spends my dowry on his mistresses and… Ouch!" She gasped when her mother pinched her.

Lady Margaret hissed, "If we were not going to the Wentworth ball tonight I would slap you. A lady does not speak of such things." Her eyes narrowed. "Now stop these hysterics immediately! I suggest you compose yourself while I fetch Liza to bring your gown and fix your hair."

After her mother left, Angelica rubbed her burning eyes, meagerly proud that she had managed not to give her mother the satisfaction of tears. Needing reassurance on the state of the rest of her collection, she peeked under her bed. At least her copy of Mary

Shelley's *Frankenstein: Or, The Modern Prometheus* was safe. Mary Shelley, daughter of Mary Wollstonecraft, was Angelica's personal hero. If Margaret had burned *Frankenstein*, Angelica would have screamed.

She frowned at the growing pile of books languishing in the dark recesses. A better hiding place for them was in order, but she didn't dare move them now. *This is completely unfair!* Angelica quivered in outrage and despair. Literature was a precious gift. One shouldn't have to hide it from others. The written word should be revered and shared by all, no matter their sex or station in life. Her gaze strayed back to the fireplace, rage curling in her belly at the destruction of a precious book.

"I will do it," Angelica vowed to the ashes. "I will ruin my reputation and gain my freedom." Her voice quavered and she felt like she could taste the smoldering paper.

She turned from the scene of the crime and approached her writing desk, stopping for a moment to caress the polished mahogany surface, resisting the urge to open the secret compartment and look upon her other hidden and oppressed rebellion... the pages of her ghost stories.

Ever since she could pick up a quill, Angelica had loved to write. The falsehoods of fiction were much preferable to those of society. Her father encouraged her talent, but her mother, naturally, despised her writing *and* her father's support of a habit that she deigned "for the lower classes."

"You inherited such common traits from *him*!" she complained constantly. "I swear I shall always regret marrying a mere mister instead of a title. Perhaps then I would not have had such an unnatural daughter."

A confusing combination of anger and pity for her mother always struck Angelica at those words. When Margaret married a common banker, the Earl of Pendlebur had been infuriated. He had cut off his daughter's money and promised to withhold the funds until Angelica made a proper marriage.

Now Margaret was determined to arrange the match of the season between her daughter and some indolent lord. Whether she intended the marriage to mend fences with Grandfather or if it was only for the money, Angelica didn't know. Either way, the pressure for a titled husband, a wealthy one if possible, was upon her tenfold more than the average debutante. The concept was sickening. One's merit should be separate from one's parentage.

She lifted her chin melodramatically and quoted, "'What's in a name? That which we call a rose by any other name would smell as sweet.'" Shakespeare had a valid point. Of course, that was as far as she could identify with his heroine. After all, Juliet actually *wanted* to get married.

The concept of marriage and being a proper society matron was anathema to Angelica. She longed for adventures such as Mary Shelley had embarked on when she was Angelica's age. Her imagination spun as she read of the author's journeys across the continent, taking her from Paris to Italy, even to Switzerland. It was in the evocative setting of Lake Geneva, during an exhilarating thunderstorm, that Mary had penned her gothic masterpiece, *Frankenstein*.

Amidst the company of such masterful writers as Lord Byron, John Polidori, and Percy Shelley, Mary had been completely free to be herself and write what she wished. Angelica longed for such freedom. She knew her work would thrive if she were away from the stifling sphere of the *haut ton*, the hypocritical pinnacle of England's nobility and their stringent idea of marriage.

She heaved a sigh and sagged against the wall. Even Mary Shelley had given in to convention when she married Percy. And apparently marriage had suffocated even her bold spirit. After *Frankenstein*, Mary had quit writing. Wedlock and motherhood seemed to make every woman as miserable as Angelica's mother.

A noise outside interrupted her reverie. Angelica rushed to the window and caught sight of a carriage stopping in front of the mansion across the street behind her house. Her heart leaped in excitement. *The duke was back in London!* Now, here was good fodder for her stories. Along with his predecessors, the Duke of Burnrath had always been the biggest mystery in high society. He rarely deigned to mix with the beau monde, only attending White's or the occasional ball before departing once again to places unknown.

Though His Grace was ever an object of speculation, he preyed on Angelica's thoughts only half as often as his home, the true center of her fascination. The imposing Elizabethan manor had belonged to the dukes of Burnrath for more than a hundred years. She believed Burnrath House was haunted. Angelica was unable to count the times she had seen movement or heard noises coming from the place when it was supposed to be vacant. Delicious fantasies whispered through her mind as to what sorts of ghoulish specters lurked, or perhaps floated, in its dark recesses. Many of her stories were inspired by Burnrath House, but imagination could only carry her so far.

She gazed at the ancient mansion, shivering in her thin shift. The upper floors thrust up from the heavy evening fog, the ornately columned chimneys resembling dark sentinels. Angelica *knew* if she managed to get inside, she could create a masterpiece of gothic horror to match Mrs. Shelley's. Dedicated research was the source of all great stories, after all. Mentally, she added entry into Burnrath House to her goals.

Angelica caught a glimpse of a dark figure leaving the house and entering the carriage before footsteps on the stairs announced the approach of her mother and her lady's maid. It was a pity she couldn't call on His Grace. Even if it was permissible for an unmarried lady to do so, the duke didn't move in the same circles as her family. Yet another disappointment brought on by stuffy matters of propriety and rank. Her bedroom door opened and she darted from the window to sit primly on the bed.

"I cannot wait to see you in this exquisite creation!" Margaret sang as she carried a ball gown into the room. Liza, Angelica's lady's maid, followed behind with stays and petticoats. "The suitors will be lining up to dance with you." All signs of anger from the argument had vanished as Margaret resumed her role of happy matchmaker.

Angelica sighed. If Mary Wollstonecraft had been her mother, she would be writing now instead of suffering this ordeal. The stays cut off her breath as Liza jerked the laces with a murmured apology. Angelica held up her arms for the endless layers of petticoats and, finally, the gown. One had to admit that the ensemble was exquisite. The pale blue satin shimmered, appearing to be anywhere between sapphire and the palest cornflower, depending on how the light hit the fabric. The dress was unadorned except for a trimming of darker blue lace at the oval bodice and along the hem.

"Since most debutantes will be wearing paler colors, I believe this will help you stand out, especially with the right coiffure." Margaret's tone forbade argument.

When Liza had finished her hair, Angelica surveyed her reflection in the mirror. Her dark brown tresses were piled atop her head and threaded with pearls, while a few curls tumbled artfully down her back. Ebony eyes fringed with sooty lashes peered shyly from her heart-shaped face. Her full lips formed a slight smile. Why, she looked at least twenty years old!

Margaret nodded in approval. "You shall make a fetching picture indeed, my dear. I expect you to draw a line of titled young bucks within moments of our arrival." Angelica grimaced as her mother pinched her cheeks to bring some color. "There, now I must see if your father rang for the carriage."

The moment her mother left the room, Angelica frowned at the maid. "Why does she have to be so mercenary? I feel like a horse or a painting up for auction."

Liza sighed. "Lady Margaret just cares for your future. She merely wants the best for you."

Angelica snorted. "What future? She wants to sentence me to life in a cage more gilt than this one." She leaped from the stool and paced the room like an angry feline. "That's all marriage is for a woman. Hell, it's all that *life* is for a woman. A prison! Well, I shall stand for this horrid slave-trade no longer! I shall—"

"You shall what?" Liza inquired, immune to the unladylike outburst.

"Never mind." Angelica was tempted to inform her maid of her intention to ruin herself, but then considered the wisdom of doing so. Liza was like a friend to her, but she was still a servant, dependent on her parents' good opinion to retain her position and the roof over her head. If Angelica succeeded in ruining her reputation and Liza knew about the scheme, her poor maid would likely be thrown out into the street without a reference. Liza was an agreeable accomplice to many of Angelica's adventures, but it would be best if Angelica acted alone on this mission.

To evade her maid's suspicion, she charged over to her bed and pulled a black silk garter from beneath her mattress.

Liza sighed again as she watched Angelica hike up her skirts to slip on the scrap of fabric. "Yer still wearin' that bleedin' thing? You never even met that poet."

"Of course I am still wearing it. John Keats has only been dead a week. A creator of great works should be mourned. Since Mother will not let me mourn him in public, I shall wear this garter until a decent period has passed, perhaps even the requisite six months."

Liza nodded. "At least you found the sense to mourn

the penniless sod in secret now." She obviously considered her station to be above that of the poet. "I'll never forget the look on your mother's face when you tried to wear black plumes in your headdress for your presentation to the King last Tuesday. She nearly ran mad!"

Angelica raised a brow. "What else could I have done? She burned my black dress."

"The hem was too high, and even if I'd let the bodice out to its limits, the dress wouldn't have fit," Liza countered smoothly before she helped Angelica with her cape and shooed her out the door.

Papa greeted Angelica at the bottom of the stairs. "Could this enchanting creature truly be my little daughter?"

She grinned at her father and dropped into a low curtsy. It was not hard to believe that her mother had once lost her heart to him. Though Jacob Winthrop was forty years old, his ebony hair had not the slightest touch of gray and his gypsy eyes, which he had passed onto Angelica, were framed by only the faintest of wrinkles. Despite the fact that he was untitled, many ladies of the Quality blushed and simpered over him. How was it possible that Mother no longer loved him?

A touch of apprehension caught her at the sight of her father's beloved visage. Would her ruination hurt him? She knew her mother would be devastated, and was surprised at the guilt that arose at the thought, despite her anger at Margaret's betrayal. Surely Papa would understand. He'd never been one to care much for the opinions of others.

She lifted her chin and quoted, "'*To hold a pen is to be at war.*'"

Jacob beamed. "Voltaire, correct?"

Angelica nodded. Even if Mary Shelley had forgotten that writing was war, she wouldn't. And war meant making sacrifices. She must remember that.

As Papa escorted her outside, she peered at Burnrath House, visible through the naked branches of the hawthorn trees. The forbidding structure seemed to beckon her from the darkness. An intoxicating tremor ran all the way down to her toes. She pulled the fabric of her cape tighter around her bared shoulders.

"Well, we had best be off before your mother has an attack of the vapors," Papa said with a slight smile that didn't quite reach his eyes.

Angelica sighed and cast the house one last longing look before allowing a footman to assist her into the coach. She *had* to find a way in there.

Her mother lectured her for the entire ride to the Wentworth ball. No dancing more than twice with the same man, else she'd be ruined. If she forgot herself and drank too much champagne, she'd be ruined. Ruined... *ruined*. The word grew more tantalizing every time she heard it.

Ruined meant that no man would want to marry her.

Ruined meant that she could abandon this shallow facade of belonging with polite society.

Ruined meant her dowry would be her own. *Ruined* meant she could write as much as she pleased.

Angelica smiled in the dark carriage. She would embark on her quest tonight. Surely the mission couldn't be that difficult.

Two

IAN ASHTON, DUKE OF BURNRATH AND LORD Vampire of London, threw down the latest issue of *The Times* with a curse. *The Vampire, or Bride of the Isles* was to have a second run in the theaters due to the popular demand. The craze spawned by Dr. John Polidori's tale, "The Vampyre," was reaching new heights. That foolish physician-turned-writer had jeopardized Ian's life with his scribbling and he wanted to know why. Did the man know of Ian's kind? Or was he merely playing with the old legends? Either way, the story had done a measure of damage.

As Polidori's tale read, "His peculiarities caused him to be invited to every house; all wished to see him, and those who had been accustomed to violent excitement, and now felt the weight of ennui, were pleased at having something in their presence capable of engaging their attention." The nobility had latched on to this vampire fanaticism with the same zeal in which they embraced every new trend. Speculations about Ian's odd hours and habits had already begun to circulate, though the duke had only been back in Town for two nights.

He'd recently returned from a wasted trip to Italy in pursuit of Lord Byron, to whom the tale had originally been attributed. Once he discovered Polidori was the author, Ian had rushed back to London, but he had yet to find the man. For now, Ian was biding his time and doing what he could to undo the damage.

He wasn't concerned that the vapid aristocrats would discover what he was, for they were too jaded to *truly* believe. But when the lampoons and gossip articles in the papers made their rounds through the general London populace, somebody would take the jest seriously. He hadn't been stalked by a vampire hunter since his third "incarnation" as the Duke of Burnrath and did not care to repeat the experience. That was why he was at this silly ball tonight. He had to protect his reputation.

"The guests are arriving, Your Grace," the Duke of Wentworth announced. "Surely you do not intend to spend the evening in my library reading the papers? There will be some stiff gaming after the dancing, I assure you."

"I am finished in here," Ian replied, rising from his chair.

Wentworth picked up the newspaper and spied the story's heading. "Egad, they will really give you a rough time now. It's ridiculous how such a silly story can stimulate the imaginations of the gullible."

Ian smiled, concealing his fangs. "How very fortunate that your ballroom is full of mirrors."

Wentworth laughed. "I hope you do not mind, but

I had Cook prepare her baked garlic and bread for our appetizers. The guests will leave with horrid breath, but I am sure the ball will be a smash and hopefully deter these ridiculous rumors. By the by, why *do* you refuse to come out during the day? If you would only ride through Hyde Park, or participate in a race or two, the talk would cease immediately."

Ian frowned and brushed a lock of inky hair away from his face. "My physician advises against doing so. I have a skin condition, you see, and if any ladies saw me burned and blistered, they would take to their beds with their hartshorn for a week."

"That bad, eh?" his friend inquired with raised brows.

Ian feigned a tragic sigh. "It is a family malady."

The Duchess of Wentworth burst into the library. "There you are. Come out this instant! It is a veritable crush out there and I need help greeting the guests." She lowered her voice. "You would not believe the obscene toupee Sir Hubert Huxtable is wearing. At first I presumed something had died on his head! And the Winthrop heiress is wearing a gown far too mature for an unwed girl."

Ian stifled a laugh at the note of censure in her voice. "We shall keep you waiting no longer, Jane."

As he followed the Wentworths down the staircase and into the crowd, he spied the aforementioned heiress. Her lush, dark beauty made the reigning insipid blondes look blandly faded. His loins tightened at the sight of her ripe figure and shining locks. Perhaps the gown *was* too mature for the debutante. Or perhaps too much time had passed since his last visit to a house of pleasure. Either way, he would do best to avoid her for her sake.

Ian took a deep breath as he plunged into the crowd, bowing and renewing introductions. It was fortunate that he had fed tonight; else the scent of so much fresh blood would drive him mad. Unbidden, his gaze rested once again on the Winthrop girl, then narrowed. There was something amiss with the look in her eyes.

Though he was unable to read minds, Ian's gift lay in detecting the subtle nuances in a human's move-ment, gestures, expressions, and voice. If he desired, he could win any hand of cards he played. Every instinct in his body told him the debutante was plan-ning something. It wasn't merely the lack of avarice in her eye that most girls of her age and status possessed; her mother had enough of that for the pair. But the impish twinkle to the beauty's subtle smile told him that she was up to mischief.

The girl downed a glass of champagne with unlady-like haste. Whatever she was going to do must take courage. He would have to keep a discreet eye on this intriguing creature. Lord Wentworth was quite a good fellow for a mortal, and it would be a shame for his party to be spoiled by some foolish chit.

❧

Angelica stifled a yawn with a sip of her third glass of champagne. She had danced her slippers off with eligible and ineligible gentlemen alike. On the ball-room floor, she'd executed the first part of her plan to scandalize the *ton*. Instead of exchanging mild pleasantries about the weather and her family's health, she'd attempted to shock her dancing partners by speaking her mind.

To a foppish baronet, she'd mocked male fashions, comparing the brilliant colors of satin knee breeches and bright waistcoats to the plumes of strutting peacocks. With a wealthy earl, she'd pried into his business ventures, discussing shipping investments and banking practices as if she were about to plunge into a wealth-making endeavor. With a dull viscount, she went as far as to go into gory details about the exhumation of corpses in *Frankenstein*. The abrupt manner in which the man's face had turned green was most satisfactory. She even danced twice with each of them.

Proud of her daring, she anxiously waited for the dance offers to cease and the gossiping to commence. To her vexation, gentlemen became more ardent in seeking out her company. She finally had to plead exhaustion and quit the floor, praying that no gentlemen would seek out her father to offer for her hand.

Angelica's lip curled in disgust as she fanned beads of sweat from her forehead. *Why will these bloody fops not leave me alone? Last week Lady Dranston's daughter was a complete wallflower because of her incessant prattle about horticulture. What could I be doing wrong?*

A viscount bowed before her. "You look over-heated, Miss Winthrop. If you would permit me to escort you, I know of the most pleasant alcove in which you could cool off." He licked his fat lips and ogled her bosom.

Her stomach roiled in revulsion, but she forced herself to meet his gaze. No doubt he would try to steal a kiss from her, and if she were caught, she would definitely be ruined. On the other hand, often a man would marry a girl he compromised. Especially a girl with a dowry of her size. The thought of being leg-shackled to this lecher for the rest of her life, much less allowing those fleshy lips anywhere near her person, made her skin crawl.

"No thank you, my lord. I am quite comfortable as I am," she said coolly.

He bowed once more and strutted off in search of other prey. Angelica felt sorry for the next poor girl.

"I absolutely adore your gown." A voice intruded on her thoughts.

She turned to see a lady in a shockingly low-cut gown of emerald silk smiling down at her. Angelica had seen the blonde before at other engagements but could not remember her name.

"Thank you." Before she could return the compliment, a girl her age in a classic gown of virginal white approached. She also looked familiar with her golden curls and cherubic lips.

The girl curtsied to Angelica before she turned to the older woman. "Oh, Victoria, Lord Branson danced twice with me tonight! He is so very hand-some and dashing."

The lady in the green gown rewarded the girl with a bitter smile. "Then you must ignore him for the rest of the evening."

The girl's face fell in disappointment. "But…"

"But nothing, Claire. He is in debt up to his ears and only has an income of four thousand per annum besides." Victoria fluttered her hand. "Oh, forgive us. I did not introduce myself. I am Lady Victoria Wheaton, and this is my sister, Miss Claire Belmont."

Angelica curtsied. "How do you do? I am Miss Angelica Winthrop."

Claire gasped in dismay. "Not the Earl of Pendlebur's granddaughter?"

Victoria smacked her sister on the arm with her fan as Angelica replied, "I am. Is there something amiss with the fact?"

Claire was shocked at her candor. "I do apologize. It is just that I thought your come-out would be next year. I, um… was not expecting such competition for the season."

Victoria chuckled. "She was betting on landing the most titled gentleman this year. My friends and I made a wager on it as well. Your presence will tilt the odds."

Angelica was stunned that these young women sounded just as obsessed with money and titles as her mother was. She didn't bother to point out that she did not want to "land" anybody. "What about love?" she blurted.

The ladies giggled and Claire replied, "I would *love* to be a duchess!" Her voice lowered conspiratorially. "The Duke of Burnrath is here tonight. Ooh, just imagine if I could get *his* attention!" She rose up on her toes and craned her neck, searching the crowd.

Victoria frowned at her sister. "Do not consider it for a moment, Claire. The dukes of Burnrath have long since held a tradition of wedding foreign brides. Plenty of naive girls and widows have tried to lure him into defying that custom, with only a broken

heart and ruined reputation to show for the effort."
She smiled. "Besides, I hear that he is a vampire."

Angelica's breath halted. She'd devoured John
Polidori's tale with nearly as much gusto as Mary
Shelley's. Could such creatures be real? If so, that
would mean her neighbor was one!

Claire tossed her curls and asked, "What is a vampire?"

"I did not know Mother sheltered you *that* much.
A vampire," Victoria explained, "is a creature that
looks like a man and steals into ladies' bedrooms and
drinks their blood. The stories are all the rage." Her
shining blue gaze belied the seriousness of the subject.

Claire shuddered. "How very ghastly." Then her
eyes lit up and she rose up on her toes once more.
"There he is, with the Duchess of Wentworth!"

Angelica scanned the crowd with bated breath. Was
the Duke of Burnrath really a vampire? Her imagination spun. It was too delicious for words. She spotted
him and realized this was the first time she'd seen His
Grace in the light. He towered above nearly every
man in the throng. His hair, dark as a raven's wing,
was unfashionably long, caressing the broad shoulders
of his black evening jacket. She shivered. His silver
eyes met hers, and Angelica felt as if her stays had been
tightened. The duke raised a sardonic brow at her and
inclined his head slightly before taking the Duchess of
Wentworth in his arms for a waltz.

Her cheeks heated and shame flooded her at being
caught staring. She shifted on weak knees and opened
her fan, hating the strange discomfort rising up at the
sight of him dancing with the Duchess of Wentworth.
She scanned the crowd for a distraction.

"He cannot be a vampire, Lady Wheaton," Angelica said, frowning as she eyed the mirrors that adorned the ballroom, the glow of the candlelit chandeliers reflected within. "Look at the mirrors. He casts a reflection."

Victoria followed her gaze. "So he does. No matter, I was only teasing. With the popularity of the tale of Lord Ruthven, many have been speculating about the duke's nocturnal leanings."

"What does a reflection have to do with vampires?" Claire asked, plying her fan and fluttering her eyelashes as she tried to get the duke's attention.

At any other opportunity, Angelica would have eagerly explained every detail of the vampire myth to a new audience, but her reaction to the duke had unsettled her. She struggled to find a meaning for the disturbing feelings he evoked. Taking another glass of champagne from a passing footman, she sipped the bubbly vintage in silence as Victoria prattled to her sister about garlic and crosses.

"What is his name, I wonder?" she murmured more to herself than for any edification.

"Ian Ashton," Claire answered. "Oh, if only he did not have that stupid family tradition! He would be the catch of the century. Imagine being the Duchess of Burnrath!"

Ian. The name sent a strange thrill through Angelica's body.

A young gentleman approached her with obnoxious mincing steps. "Would you care to dance, Miss Winthrop?"

She tore her gaze from the duke and saw that a line

had formed behind the lace-bedecked Corinthian. Her original problem returned to her. She must avoid marriage to one of these mindless dandies. To do so, she needed to focus on how to best destroy her reputation, *not* staring at a handsome duke, one who wasn't even a vampire.

"Not right now, thank you," she said to the gentleman. She raised her voice so the other contenders could hear. "I fear I am getting a headache." Her eyes scanned the area, looking for an opportunity to escape.

She saw the Duke of Burnrath leave the dance floor and go into the gaming room. At first, she was chagrined to find her attention upon him once more, but then she was inspired. A debutante wouldn't be caught dead there, especially if she were following an unmarriageable gentleman inside. Such an action would ruin her for certain. And if she happened to get a closer look at His Grace, well, it would be more than worthwhile.

She checked to make sure her mother wasn't watching. Relief and irritation warred as she saw Mother chatting cozily with Lady Osgoode and Lady Makepeace. No doubt attempting to auction her to the highest bidder! Angelica suppressed a derisive snort and headed for the card room.

The second she entered the smoky room, each gentleman looked up from his cards and stared. As a few awkward coughs echoed, her face heated and she was overcome with the urge to flee.

"I *thought* I saw you come in here," Victoria said from behind her. "This is really not the place for an unwed lady, but I am sure you are merely curious."

Her voice was oddly triumphant. Angelica smiled in

comprehension. Victoria wanted Angelica's reputation ruined to raise the odds of her sister making a better match. *Let Claire have them all!* She stifled the urge to giggle. Champagne, she decided as liquid euphoria tinged the edges of her consciousness, was ever so nice.

She spotted a group of ladies clustered around the faro table, watching the high-stakes play. They waved at Victoria and smirked at Angelica, whispering behind their silk fans.

"Well, I suppose that as long as you are with me, you should be suitably chaperoned," Victoria said, tugging her farther into the room.

True to her words, the male audience seemed to relax as Angelica joined the group of women. By their presence in this room, they must be of the "fast" set. *Mother will have an apoplexy if she sees me here!* For some reason, the thought brought back her giggles as she fetched another glass of champagne from a passing footman. The other women looked at each other and laughed. The room tilted and for a moment it seemed that there was two of everything. She blinked and looked back at the women. The way that the jewels at their throats caught the light was extraordinary.

⤜⤝

For the first time in over two hundred years, Ian was losing a game unintentionally. The Winthrop girl was distracting him. At first he thought she had purposefully followed him into the card room, but since she hadn't looked at him since she'd come in, he was not so certain. His gaze surreptitiously flickered over her in annoyance. Whatever could she be planning?

"I daresay," Lord Ponsonby drawled, tapping out his cigar. "That little minx over there is diverting my attention from the game. I am tempted to quit the table and endeavor to receive an introduction."

"Unless your aim is marriage, I would not consider it." Lord Makepeace scratched his muttonchop whiskers. "That's the Pendlebur heiress."

Ponsonby shook his head. "She couldn't be. An heiress would not risk her reputation coming in here."

"I am certain that my wife is responsible for this," Viscount Wheaton's brows drew together in consternation. "This has the signature of one of Victoria's pranks. The poor miss likely has no idea she is doing anything wrong."

"Well, if the damage is already done…" Ponsonby stood. "My breeches haven't been this tight in years. Anyone care to wager that I can seduce her before the night is out?"

"You will not," Ian countered with a growl and rose from the table, confused that he felt so strongly about a girl naive enough to allow her reputation to be ruined. Or maybe the thought of Ponsonby's limpid hands upon her silken flesh was what vexed him.

Ponsonby raised a brow. "God's teeth, Burnrath, I thought you didn't dally with maidens."

"I do not." He crossed the room behind Ponsonby. "I merely believe someone should be mature enough to put a stop to this foolishness."

Ponsonby ignored him and approached the girl. "And who is this beautiful lady?" he said, straining to peer down her bodice.

Ian followed close behind, ready to throttle the

sod if he so much as touched the innocent beauty. Oblivious to the tension filling the room, the debutante hiccupped and retrieved a smoldering cheroot from the table. Her gaze was laced with scorn as she, unbelievably, put it to her lush lips and inhaled.

All eyes fixed upon her in stunned silence as she blew out a cloud of smoke and quoted, "'Taught from infancy that beauty is woman's scepter, the mind shapes itself to the body, and roaming round its gilt cage, only seeks to adorn its prison.'"

Ian couldn't suppress his laughter. He didn't know what was more amusing about her quote: the fact that the chit was well-read, or that a beauty such as she was reciting the words of the infamous Mary Wollstonecraft.

She swayed on her feet and his amusement dissipated as he realized that the girl was foxed. Frowning, he extracted the cheroot from her dainty fingers and took her hand.

"I believe I owe you a dance." He forced a casual tone, hoping to get her out of the card room and back to the ballroom without a scene.

"Oh… huh?" she stammered, blinking up at him with huge dark eyes.

Behaving as if that were an assent, he took her by the elbow and escorted her out of the gaming room amidst the accompaniment of brittle titters from the "ladies" and guffaws from the "gentlemen."

"I must inform you, Miss Winthrop, that the gaming room is not the place for virtuous young ladies." He tried to sound stern and keep his eyes from drifting down to her lovely breasts. But her face was just as captivating. He nearly lost his footing as he escorted her down the stairs to the ballroom.

The girl nodded and fixed her ebony eyes on his. "I *know* what I am doing. 'In fact, it is a farce to call any being virtuous whose virtues do not result from the exercise of its own reason.'"

Ian choked back a laugh as he tried not to drown in her dark gaze. "Touché, my dear. I also found Mrs. Wollstonecraft's work to be invaluably stimulating. Pray tell, do you believe *Frankenstein* to be the work of her daughter, or did her husband pen the novel, as most conclude?"

"My name is Angelica, not 'my dear,' and only a complete bird wit would not recognize hereditary genius when they read it. Or perhaps, society does not believe a woman is capable of writing a passable gothic tale."

Angelica. The name fit her ethereal beauty. At least until she opened her mouth. This was not the typical, vapid product of a successful launch into the Quality. This woman was an intriguing creature, fascinating in her combination of astuteness and naive rebellion against convention. And her dark forbidden beauty was driving him mad.

Rather than release her to a suitable dance partner as he had intended once they entered the ballroom, he took her in his arms for a waltz. It was painful to keep his gaze from the tempting swell of her breasts above the blue satin, the subtle rhythm of her delicate pulse beating at her throat, or to endure the warm feel of her tiny waist beneath his hand as he guided her in the close dance.

"I heard that you are a vampire," Angelica said, gazing up at him with candid gypsy eyes.

He threw back his head and laughed, oblivious to the scandalized stares cast their way. "I am a man."

The girl nodded. "I assumed so."

"And why is that?" *Ah, now shall come the contrived flirtation.* Ian settled his features into an expression of detached boredom that was guaranteed to send ladies scurrying.

"I saw that you cast a reflection." She was either too drunk to notice his disdain or very brave.

Her lush lips curved into a smile, and he found himself asking, "And if my image were not captured in the glass, what would you do?"

She grinned up at him. "I would of course ask you what such a thing is like, to be a vampire."

Ian fought to conceal his shock and keep his voice level. "Why would you want to know such a thing? Would you want to be one?"

Angelica smiled as if they were discussing the latest Paris fashions. "I did not think about that. I only thought it would make a good story. I am a writer, you see."

A good story. His jaw clenched in irritation as he thought of Polidori's fabrication. A good story was what had landed him in this mess.

Thankfully, the music ended before she could continue her unconventional banter. "Thank you for the dance, Miss Winthrop." He took her arm and escorted her to her mother.

"Mother, I believe you have met Lord Burnrath." Angelica hiccupped.

Lady Margaret Winthrop nodded. "Y-your Grace," she murmured. Her throne-room curtsy contrasted oddly with her panic-stricken face.

Ian smiled wryly as he bowed. "Lady Margaret." No doubt she was terrified to see her delicate flower in the company of one with his questionable reputation.

The Duchess of Wentworth beckoned him with a nod and he obeyed the summons, hoping to reassure the frightened mama. But Angelica seemed to command his attention for one last look. To his disbelief, the outrageous woman actually grinned at him.

He forced the impertinent baggage from his mind as he finished his dance with the hostess and bid her farewell.

Tonight he would gather together all of London's vampires and command them to search for Dr. John Polidori. He must find out if this man knew the secrets of his kind. For if he did, the physician would have to be silenced... one way or the other.

His lips curved into a rueful smile as the butler handed him his topcoat and hat. It was unlikely that he would kill Polidori for the crimes of his wayward pen. The Elders frowned upon that practice in these modern times. Likely he would be required to Mark the upstart and have him watched for the rest of his life, or perhaps Ian would be encouraged to Change him. Still, wisdom dictated him to tell his subordinates as little as possible, the better to keep his options open.

Three

ROSETTA PACED THE UNDERGROUND CHAMBER, FANGS abrading her lower lip as she nibbled on it, a nervous habit left over from her mortal days. Sleep was impossible this day. She had deceived her lord last night, and he wasn't merely any Lord Vampire. Ian Ashton was the Lord of London! Her punishment could be death, rather than banishment. Running a slim hand through her cropped jet hair, she approached the bed to gaze down at the cause of her folly.

John. She smoothed dark curls from his brooding face, noting with a soft smile that his color seemed better. She'd met Dr. John Polidori in Switzerland on her grand tour, which all new vampires took. Hers had been delayed a few years due to the execution of her maker, who'd Changed her without permission from the Elders. Lord Burnrath had sent her off with generous funds as soon as the ordeal was over, telling her that the trip would help her get over the pain of losing her maker. Rosetta took the money gratefully. In truth she was happy her maker was gone. He was an autocratic boor with no imagination or appreciation for the beauty of life. The bastard hadn't even been able to read.

Rosetta enjoyed her travels like nothing else, and when she heard that there was to be a great gathering of writers at Lord Byron's villa on Lake Geneva, she had dashed off to Switzerland as fast as her funds permitted.

On her first night there, she came upon a man wandering the ruins of an ancient castle. His rich voice murmured a delightful combination of words, forming a rhyming melody that tickled her senses in the most pleasing manner. Every once in a while, he'd frown and say the line again, replacing a word or two with others that made his verse sing. He was composing a poem. She smiled and silently climbed a stone parapet above him to hear him better. Rosetta loved poetry with an intensity that bordered on obsession.

When the man stepped into a shaft of moonlight, her breath caught as he came into view. From his rich dark curls and cinnamon-tinted skin to his ebony, slumberous eyes and lithe form, he was the most beautiful man she had beheld. Rosetta leaned forward, licked her lips—and a stone came loose under her hand. She lost her balance and tumbled down from the ruins with a startled shriek.

She struck the cobblestone surface of the remains of the bailey. Her leg broke with a sickening snap and she fainted.

When Rosetta awoke, she was lying in a sumptuous bedchamber and the man she had been spying on was poised over her leg, inspecting the injured limb with scholarly studiousness. He raised his head and their eyes met. A frisson of heat passed between them and left her breathless.

"That was quite the fall you took, miss." His voice was like dark Swiss chocolate. "Whatever were you doing up in those ruins?"

"I was listening to your poem," she confessed. Then, before he could ask more, she said, "My name is Rosetta. Who are you, my lord?"

He chuckled ruefully. "I am no lord, only a mere physician. Dr. John Polidori, at your service, dear Rosetta. I am here as companion to Lord Byron. And, speaking of my position, I must see to your leg."

Polidori turned and removed a brown bottle and a spoon from his bag. He poured a thick liquid with the heavy aroma of poppies into the spoon and bade her to take the medicine with a stern expression that would not tolerate refusal.

He set her broken leg and recited his poetry to distract her from the pain. The dark odes he composed were like beautiful music to her ears. By the time he finished, dawn was creeping near.

"Now you must rest and I will see you home in the morning," he said.

"I'm afraid that's not possible," Rosetta countered. "I must go now!"

"But your leg!" he protested.

"I will survive," she said as she struggled to get out of the bed.

Polidori helped her to her feet despite the mutinous expression marring his handsome features. Reluctantly, he handed her a crutch. "But when may I see you again?"

"I don't know." The words made her ache dreadfully, but no other answer was allowed. Getting too close to mortals was dangerous. "Really, sir, I must go!"

Somehow, the dear man understood the urgency in her voice and reluctantly summoned a servant to drive her to her inn. She had barely closed the wooden chest she slept in before the sun's deadly rays streamed through the window. Her day sleep was filled with dreams of the handsome doctor, and when she awoke, she still couldn't get him out of her mind. Though every instinct screamed at her not to, she limped off to Byron's villa to spy upon him once more.

Rosetta had followed him everywhere since. She even kept the cast on her leg long after it healed in case he spotted her. The more she watched him, the deeper he crawled into her heart. His compassionate care for his patients fascinated her as well. He seemed to be too good to be a real person. Indeed, the man had a passion and capability for love that eclipsed that of the usual mortal man.

John Polidori never lacked bed partners, male and female, and he treated all with tenderness and regard from the beginning to the end of his affairs. Before she became fully aware of the fact, Rosetta found herself longing to be one of those who came into his arms. Unfortunately, his current lover was the tempestuous poet, Lord Byron. And when the arrogant bastard sent her dearest John fleeing back to London to nurse his broken heart, Rosetta's urge to kill the poet was terrifying in its viciousness. But it was forbidden to kill a mortal in these times when modern science threatened to reveal her kind.

So she contented herself with watching over John like a dark guardian angel, aching with desire to comfort him as he plunged himself deeper and deeper into debt with his drinking and gambling, trying to drown his sorrow. While he slept, she'd slip into his room to stand over him and watch the lines of worry smooth from his handsome face. Every night she whispered words of love and encouragement to him, urging him to continue to write and support himself. After awhile, her will seemed to affect him, for he had pulled out his parchment at last. But this time, John did not pen another poem but a story—a story about a vampire.

Her heart thudded in her breast as she spied the story's title page. *Could he know?* She gave his slumbering form a worried glance before scooping up his pages and fleeing to her lair to discover what secrets he'd gleaned of her kind.

Rosetta devoured Polidori's tale in less than an hour. As she read, her terror dissolved into gales of surprised laughter. This wasn't a story about her kind at all! The work was a satire, albeit a morbid sort of parody. The so-called "vampyre" was in truth a symbol for Lord Byron's dissolute and sometimes perverse nature.

She hugged the pages to her chest, shoulders still shaking in mirth. Why, "The Vampyre" was a work of genius! And best of all, it was the perfect way for John to thumb his nose at Lord Byron. All of England would be laughing at the man who broke Polidori's heart if they read the tale. The local vampires would have a good chuckle as well. Rosetta returned the story to John and whispered to him that he should publish it at once. Unfortunately, he heeded her words. And that was only the first thing to go wrong.

When Polidori anonymously published his story, vampires became Europe's favorite trend. Nobody seemed to realize that the story was a satire. The local populace of blood drinkers were irritated, especially the Lord of London. He thought the story was about him! And to Rosetta's everlasting fury, the tale was mistakenly accredited to Lord Byron. However, when the Duke of Burnrath made a trip to Italy to make discreet inquiries about the man, Rosetta was relieved, for he would be looking in the wrong direction. Though the Lord of London seemed more annoyed than enraged about the story, she was worried that it had attracted his notice at all.

Her heart clenched in agony with the knowledge that she wasn't old enough to have the power to Mark the man she loved. If she were able, he would belong to her and all others of her kind would know that to harm him would incur her undying wrath. He could be her mortal companion and eventually she could petition her lord to Change John. Then they could be together forever, and her love would be safe. But after what she'd done, her hope for such an easy solution lay in tatters.

Her worries bore fruit when Lord Burnrath convened with all of his vampires one night. Not only had he discovered the identity of the author of "The Vampyre," but he was furious about the story's growing popularity and the suspicions it created regarding his identity. Since he mingled with the mortals of the *haut ton* as the Duke of Burnrath, his reputation was in danger. Rosetta fought back feelings of guilt. In truth, he was a fair, if not kind, Lord Vampire.

"I want you all to search for this Dr. Polidori," the duke had commanded, his powerful strides circling them all. "When you find him, bring to me alive. Until this matter is resolved, all petitions to change territories will be held in abeyance. I need all of you with me now."

Rosetta had kept her head down in feigned obeisance, struggling to keep her features composed and not to tug at her cravat or fidget in her male garb. She'd been terrified he would see that she knew where John was, even as her mind screamed at her heart for betraying her master. But she was trapped now, forbidden to leave the city until the duke allowed petitions once more.

Still, she was almost too late. With the deadly fingers of dawn crawling into the sky, Rosetta found Polidori unconscious in an alley behind one of his favorite gaming establishments. He didn't stir as she carried him to her lair and she feared blood poisoning from too much drink. He was deathly pale and emaciated, so she bit her finger and gently coaxed a few drops of her blood between his sculpted lips. His color returned and his breathing steadied, but still he did not awaken.

Rosetta lay down and took the sleeping man into her arms to warm him. She had to find a way to stop the Lord of London's quest to find John. Her thoughts raced as she reviewed and discarded plans.

Before she fell asleep, she kissed his brow and whispered, "I will keep you safe, my love. I promise."

❦

Angelica wished the day would end as soon as she opened her eyes.

"You have three callers!" Margaret announced as the breakfast dishes were cleared from the table.

"Ughhh…" Angelica groaned. Her mother's strident voice was more piercing than the morning light streaming in the windows. Champagne, apparently, was not so nice after all. How she longed to go back to sleep, but no, her mother just *had* to drag her out of bed at an uncivilized hour to break into yet another grating lecture about her conduct last night. As if her mother hadn't blistered her ears enough on the carriage ride home the night before. *If I never have to hear about marriage again, this will be worth it.* She tried to keep up the litany, but her head ached too much for the thought to be even moderately convincing.

"My goodness, Lord Makepeace, Lord Ponsonby, *and* Sir Albert Brighton are here to pay calls to you," Margaret continued, oblivious to her daughter's agony. "Angelica, attend to your hair at once! This is a better opportunity than I anticipated. We must contrive a way to allow all three to escort you to the park." In a rare burst of affection, she kissed her daughter's cheek. "Whatever you did, dear, was an absolute success. If only your sainted grandmother were alive to see this day!"

Angelica managed a wan smile at her mother's cheer—until the news sank in. *Callers.* That meant she had failed in her endeavor to render herself unmarriageable. She longed to sink through the floor.

Margaret patted down Angelica's hair and shoved

her into the drawing room. Three bouquets of flowers were thrust in her face as the fops bowed before her. *Dear God, they look ready to ask for my hand already!* She fought the urge to flee to her room and vomit into her chamber pot. Only one thing settled her rebellious stomach, and she focused on the thought with all her will as clammy lips were pressed to the back of her hand. Today she planned to resubmit her first complete ghost story to *The New Monthly Magazine*.

While writing the haunting tale of the ghost of a highwayman haranguing travelers as they crossed Hounslow Heath, Angelica had been busy gathering a disguise. She had acquired the costume piece by piece and hid the collection under a board that she'd painstakingly removed from her closet floor.

For she couldn't submit her story as Angelica Winthrop. To her undying dismay and bitterness, she'd learned that Mary Shelley's success as a gothic authoress was the exception, rather than the rule, owing much to the fact that she and her family were connected to the publishing business.

When Angelica went to the office of *The New Monthly Magazine*, the editor had nearly laughed her out of the establishment. She ground her teeth at the injustice. Her merits as a writer should stand on their own, having nothing to do with her sex. On a flight of inspiration, she decided to beat them at their own game. She would see if "Allan Winthrop" had better luck. The tiewig she'd ordered was the final piece to her costume and should be in the shop today. And if her writing gained enormous popularity, she'd whip off her wig and expose herself before Mr. Colburn, the publisher himself, with a triumphant laugh! But first, she had this obligatory nonsense with her suitors to contend with.

The morning jaunt through Hyde Park represented the most unendurable two hours of her life. And Liza's mildly amused smile didn't help matters. Every bump the carriage wheels hit jarred her bones and intensified her agony. The gentlemen crowded her, making it hard for her to breathe as they vied for her attention. Her mouth tasted like a sweaty stocking and her head throbbed with the effort of making small talk. She supposed they thought she was behaving with admirable maidenly modesty, when truly her skull ached with every word she spoke. And if the birds didn't stop chirping, she swore she would take up shooting.

When the trio brought her and her maid back home, she strained every ounce of her patience saying good-bye politely to each one instead of bolting from the carriage as if the conveyance were on fire.

Angelica heaved a sigh of relief as Liza shut the front door behind her, silencing the platitudes at last. But the peace was not to endure.

Her mother practically charged at her in the foyer, breathless with excitement. "You must tell me at once everything that happened!"

She looked so girlish in her enthusiasm that Angelica could not suppress a chuckle. "Mother, we have only now returned."

Margaret sobered and straightened her back. "Of course, I'll allow you to get your breath and Liza may bring us some tea. Three suitors in one day! I am so proud of you, my dear."

Before Liza had set down the teapot, her mother fixed Angelica with an eager, inquisitive stare. "Now, tell me *everything* that transpired."

Angelica lifted her gaze heavenward as she poured her tea. "There was nothing of note. We discussed the weather. I inquired of their families, complimented Makepeace's phaeton and horses, and greeted our acquaintances in the park."

Margaret's eyes twinkled. "I hear that Makepeace is one of Claire Belmont's suitors. It appears you have pulled him from her grasp."

Angelica closed her eyes at her mother's mercenary tone. "I didn't intend to do so."

Margaret harrumphed. "She has plenty of other suitors. I daresay she is your biggest competition this season. Your dowry may be larger, but blondes are all the rage."

Angelica felt an unexpected wave of pity for Claire. Like any respectable debutante, the girl was utterly consumed with the obsession of seeking a husband with the most elevated title and greatest wealth. Angelica had no doubt that the beautiful girl would succeed. But then what would become of her? After she went through the unpleasant business of producing the requisite heir, Claire's life and purpose would be over. Angelica's hands clenched into determined fists under the table. *That must not happen to me.*

Margaret interrupted her reverie. "Daydreaming about your suitors, I see. You didn't favor one more than the others with your attention, did you?" Her voice sharpened.

"Of course not. In fact, I hardly said a word and allowed them to talk about themselves, which they were pleased to do." Angelica refrained from saying that her head ached so badly that speaking took far too much effort.

Her mother nodded. "Good. I am glad you are seeking to atone for your scandalous behavior last night, though it seemed to benefit you greatly."

"What do you mean?" The only thing Angelica regretted about last night's conduct was that she drank too much and failed to scandalize anyone.

Margaret leaned forward conspiratorially, though they were privately ensconced in their own home. "I think your popularity is highly due to the fact that the Duke of Burnrath paid some attention to you last night," she whispered. "He has never been known to do so to an unmarried lady, so all gentlemen, naturally, will seek to discover what he found so entrancing about you. Men are like that, my dear. Where one goes, the others will follow. You must endeavor to keep his interest, but do not, under any circumstance, allow him an opportunity to get you alone. Then you would be ruined."

Angelica laughed at her mother's contradictory instructions. "How is it that a man can bolster my reputation with one hand, yet destroy it with another?"

"Do not be glib." Margaret's eyes narrowed. "Everyone knows that he will never marry an English girl. Great catch though he would be, he would only offer indecent things to you."

"What sorts of indecent things?" Angelica leaned forward. It was the closest her mother had come to discussing anything that went on between a man and a woman. A sudden and alarming dizziness and warmth curled through her body as she remembered the duke's hands upon her during their waltz last evening.

"A *lady* would not endeavor to know," her mother said primly. "Now you must take a nap and restore your color. You are much too pale."

Angelica slumped in disappointment and changed the subject. "Lady Wheaton told me His Grace is rumored to be a vampire."

Her suggestion had the desired effect, for Margaret's agonized sigh heaved through the dining room.

"I was afraid you would hear that foolishness." She frowned. "Put that twaddle firmly out of your mind. Vampires are nothing but the product of a drunken physician's twisted imaginings."

"Actually," Angelica countered, "there have been legends of such creatures for centuries. I have researched—"

Margaret bristled. "I will hear no more of this foolish drivel."

"Yes, Mother." She struggled to keep the mutinous tone from her voice as she turned back to more important matters. "May I take Liza with me for some shopping this afternoon?"

Margaret nodded. Her gratitude for the shift in topic was apparent. "You must purchase a new fan. The one that matches your gown for tonight is frayed. Now hurry on to bed. I cannot have you looking like a corpse at Almack's tonight."

Angelica grinned. "A corpse at Almack's... now *that* would be a great story!"

Her mother's eyes narrowed. "Don't you dare start in on that morbid nonsense again!"

As Angelica made her way up the stairs, she shook her head when Margaret murmured, "It is a pity His Grace will not be there."

A small part of her agreed. If she allowed him the opportunity to get her alone, she could be ruined, her mother had said. Now that was a tantalizing thought… too tantalizing. If her fascination with His Grace last evening was any indicator, such an endeavor would be far too risky. Besides, he'd seemed to have grown bored with her quite rapidly once she began to speak of her writing. Angelica frowned as she lay down for her nap. It was a shame the Duke of Burnrath wasn't really a vampire. He was certainly handsome enough to fit the role perfectly.

Four

WHEN ANGELICA ARRIVED AT THE HEADQUARTERS OF
The New Monthly Magazine, not only was the owner,
Henry Colburn, present but he was also unoccupied
and eager to read new material. Best of all, her
disguise seemed to pass muster. Without the slightest
odd glance, an assistant served her a cup of tepid
tea and bade her to wait in the outer office while
Colburn retired to his private office to read. Out
of the corner of her eye, Angelica peered out the
window and watched Liza's pacing, envious that her
maid was allowed to indulge in an outward display
of nervousness.

Angelica lounged in her chair instead, trying to
look bored and resisting the urge to pick at invisible lint on her coat. Just as she was ready to tap
her uncomfortable Hessians in impatience, Colburn
emerged from his office.

"I like it," he said.

"You do?" Angelica held back a whoop of joy.

As if sensing her restraint, Colburn's thin lips
twitched in a slight smile. "Indeed. These tales are all

the rage and I admire your descriptive ability. I'll give you six pounds."

Six pounds! Angelica could hardly contain her glee. Finally she was a real author, paid for her work.

The money exchanged hands, and her joy was compounded when Colburn asked, "Do you have any more?"

Angelica coughed and stammered, "W-well, I do have an idea about a haunted mansion."

The editor nodded stiffly. "Excellent. Have the manuscript ready by next week and I'll pay you double. That is, if this first one sells, which I believe it will. Good day, Mr. Winters."

Angelica grinned and almost curtsied. She recovered herself and shook his hand, squeezing with all her might. "And a good day to you, Mr. Colburn!"

Once she and Liza were settled in their rented hack, Angelica bounced up and down as she changed back into her dress and recounted the events to the maid, punctuating each sentence with, "I will be a published author!"

"'Ey, there'll be no 'anky-panky goin' on in my coach, gov'ner!" the driver shouted.

"We're behaving,'" Liza called back as she untied Angelica's neckcloth.

Changing back into her dress was a struggle, but the task was managed by the time the carriage stopped. Angelica patted her reticule containing her disguise, her head spinning in delirious glee as they walked around the block to her home.

"Whatever took you so long?" Margaret demanded the moment they entered the front parlor.

Not even her mother's anger at the lateness of
their arrival dampened Angelica's spirits. "I am
sorry, Mother. The traffic was a veritable stalemate
out there."

Margaret sighed and looked at the mantel clock.
"Very well, just do not let it happen again. Now,
hurry up to your bath. The doors close at Almack's at
eleven o'clock sharp, and not even the King himself
would be admitted one minute after."

Liza helped her into her ivory silk ball gown while
Angelica muttered, "I wish I didn't have to spend
the evening being paraded about the marriage mart
drinking lukewarm lemonade and making small talk
to the dandies as they sniff out my dowry. Do you
think Mother would let me stay home and write if I
plead the sick headache?"

The maid chuckled. "She wouldn't believe the lie
for a second, miss. Now I'll see to your hair and you
can tell me about your next chilling ghost story."

Angelica's heart warmed when she entered the
dining room to see her father seated at the table in
evening wear. As her eyes met his, she realized that
Jacob Winthrop was a noble man, no matter what
the *ton* said.

"You look stunning, my dearest," he said and rose
to pull out her chair.

She smiled and curtsied. "Thank you, Papa."

"Well, Jacob," Margaret said, her voice trembling
with ill-concealed excitement, "are you going to tell
her the good news?"

Her father cleared his throat with authority and winked at Angelica. "Your season is already a success. While you were gone, I've received three offers for your hand today."

"What?" Angelica gasped as her veins seemed to fill with ice.

He nodded. "Yes, apparently Lord Makepeace, Sir George Wiltshire, and Baron Osgoode are quite taken with you."

"An earl already!" her mother exclaimed.

"Wh–what did you say to them?" Angelica kept her shaking hands in her lap and out of sight.

"I told them I would consider their offers, but I would like for you to enjoy a full season as this is the only opportunity a girl has to be courted. I placated them by giving them full permission to call upon you in the meantime as I believe it's only fair that you should have the opportunity to get to know them better." He raised his glass in a toast to her. "I intend for you to have some opinion in the matter, my dear."

Angelica almost opened her mouth to say she wanted none of them, but her mother silenced her with a glare and a shake of her head. Instead, she regarded her father's loving smile and managed a wan one of her own.

"I appreciate your consideration, Papa." She struggled to keep her dread from showing.

Margaret nodded in approval. "And just think, that gives us time to see if we can wring an offer from someone better, perhaps even a duke!"

❧

Ian growled low in his throat as he viewed the most recent entries in the White's betting book. Usually the bets were harmless, ranging from the commonplace, such as horse races and boxing matches, to the ludicrous, such as when one of the patrons would catch a cold. However, two wagers had him grinding his teeth. One was that he, the Duke of Burnrath, would bed the saucy Winthrop heiress.

The bet was only for one hundred pounds, but it still left a foul taste in his mouth. He had done little more than dance with the young lady. Ian was somewhat placated to see counter-bets that Ponsonby or Wheaton would do the deed, for at least he was not singled out. Even better, there were wagers to see who would marry her, those raised already as high as one thousand pounds.

What truly enraged him was the betting that he was, indeed, a vampire. Apparently, his appearance before mirrors and dining on garlic were not enough to still the wagging tongues.

Lord Makepeace nudged in to write his wager on that very line.

"And just how am I to prove this silly speculation one way or the other?" Ian asked.

Makepeace jumped, face white as his cravat. "I-I say, Burnrath, I did not recognize you at first!" He managed a nervous chuckle. "I implore you not to drink my blood."

Ian laughed. "According to the stories, I think I am supposed to prefer the blood of innocent maidens."

The earl looked at him in confusion before comprehension finally dawned and he let out a hearty guffaw, clapping Ian on the back. "Quite so."

Makepeace returned to the betting book and wagered six hundred pounds that Ian Ashton, Duke of Burnrath, was *not* a bloodsucking fiend. He then wagered eleven hundred that *he*, Lord Makepeace, would wed Miss Winthrop.

The earl clapped Ian on the shoulder. "I've enjoyed chatting with you, Burnrath, but I must leave for Almack's and pay court to a certain lovely young lady."

As the earl left, Ian suppressed the urge to wrap his hands around the fop's scrawny neck. Surely a lady as witty and beautiful as Angelica could do better than a mutton-headed cad like Makepeace. He shook his head, frowning. The decision would be in her parents' hands as it always had been in the upper classes. The poor girl would be lucky to wed a man young enough to give her pleasure. A full-blown image of the little temptress struck him. Ian cursed himself for wanting something he could never have and vowed to keep Angelica Winthrop from his mind.

Ian sat down at one of the green felt tables to play a hand of cards. He may have dissuaded one man's suspicions tonight, but apparently he would have to do more to stop the talk altogether. He hoped his informants would track down Polidori soon.

As the game progressed, Ian found it more and more difficult to focus on his cards and the conversation with his opponents. Something hadn't been right when he met with his subordinates the night before. Nothing obvious had appeared to be amiss, but the more he pondered, the more he couldn't

shake the feeling that something was wrong. A detail
of that conversation teased his memory with infuriating vagueness. Perhaps he should discuss the matter
with his second in command. Rafe was ruthless in
ferreting out mischief.

Ian gave up on the game with a sigh, turning in
his markers. As he turned toward the door, lukewarm
liquid splashed in his face. The slight odor of beeswax
and incense revealed the liquid to be holy water.
From the corner of his eye he spied the young Baron
Osgoode stuffing a flask in his pocket, trying to look
inconspicuous, and failing miserably. He seized the
boy by the shoulder and spun him around.

"It w-was an accident, Your Grace!" Osgoode
stammered. Sweat beaded on his upper lip.

"You lie, you little fool," Lord Wentworth
countered, approaching him from behind. "I saw the
whole thing. What did you expect to happen? Did
you think His Grace would burst into flame?"

Ian wiped his face with a handkerchief, resisting
the urge to bare his fangs. Those who weren't staring
at the altercation swarmed to the betting book to
place wagers.

"Name your second," Ian snarled. "I expect to see
you at Chalk Walk in one hour!"

A white-faced fop came forward and put a hand
on Osgoode's shoulder as he faced Ian. "Er... Your
Grace? Shouldn't we be doing this at dawn?"

"I am disinclined to wait." Ian spun on his heel
and left. His temper made his blood thirst rise to a
furious pitch.

The incident went off without a hitch. As was

expected, the baron deloped, admitting guilt. Ian accepted the apology, and the seconds heaved sighs of relief. Both gentlemen tossed the yawning Dr. Sampson a sovereign for his troubles. There were a few grumbles of disappointment from the more bloodthirsty spectators, but most were eager to get back to their drink and games.

As Ian shook hands with his opponent before departing, he whispered, "Let this be a lesson to you to curb your impulses, Osgoode. And know this: I could have your blood if I wanted it."

⊱⊰

Word of the duel spread like a conflagration through every drawing room, gaming hall, and brothel in England's hallowed capitol. Violent arguments broke out about the cause of the delicious incident. The more fantastical members of the *ton* averred that the duke was enraged at having holy water thrown at him because he felt his dastardly secret was at risk of exposure. Others were of agreement that purposeful damage to one's neckcloth more than merited pistols at dawn. Many wielded their copies of "The Vampyre" as they again debated about Lord Burnrath's status. Was he man or monster?

"Listen to this," Lord Makepeace demanded of his inebriated audience as he opened the book and read, "'It happened that in the midst of the dissipations attendant upon a London winter, there appeared at the various parties of the leaders of the *ton* a nobleman, more remarkable for his singularities, than his rank.' That describes Burnrath right from the start!"

"Ah, but that is not quite accurate, for Burnrath is a duke," Viscount Wheaton countered with a slight slur. "If you ask anyone, especially the mother of a debutante, she would say his *rank* is far more remarkable than his 'singularities.'" Brandy sloshed over the rim of his glass as he raised it to his lips. "I daresay m'mother-in-law would welcome a match between Burnrath and Claire, even if the chap were to drain the chit's blood on their wedding night!"

Makepeace glowered as the intoxicated group roared with laughter at Wheaton's sally. Still, there were a few grumbles from those who were envious of Lord Burnrath's wealth, title, and desirability. Lord Ponsonby, still slighted over Ian's monopolizing of the Winthrop heiress, rose to the debate.

"Edward may have the right of it." He nodded at Makepeace. "Duke or not, Burnrath has never been seen buying horses at Tattersall's, racing at Rotten Row, or even boxing at Gentleman Jack's."

"Perhaps His Grace does not ride, and not all gentlemen are avid pugilists," the Marquess of Wakefield argued, waving his cigar impatiently. "However, he does sponsor a boxer in Cheapside, I've heard."

Ponsonby refused to be thwarted and tore John Polidori's tale from Makepeace's grasp. "What about this, eh?" he said, starting to read. "'Those who felt this sensation of awe, could not explain whence it arose: some attributed it to the dead gray eye, which, fixing upon the object's face, did not seem to penetrate, and at one glance to pierce through to the inward workings of the heart; but fell upon the cheek with a leaden ray that weighed upon the skin it could not pass.'"

All shivered at the ghastly, yet visceral description. Ponsonby smiled in triumph. A young viscount nodded in eager agreement, swept away by the imaginative speculation going on in the club. "Yes, that's exactly how I feel when he looks at me!"

"His eyes are silver, not gray," another man argued skeptically.

"All the more inhuman!" Ponsonby declared and continued reading, "'He gazed upon the mirth around him, as if he could not participate therein. Apparently, the light laughter of the fair only attracted his attention, that he might by a look quell it and throw fear into those breasts where thoughtlessness reigned.'"

The men continued to drink and argue. The further into their cups they fell, the more convoluted their logic became until thoughtlessness did indeed reign.

Castlecoote, Ireland

Ben Flannigan groaned as he pulled on the stake, using all of his strength to work the sharpened piece of ash out of the monster's breast. The stake came free with a squelch and a crunch of bone. He took a moment to wipe the sweat from his brow before he squared his shoulders and turned back to the corpse. His work was only half finished. Now he needed to drag nearly two hundred pounds of deadweight out from the crypt and into the sun.

By the time the task was complete, the hunter was

gasping for breath. He pulled a flask of good Irish whiskey from his pocket and settled back against a tombstone to watch God's light do its work.

Contrary to the legends, a vampire did not burst into flames the moment the body came into contact with the sun's rays. The body's pale visage pinkened as if embarrassed by its predicament, then slowly darkened to a red not unlike that of a boiled lobster. Steam rose from the corpse with a hiss, emphasizing the comparison.

Ben chuckled and raised his flask in a toast to the sun before taking a deep drink. This was his favorite part. The vampire's crimson flesh now began to blacken and crackle. Tendrils of acrid smoke curled up and out of the body. Moments later, the first flames flickered out of the melting eyeballs as well as the thing's nostrils.

Once the body was engulfed in flames, Ben retrieved two large jugs of holy water from his bag. The first he poured out in a circle around the corpse to keep the flames from spreading. The second he would use when the creature had been reduced to ashes.

While he waited, the hunter logged the details of the kill in his journal. His count was now fourteen, one of the highest of all hunters. He was not as pleased with those accomplishments as another might be, however. This vampire, as well as the other that he had destroyed in Windsor, had been a disappointment, no older or craftier than his last thirteen kills. Since he had failed at attaining the priesthood, Ben Flannigan was determined to excel at this profession and it was past time for more challenging quarry.

He rummaged in his pack until he found his

tattered copy of "The Vampyre" by John Polidori. Ever since he had read the story, a question had invaded his mind and refused to be ignored. Could a vampire truly pose as a member of the nobility?

The more he thought about it, the more he concluded such a thing was indeed possible. He'd read that those in the ranks of high society engaged in mindless revelry until dawn and then slept the day away during the social season. The rest of their time they spent sequestered on their country estates. A vampire could do very well in such an environment if it were very powerful and extremely clever.

The last line of the story was a whispered echo in the back of his mind, filling him with an odd mixture of dread and predatory titillation: "The guardians hastened to protect Miss Aubrey; but when they arrived, it was too late. Lord Ruthven had disappeared, and Aubrey's sister had glutted the thirst of a VAMPYRE!"

Ah, to face such a clever enemy, to cast off its mask and expose its deception to all before dispatching the abomination back to hell. The thought warmed Ben like the flames of a Yule log. He longed to try his hand at such prey.

Aside from the fact that travel to London, not to mention lodgings, would be costly, Ben had put off his decision to go there for well over a year. After all, facing an ancient vampire would be nothing like the younglings he had slain. His teacher, God rest his soul, had told him such stories.

But now, after fourteen kills, nine of those in the last year, Ben was ready. He could feel it down to the marrow of his very bones.

Five

ANGELICA BLINKED IN JOYOUS DISBELIEF AS SHE watched the last servant leave Burnrath House for the evening. The maid had left the door ajar! Fate must be smiling down upon her this day. She sent a silent prayer heavenward in thanks for the duke's eccentric policy of leaving his house unstaffed after the day's chores were finished.

Today she would finally get inside the place that had held her imagination in thrall for years. She scooped up her pocket watch from the bureau and checked the time. Liza would be up to wake her from her nap at dark. That would give Angelica nearly two hours to explore the house safely.

With desperate speed, she changed into her men's clothing and packed writing paper and a quill into a sturdy bag. After a few failed attempts with the neck-cloth, she cast the linen aside. Not having time for the tiewig, she tucked her hair into a cap. She slowly worked her window open, wincing as the wood frame creaked. Holding her breath, she placed one foot on the rose trellis, then the other, clinging to the window frame for support. She carefully made her way down the trellis, cursing under her breath as the rose thorns poked through and caught at her clothes.

Once she reached the ground, she scanned Rosemead Street through the gate for passersby. Satisfied that the street was empty, she scrambled over the fence, grateful that she wasn't wearing skirts to hamper her already fumbling progress. Angelica straightened her disguise, lifted her chin, and crossed Rosemead to Number 6, Burnrath House, trying to appear casual. Her heart pounded in her ears as she made her way up the cobblestone walkway, forcing every vestige of her will to maintain her casual stride and keep her from breaking into a run.

The Elizabethan mansion looked ominous and imposing even in the waning daylight. Gray clouds overhead made the chimneys cast strange-moving shadows. Carved of sandstone and roofed with slate, the house was in the shape of an enormous letter *E* turned on its side. Angelica wondered if the design was intended as a tribute to the virgin queen, or if it was merely a sign of the death of the enclosed courtyard structure that had been favored in medieval times.

Her eyes narrowed at the darkening sky. *I pray the rain holds back until I return home. I don't know how I'd explain wet hair to Mother.*

After what seemed an eternity, she cautiously opened the front door, holding her breath as she waited to hear a voice cry out, "Intruder!"

The house was silent, dark, and empty. Mouth dry, she closed the door behind her, wishing she'd brought a candle. She let out the breath she was holding and started forward, skin tingling in anticipation. *I am inside Burnrath House at last!* She smiled. *I wonder if I'll encounter any ghosts.* The thought didn't bring as much cheer as anticipated, now that she was within the setting of her fantasies. Instead, tiny shivers raced up and down her arms and legs.

Plush Aubusson carpets covered nearly every inch of the smooth hardwood floors. Ornate furniture from the Renaissance graced the place like somber skeletons. No modern Oriental items for this stately home; however, the duke had gone to the astounding expense of installing gas lamps throughout the place.

Angelica stared at the iron and glass devices in awe. She'd never seen gas lamps outside of the theaters and Pall Mall. They must make the rooms as bright as day. Her fingers trembled with the urge to light one, but she hadn't the slightest idea how to do so. She shook her head, realizing that if she had known, she wouldn't dare, for someone may see her through the large windows.

All stories and legends of haunted houses took place on the upper floors, so with a nervous smile, Angelica darted up the stairs. The long corridor was dark and abandoned, apart from tasteful paintings decorating the walls. Her heart leaped into her throat with every door she opened, then fell in a mixture of relief and disappointment when she saw the empty rooms with sheet-draped furniture. Cobwebs clung to every angle and corner. The stale, musty odors tickled her nose. Still, her eager imagination conjured up howling specters rising out from the fireplaces, angry at having their rest disturbed. The writer in her demanded a story for these ghosts, and while she explored, she named them and constructed the tales of their gruesome murders.

Her imaginary constable was just collapsing into a faint after seeing the blood-drenched ceiling when she found the library.

"Oh my…" Her breath caught suddenly, and a thrill rushed through her body at the vast array of books in the mammoth chamber. The meager light from the windows gleamed on the high shelves and wheeled ladder. Gas lamps stood in every corner of the room, and two overstuffed wingback chairs sat companionably before an elaborate carved marble fireplace. With such light, one could read all night long if she desired. Angelica let out her breath in a reverent sigh. Burnrath's library was the most beautiful place she'd ever seen. Like the main room, the library seemed immaculately clean. There was not a cobweb in sight, and the chamber smelled of fresh polish.

The duke must spend all of his time here, she mused, having greater respect for the man, given his obvious love of the written word. She tiptoed to the shelves to see what captured his fancy.

Her eyes squinted in the darkness, but try as she might, she couldn't read the titles. To her dismay, dusk was quickly closing in. She needed to hurry home. With a reluctant sigh, she hurried out of the library, closing the door softly behind her.

As she made her way down the thickly carpeted stairs, she glanced at the paintings of the previous dukes of Burnrath. Something about the paintings gave her pause. There were no portraits of the wives or children. In fact, the pictures were painted when the men were the same age. No doubt another eccentric family tradition, Angelica thought with a snort. Then her brow furrowed in contemplation as she leaned closer to examine each one. Despite the differences in artists' styles and the subjects' clothing, she could almost believe that they were all of the same man.

"How very odd…" she whispered aloud.

Something squeaked and brushed past her ankle. Angelica shrieked and jumped, losing her footing on the stairs. As she tumbled down, pain jarring her from multiple impacts, she saw a small rat scurry away. Shame washed over her for acting like such a ninny. Then everything went black.

Ian's eyes snapped open as he heard a thump. There was an intruder in his house. *Who would dare?* He lurched to his feet. The blood hunger tinged his vision with red and he grinned. *No matter, I have an easy meal.* He threw on a pair of black trousers and hurriedly fastened the first few buttons on a white lawn shirt, scorning his boots. He yanked open the secret door and ran up the cellar stairs, licking his fangs in anticipation.

With the silence only a nocturnal hunter could muster, he stalked on quiet feet through the kitchen and into the drawing room. The staircase came into view and so did his culprit, a young, slim boy who had apparently taken a spill and was struggling to sit up. The absence of a stake and the presence of a satchel indicated that this was a common thief who'd invaded his sanctuary, rather than a vexing vampire hunter.

The thief saw him and his black eyes widened in

shock. There was something familiar about the boy, but Ian's hunger chased away further speculation. All street urchins looked alike anyhow. He could hear the pounding of the lad's heart and taste the fear on his tongue. Ian inhaled deeply as the thirst within him surged in triumph to be so soon abated.

❦

Terror coursed through Angelica as she saw the Duke of Burnrath approach. He seemed carved from shadows, and his eyes glowed molten silver like those of a ferocious beast as he moved ever closer with deadly fluid grace.

"You made a poor selection of a residence to rob, boy," he whispered. His hair hung in his face, making him appear dangerous and rakish.

Relief flooded her with the realization that he didn't recognize her, and she struggled to gain her feet. Pain erupted in her ankle and Angelica collapsed, watching in helpless trepidation as he slowly stalked nearer. He seized her by her upper arms, and she whimpered at the pressure of his fingertips digging into her flesh. Those inhuman silver eyes locked onto hers, holding her spellbound.

"You will pay a price for your clumsiness, I am afraid." His sculpted lips parted to reveal gleaming sharp fangs.

A scream caught in her throat as he bent his head toward her. His hair caressed her cheek, smelling of wild spices.

As he sank his teeth into her neck, Angelica's last rational thought before she fainted was: *My God, the duke really is a vampire! What a story that would make…*

Six

THE SECOND THE BLOOD TOUCHED HIS TONGUE AND
the delicate perfume of lilacs infused his senses, Ian
knew his victim was female. As her life and emotions
began to flash through his mind, he realized that he
held Angelica Winthrop in his arms. But he could not
stop drinking, for his hunger was too strong. *God*, she
was sweet!

Out of respect and to avoid getting too close to her,
he shut his mind off from hers, only taking her blood
and allowing her incredible passion for living to feed
him along with her vitality. When he was sated, he
released her and bit his finger, using his blood to heal
the puncture wounds at her delicate throat and feeling
like a monster for touching that pure ivory skin. He
hoped she was uninjured from her fall.

Ian scooped her up and carried her to the sitting
room, marveling at how light and perfect she felt in
his arms. Angelica's cap fell off, letting the dark silken
tresses tumble out to caress his chest. The scent of
spring flowers wafted from her shining locks. After he
lit a lamp and laid his delicate burden on the sofa, his

fingers combed through that lovely hair as he felt for lumps. He frowned when he found a small one at the base of her skull.

After he unbuttoned her frayed frock coat, still perplexed as to why she was dressed like a man, he felt for broken bones. Unbidden, his hands lingered on her breasts through her coarse linen shirt before continuing his examination. He felt her buttocks and thighs through her trousers, and his own grew tight as he stiffened with arousal. Ian shook his head to clear it and ran his hands down her calves. When he touched her swelling ankle, she gasped in pain and bolted upright. As her gaze met his and widened with fright, Ian cursed under his breath. He'd forgotten to erase her memory of him feeding on her.

~∘∾

Angelica fought to see past the white spots of agony pulsing up from her ankle. Her vision cleared, revealing the Duke of Burnrath poised above her. His silver eyes reflected the brilliant flame of the gas lamp, making him resemble an unholy specter. She opened her mouth to scream, but his hand clamped over her mouth. Her senses swam as his masculine scent enveloped her. She tried to struggle, but she was too weak from blood loss to manage more than a feeble squirm.

"Please, do not scream, Angel," he said in an unbelievably gentle tone. "I promise not to hurt you. Now, if I let you go, will you be calm and explain what you were doing in my home?"

She nodded, believing him for now. Perhaps it was

the sincerity in his voice, or the fact that he called her such a sweet endearment as "Angel." After all, she could always scream later.

He held up his other hand and fixed her with an intense stare. "I will know if you lie."

She believed that, too. He released her and she sat up. Her head swam with dizziness, but she remained upright, clinging to the arm of the sofa for support.

"You *bit* me!" she cried in frightened outrage. "You drank my blood!" She placed a hand against her neck, her eyes widening when she realized there was no wound.

To her disbelief, he looked ashamed. That put her at ease more than anything.

"I thought you were a burglar." He ran his hand through his coal black hair, appearing nervous. "And I am hungry when I wake. Please believe me when I tell you, I never would have drunk from you if I had known your identity." His brows drew together sternly. "Your clothing did not help matters. Would you be inclined to explain why you were in my house dressed as a male?"

Perhaps her mind was still fuzzy from the blood loss, or perhaps it was the way he'd changed from a frightening monster to a gentleman in mere moments. Her fear abated. As Angelica searched for the right words, the situation suddenly seemed comical and she erupted into giggles. Ian's perplexed expression made her laugh harder.

When she at last composed herself, she said, "You will probably find this to be amusing."

"I am certain I will be delighted," he said dryly.

The sight of him lounging back against the sofa cushion with his shirt open sobered her. She had never seen a man's bare chest before, and this glimpse of Burnrath's made her breath catch. Vampire or not, he appeared even more handsome barefoot and disheveled, his lips curved in casual humor.

Fighting to maintain her composure, she explained, "As I told you at the Wentworth ball, I have always wanted to be a writer."

"Ah, so I am looking at the next Duchess of Devonshire?" His indulgent tone seemed mocking.

Angelica bristled at the assumption. "Just because I am female does not mean I write thinly veiled gossip like *The Sylph*. I desire to be a gothic authoress, like Mary Shelley."

His brow rose. "I imagine your mother doesn't approve."

She was about to retort, but there seemed to be a glint of sympathetic understanding in his eyes. "Yes, I have to hide my stories from her. However," she added with a lift to her chin, "my father does not object and Liza, my maid, is my most faithful reader."

"Have you been published yet?" the duke asked with what seemed to be genuine interest.

Angelica nodded. "Yes, though that at first posed a trifle of a challenge, for 'Angelica Winthrop' was laughed out of the offices of *The New Monthly Magazine*. However, they were quick to welcome 'Allan Winthrop.'" She smoothed the lapels of her waistcoat and laughed, though she couldn't keep the bitterness out of her feigned mirth.

"Ah, so the reason behind your disguise is becoming

clear." The vampire nodded, eyeing her intently. "But what were you doing in my home?"

Angelica grinned. "Now we come to the amusing part of my tale, Your Grace. I have been fascinated with Burnrath House for many years. With all the odd sounds and coming and goings in the night, as well as the conspicuous absence of servants at such hours, I could only reach one conclusion."

The duke leaned forward, silver eyes glittering ominously. "And that conclusion was?"

"I believed your house was haunted," she explained with burning cheeks. "I never imagined this place was haven to a vampire."

Burnrath's sharp crack of laughter resounded through the chamber.

"So," Angelica continued, chuckling. "When Colburn offered me double if I could finish another story, I was determined to write one about this house."

For some reason she left out the part about needing the money to run away to avoid marriage. Though Burnrath was a vampire, he was still a nobleman and would no doubt disapprove of her shirking what he would see as her duty. "And when your maid left the front door ajar," she explained, "I thought it was the only opportunity I would receive to see the inside of the famous Burnrath House."

The duke's brow rose. "Your interest in my tomb of a home and things that stalk the night is peculiar. I should think a pretty young thing such as you would be more suited to picking flowers in a sunny meadow."

Angelica smiled and quoted,

"Sing to me no songs of daylight
For the sun is the enemy of lovers.
Sing instead of shadows and darkness
And memories of midnight."

"That was Sappho, correct?" he asked.

She nodded. "Yes, I—"

"You are not in the slightest bit afraid of me, are you?" he interrupted, staring at her as if she were an exotic animal.

She regarded him with a measure of surprise, realizing that she was not. "Should I be?" she reasoned aloud. "You are not the soulless creature the myths portray."

"What makes you say that?" He seemed to be genuinely curious, as if what she thought mattered to him.

Angelica shrugged, unused to a man taking her seriously. "Well, you have a reflection, for one thing."

The vampire's lips twisted in a wry smile. "A stone has no soul, but if you hold one before a mirror, will it not cast its reflection?"

Angelica's eyes widened in astonishment at his logic and she nodded quickly. Her shoulders hunched as fury radiated within. *Of course! Even a fool would realize that!*

"You are angry and ashamed." He sounded surprised. "Why?"

Her voice was ragged with self-contempt that she could not conceal. "I should have known that. The logic is stupidly apparent."

"I do not believe I have ever seen a woman react in such a way over her ignorance." The duke peered at her like she was an odd curiosity displayed for his entertainment.

His musing tone fueled the conflagration. A small

measure of the contempt in her gaze was now directed at him. "Perhaps *they* hide it better than I do."

Burnrath did not reply and instead continued to stare at her as if he could peer into her soul. Angelica shivered and brought the conversation to a more comfortable topic.

"All that aside, I do think it is now too late to fear you." She forced an airy lilt to her tone. "After all, I should think if you had meant to kill me by now, you would have."

The vampire leaned forward. "Death is not your only danger in being alone with me, little Angel." He was so close that she could feel his breath on her lips, and her body, unbidden, began to tremble. He was going to kiss her! She closed her eyes and...

∼⟡∼

There was a knock at the door.

"Dammit!" Ian growled, leaping up from the sofa as the reality of the situation crashed upon him. "It is my coachman."

He strode to the door, teeth clenched in irritation at the interruption.

"Your Grace?" Albert inquired, taking in the sight of Ian's open shirt and bare feet. "I thought you were wanting me to take you to your club."

"My plans have changed," Ian said, prepared to dismiss the coachman. Then he remembered Angelica's injuries. If she had not awakened so quickly, he could have healed her with his blood, but he didn't dare frighten her further. "Would you be so kind as to fetch a doctor?"

"Why, are you unwell?" Albert asked anxiously.

"It is not for me." He shut the door in the coachman's face.

His foul mood faded as he returned to the beauty reclining on his sofa. He had never before met anyone as fascinating as Angelica Winthrop. Her passion for her writing humbled him even as the rich descriptions of her stories captivated him. His gaze caressed Angelica's face and form, noting her fine-boned features and luscious lips that caused him to nearly forget himself and capture them in a devouring kiss.

"Is everything all right?" she asked nervously, her fists clenched in her lap.

"I sent for a doctor to see to your ankle, Miss Winthrop," he said with forced formality even as he longed to return to their engaging conversation.

"Oh. Thank you." Her long lashes swept her cheeks as if perhaps she regretted the return to propriety.

The cozy spell was broken and they spent the next half hour struggling with stilted small talk, not daring to meet each other's gazes.

The doctor arrived, not batting an eye at the young lady in male garb.

"Miss Winthrop is a neighbor and dear friend of mine." Ian had worked out a plausible lie. "She had a quarrel with her mother and sought a confidante. Unfortunately, she was so overwrought that she tripped on my doorstep." He shook his head at the idea of such female silliness, ignoring Angelica's snort of disgust.

"I want you to say she was found on the sidewalk," Ian concluded. "She is well-bred and I do not want her compromised. You will be well compensated, naturally."

Dr. Sampson nodded and patted his black medical bag. "Just the thing. Now I shall see to the little patient, and then we may get her home to her worried parents."

Ian paced the hallway, hoping Angelica's ankle wasn't broken and that her foolish stunt wouldn't get her into too much trouble. As his jaw clenched, he was disturbed about how much he cared, especially with the new concern that she'd reveal his secret. He frowned. Surely she couldn't be so foolish. And if she was, what would he do then? He couldn't kill her, and he sure as hell couldn't Change her.

An hour later, the doctor brought Angelica to the foyer, half carrying her. "Hellloooo again, Your Grace," she slurred with a silly smile on her lush lips.

"The young lady's ankle is not broken," Dr. Sampson announced briskly. "But it is badly sprained. I've given her a dose of laudanum, and I will instruct her parents that she must stay off her feet for at least a week. She may have use of a crutch by tomorrow, God willing." He inclined his head in gratitude as Ian handed him a banknote. "I will take her to the carriage now."

"Good-bye, Miss Winthrop." Ian kissed the back of her hand.

"I shall miss you, Your Grace," Angelica giggled, swaying from the effects of the laudanum. "Even though you bit me."

The doctor raised a brow, and Ian shrugged his shoulders as if he had no idea what she meant.

He watched as she was loaded into the waiting carriage. *I think I will miss you too, Angel.* Perhaps he would steal a dance when she was healed.

❧

Albert, Burnrath's coachman, was able to hold his silence for nearly twenty-four hours. But the news that a young lady of the Quality had been carried out of the duke's house dressed like a boy and with a sprained ankle was too juicy a tidbit to hold in. Especially since the duke himself had been partially undressed. Albert told his current ladylove, who was the Cavendish's parlor maid, while walking with her in the park on her day off.

The maid told Lady Cavendish at her first opportunity. The countess often shared her chocolate bonbons when presented with titillating news. By the next evening, the *ton* was speculating on just who the young lady was. When callers were turned away from the Winthrop house due to Angelica being abed with a sprained ankle, gossip raged through the nobility like wildfire. Since the last news one usually heard was about oneself, the Winthrops and their household were blissfully unaware of their slaughtered reputations.

Seven

ANGELICA HUMMED A MERRY TUNE AS SHE WROTE "THE End" at the bottom of the last page of her story, "The Haunting of Rathton Manor." When Liza returned, she would have her deliver the manuscript to Colburn and return with her twelve pounds. "The Ghost of the Highwayman" had already been published and had received excellent reviews to her delight and her father's pride. Her mother, for once, had kept her lips pursed in silence, only muttering her disapproval in the background. Now that she'd confessed her writing success to her parents, Angelica had renewed her hope that she could convince her father to let her use her dowry for her writing career instead of marriage.

For the tenth time this afternoon, she peered out her window at Burnrath House. The mansion loomed behind the budding hawthorn trees in silent vigilance, guarding a vampire during his day rest... a vampire who had drunk her blood then apologized for it... a vampire who had nearly kissed her and probably would have apologized for that as well. Instead of a horrid monster who slaughtered innocents, he had been a gentleman who'd summoned a doctor, seen that her injuries were treated, and sent her safely home.

Angelica smiled as she thought back to that night, five days ago, when the doctor had helped her out of the carriage and into the arms of her frantic parents. The look on her mother's face as she took in Angelica's masculine attire had been so comical that her face had burned with the effort of suppressing the giggles. She had dozed on and off as she was hauled into the house, muzzy-headed from the medicine the doctor forced down her throat and only half hearing her mother's tirade.

Papa had looked so frightened and concerned that she had longed to tell him some good news. On a flight of inspiration, she had informed them about the publication of her first story as if the happy event had occurred that very day.

"You will be a published author?" Papa's eyes had lit up once they were settled in the drawing room. "Well done, my dearest!"

"Do not encourage her!" Margaret shrieked, doubtless on the verge of hysterics. "If anyone knows she penned that story, she will be ruined beyond all hope."

Angelica's head had nodded back and forth in slow motion. It seemed that she could see everything in double. She feared she would fall out of her chair. She gripped the sides of her seat in a futile effort to stop the swaying.

Dr. Sampson must have noticed, for he'd interrupted the discussion. "The young lady has had a very trying day. I have given her a healthy dose of laudanum and I recommend that she be put to bed immediately. I will check on her tomorrow and bring a crutch with me."

The following days were paradise for Angelica. She spent nearly the entire time writing, with no Almack's, no balls, no callers, no suitors, and no lectures from Margaret to take her away from her muse. When she wasn't writing, she enjoyed meals in bed and reading her favorite novels, taking every available opportunity to look out the window at the Burnrath mansion and daydream about her encounter with the vampire. Over and over she replayed her adventure with him in her mind, relishing the tingle that ran up her spine with each remembered detail.

Angelica shook her head and fought to remain practical. She would miss having the duke as a neighbor when she moved to a modest flat and embarked on her career. Perhaps she could call on him sometime when her career was more established. Then maybe she could ask him about vampires… and maybe he would kiss her! She frowned. *Practical*, she must be practical. And yet her belly fluttered as she imagined his lips on hers… and the sight of his bare chest beneath his unbuttoned shirt.

To be truthful, her ankle had felt fine since the day before. She merely wanted more time to finish her story and enjoy her peace away from the social whirlwind.

Only moments after Liza departed with her letter and manuscript, Margaret marched into Angelica's bedchamber with Dr. Sampson. It was time for another examination. Unfortunately, this time he pronounced her healed. Angelica bit back an unladylike curse.

"Then we may go to the Cavendish ball tonight?" Mother asked him, wringing her hands.

"Just so long as she limits her dancing," he said, closing his medical bag.

Margaret beamed. Angelica groaned.

⁓

John Polidori awoke to the sound of a soft soprano singing a haunting melody. A blissful sigh escaped his lips when he felt the soothing sensation of a cold cloth bathing his forehead. He opened his eyes, and his blurred vision took in the sight of the figure before him. The cropped hair and masculine attire led him at first to believe that he was being tended by a young man. But the lilting voice and smooth luminous skin gave him pause. Was he being nursed by one of the famed *castrati* singers of his home country? The notion was dashed as he felt a pair of soft breasts pressing against his shoulder.

"John, you are awake." Her voice was cultured and gentle as an angel's.

"Where am I?" he croaked, forcing his heavy eyes to focus. "How long have I been asleep?"

She handed him a cup of water and he drank greedily. "I found you unconscious in the alley behind your usual club three nights ago." Her full lips pouted as she ran a gentle hand through his hair. "I brought you to my home and have been caring for you since. I think you were sick from drink."

He could see her clearly now. He knew this woman. How could he ever have mistaken her for a male? And how could he have forgotten her lovely voice? Her exquisite face had stayed in his memory for all time. Lord Byron and his friends had mocked him when he spent weeks searching the Swiss countryside for her. But if Byron had seen her, he would have stilled his wagging tongue.

The rich fabric of her waistcoat and cravat looked coarse against the silken glow of her face and hands. Her dark eyes were as large as a doe's, fringed with lashes impossibly long and thick and framed with thin black brows. The lady's fine-boned face was as delicate as porcelain, with ruby lips that made him groan with desire for a taste. John reached up and touched them with his finger to make sure she was real.

Excitement warred with dizziness. "It *is* you! Rosetta, my darling, what are you doing in England? I searched for you for months after we met. I set your leg. Do you remember?"

She nodded, smiling. "I will never forget your kindness. My heart is filled with joy that you remember me."

"But how did you find me?" he asked, frowning as he took in his surroundings. "And why is this chamber without windows?"

She ran a hand through his curls. "First you must eat while I heat water for your bath. I've brought you clean clothing. When you are comfortable, I will tell all."

Once he was clean and his hunger was sated, John was afraid he'd have to fight the drowsy languor. But when Rosetta opened her mouth to reveal pearly white fangs as she told her story, he was stunned. Despite the fantastical creations that spilled from his pen, he was a realist. A physician and scientist had no room for fantasy in his beliefs. He never imagined that the creatures of myth that fired his imagination and populated his stories could possibly be real.

But another thing stirred him more than her amazing story. Rosetta loved him. The fact was clear with every word she spoke, and the way her eyes glowed with adoration whenever they rested upon him. The revelation struck a chord within him that he'd long since tried to kill. Though he had often loved, no one had ever truly loved him in return. Oh, George Gordon, Lord Byron, had claimed to, but it wasn't until John's heart was lost to the poet that he learned that Byron loved a new person every week.

Indeed, Lord Byron had been the man he sought to represent as the vampire, Lord Ruthven, *not* the Duke of Burnrath, who apparently was the Vampire Lord of London! The situation would be quite ridiculous if his life were not in such grave danger.

He stood up and walked across the carpeted floor toward Rosetta. Ah, his beautiful savior Rosetta! Already, he was losing his heart to her dark passion more than he had to her tender beauty four years ago. "I see that my thanks are necessary."

"Not at all, John, I would save you all over again if I had to." Those delicate cheeks pinkened once more as he drew near. "Besides, it was my fault that you published that story. If I had not whispered my encouragement to you every night, your life would not be at risk."

"Still, you have put your life in danger to save mine," he whispered, caressing her hair. "'No poet's dream e'er show'd a form so fair; no heav'nly gleam of prophet's fire could paint e'en Virtue's grace with hues so chaste, though bright, as deck'd her face.' I wrote that about you after we met."

Rosetta's lips parted in awe. "You did? That poem is one of my favorites."

He leaned closer to her. "Rosetta, I offer you my blood, my body, my life."

His mouth slanted across hers as passion consumed them. The candles flickered as they collapsed onto the bed.

After the most passionate bout of lovemaking either had ever experienced, the pair lay entwined in each other's arms, still panting for breath as they talked. Sometimes their laughter mingled like a beautiful dream as they discovered things they had in common. Other times they fell into a blissful silence as their gazes locked, overcome with emotions too potent for words. They spoke of everything from vampires to poetry to medicine. They spoke of anything but the danger they were in.

Tonight was not for fearful thoughts. Tonight was for the rosy glow and vivid light of new love. For each had found the other half of their souls.

❧

Ian stared in disbelief at the latest entry in White's betting book. "The bet paid off?"

The duke of Wentworth nodded. "Well, of course the bet paid off. Lady Cavendish heard it from her maid who heard it from *your* coachman. Everyone knows you've had her." He toyed with his quizzing glass, eyes narrowed against the smoke saturating the club.

Ian shook his head as Wentworth narrated the week's gossip. His fists clenched in desire to strangle the coachman. Albert would be dismissed at the earliest opportunity.

"Of course, I must say I don't at all approve, Burnrath," Wentworth continued, oblivious to Ian's rage as they returned to their table. "The girl and her family will not be able to show their faces in society again after tonight. Speaking of, I must depart for the Cavendish ball."

"Why tonight?" Ian snapped, resisting the urge to bare his fangs. "Did I not 'have' her last week?"

His friend sighed and leaned back in his chair. "Well, the girl was safely ensconced in her home with an injured ankle, so nobody has had the chance to cut her yet. You know how traditionally vicious we are. It must be made official, tonight, as I understand the Winthrops will be attending the ball. Lady Cavendish will reserve first right, I suppose."

More than ever, Ian was sickened at the cruelty the *ton* seemed to thrive on. All of his predatory instincts raged at him to fly to Cavendish House and turn the ball into a massacre. He fought to keep his voice level. "I do not suppose anyone would believe I didn't touch her?"

Wentworth shook his head and sipped his glass of aged bourbon. "Not for a moment. The gossip even says you were partially undressed. Are you saying you didn't bed her?"

"I was barefoot, not undressed." Ian paused as the

severity of the matter became clear. "And no, I did *not* bed her." Guilt and self-loathing sucked at his soul. *Damn it.* Because of him, the poor girl's life was ruined.

Before, all he had to worry about was whether Angelica would reveal his secret to her peers. Now, she would have none. His hands clenched the felt-covered table until he heard the wood squeal in protest. Then again, she may yet be able to open her mouth to someone. There must be a way to silence her and also repair the damage he'd done.

A mad notion whispered in the back of his head. The more he thought about it, the more attractive the idea became. If the plan proved successful, not only could he ensure that Angelica kept her mouth shut, but she would be welcomed back into society and pampered more than ever. And, hopefully, the rest of the speculations about his nocturnal proclivities should cease as well.

Ian smiled as he handed Wentworth the quill and gestured to the betting book. "You are about to make a tidy profit, my friend."

"Why is that?" His friend blinked in confusion at the abrupt change in mood.

"I *will* bed the Winthrop heiress," Ian said with a wry grin. "However, it shall be *after* I wed her."

Eight

THE MOMENT THE WINTHROPS WERE ANNOUNCED BY the Cavendish butler, Angelica knew something was wrong. The throng abruptly fell silent as the Winthrops took their place in the receiving line. Icy stares and amused glances pelted her and her parents before the ballroom erupted in whispers and mocking laughter. When her mother led them to greet the hostess, Lady Cavendish cut her dead.

"Surely she cannot still be upset that I won her ruby earrings last month," Margaret whispered. Her cheeks flamed scarlet. "It's not my fault that she is a dreadful whist player!"

As they made their way to the refreshment table, Baron Osgoode approached them and retracted his offer of marriage.

"I am certain you understand," he said, favoring her with a stiff, mocking bow.

"Though I am happy to be relieved of your suit, I do *not* understand," Angelica replied, voice laden with deliberate scorn at his rudeness.

Osgoode swept her with a scathing glare. "Come

off the act, little miss. Everyone knows what happened between you and the Duke of Burnrath."

"Do you mean to tell me," her mother's voice quavered in indignation, "that you are refusing her simply because she danced with His Grace at the Wentworth ball?"

Osgoode sneered. "So, she lied to you as well. I assure you, madam, that she has done more than *dance* with him." With another mocking bow, he left to lead a blonde beauty onto the dance floor. He whispered in her ear, and they both glanced at the Winthrops and smirked.

"Explain yourself immediately!" Margaret hissed.

Angelica swallowed. Suddenly the glitter of the chandeliers and the bejeweled nobles around her was overwhelming to the point of nausea. "When I sprained my ankle, the duke found me, not the coachman. His Grace sent his coachman for the doctor. He did not touch me other than to carry me to his couch and check for broken bones." She did not dare confess that he also drank her blood... and nearly kissed her.

"You mean to tell me that you were inside his home with him *alone*?" her mother panted, appearing to be close to an attack of the vapors. "Do you know what you've done? We're *ruined*! No man will have you now, and my father will cut us off from every shilling of my inheritance!"

Ruined. It had finally happened. She was free. She opened her mouth to say, I told you I did not wish to wed, but the sight of her mother's pallor and the heartbroken look on her father's face gave her pause. In that moment, she knew that not only did her parents love each other, but they also *both* loved her and honestly believed a marriage would be best for her. Her belly knotted with something that felt suspiciously like guilt. *I never wanted to hurt them.* As if her intentions would make everything well again.

"We had better leave," Margaret said, practically tugging Angelica's father along. The richly garbed crowd of spectators resembled a malevolent rainbow sea.

"The Duke and Duchess of Wentworth!" The Cavendish butler pounded his cane as he announced the latest arrivals.

Her mother paled further and Angelica winced at the realization that more of their friends were arriving to hear of her family's disgrace. The duke and duchess greeted their hostess and then approached the Winthrops with friendly smiles.

"They must not have heard yet," Papa muttered, staring at the polished floor.

"That makes this disaster all the more humiliating!" Mother wailed, clinging to his arm.

I will atone for this somehow, Angelica vowed. *I shall stay with them and give them the money I earn from my stories. Perhaps I will even write romantic novels if I have to. I hear they turn a higher profit. Somehow, I will earn their forgiveness.* Yet, despite her remorse, she couldn't help but feel liberated from this false society and its perverse way of auctioning women off to the highest bidder.

"The Duke of Burnrath!" the butler boomed. The thud of the cane now sounded more like a judge's gavel.

"Oh my Lord, I think I'm going to faint," her

mother gasped, swaying on her feet. The Duchess of
Wentworth hurried to her side. The duke grinned at
her father as if everything was playing out to a satisfactory conclusion. Angelica wondered if perhaps the
man was cracked.

Angelica steadied her mother and craned her neck
to see the vampire stroll in, impeccable in his evening
finery. Her heart thudded in her chest at the sight
of his beautiful but dangerous visage. Unbidden, her
hand went up to her neck, which tingled in remem-
brance of his bite.

The whispers echoed through the ballroom like
sinister wings of bats.

"That blackguard!" her father growled. His narrow
frame shook with fury. "I am going to call him out."

"Jacob, *please!*" her mother pleaded, her face
was as white as Angelica's ball gown. "Do not do
such a thing. You will only throw more fire on this
dreadful scandal!"

"Why not? All is lost anyway. I intend to give them
something else to talk about. It is my duty to demand
satisfaction and defend my daughter's honor." He
squeezed Angelica's hand and approached the duke,
likely to the Quality's everlasting amusement.

Angelica clutched her mother's arm with numb
fingers, silently praying. *Please, do not let him hurt my
papa.* The Wentworths remained silent. Perhaps they
had heard the gossip after all. If so, she owed them her
eternal gratitude for their kindness.

A crowd gathered around and drowned out her
father's angry tirade with excited murmurs. To the
disappointment of their audience, the two men went

out the doors side by side, their backs straight as pikestaffs. Their figures were barely visible under the meager light of the lanterns strung over the lawn.

"Surely they do not intend to duel *here*?" Lady Cavendish put a shaky hand to her throat at such a momentous breach of propriety. However, Angelica swore she could see a glint of excitement in her eyes.

"Of course not, my lady," the Duke of Wentworth drawled. "Rapiers and pistols were not part of the recommended dress, after all. The worst they can do is engage in fisticuffs."

Lady Cavendish shrieked at a passing servant to fetch her some hartshorn.

"Oh, I wish I could see what is happening." Margaret's voice was shrill with panic.

"It would take a shipman's winch to lift the crowd out of the way," Angelica replied drily, trying to hide her panic.

The Duchess of Wentworth chuckled as she fanned Margaret. "I admire a woman whose wit can hold up to any situation."

In a surprisingly short time, her father and the duke returned. Burnrath possessed a satisfied expression, while Angelica's father appeared stunned. *What had happened outside?*

"Dear God, he's coming this way," her mother gasped, retrieving her own fan. "Hasn't he done enough damage?"

The crowd parted like the Red Sea as the Duke of Burnrath approached her. His gaze locked on Angelica while his lips curved in an enigmatic smile. Her chin lifted in attempt to deny her weak knees.

The whole world seemed to hold its breath as he bent to one knee and placed a hand over his heart.

Angelica frowned as her mind swam in confusion. *What in the blazes is he doing? Surely he doesn't think an apology will repair matters in the slightest.*

"Miss Winthrop," the vampire began, holding her motionless with his compelling husky voice. "Ever since I first saw you, I have been enchanted. And when I found you injured outside in front of my house and had the opportunity to speak with you, my heart was touched. I have not been able to rid you from my thoughts since. Would you please do me the honor of becoming my wife?"

The gasps from all around hurt Angelica's ears as they nearly shook the large chamber. Her stays became a cruel vise, forbidding the slightest breath of air into her lungs. The blood roared in her ears. Black and white spots danced in her vision.

"Of course she will," Margaret announced cheerfully, then immediately fainted into Papa's arms. The Duchess of Wentworth rummaged in her reticule for smelling salts. Lady Cavendish elbowed her way through the masses for a better look.

"But… you are a vampire," Angelica blurted out. *Good God, is this truly happening?*

Titters and guffaws broke out. "Surely you do not believe that nonsense, my dear," the Duke of Wentworth said, his brow creasing with worry.

Angelica blushed as she realized she'd spoken aloud. Burnrath laughed, but there was a warning glint in his eye.

"I was only jesting, Your Grace," she said faintly

and reached out to help him to his feet. He took her hand and pressed his lips to her knuckles.

"I believe I have further things to discuss with your father," he said softly. "Please save a dance for me upon my return."

The Duke of Burnrath bowed and left her. Immediately Angelica was swarmed by an array of ladies, all congratulating her as if they had not given her the cut direct only minutes ago. *This cannot be happening!* A silent scream caught in her throat as the situation finally dawned on her. *I was ruined, then in the blink of an eye I have become the toast of the beau monde. All because a vampire wants to marry me!* Everyone thought her tears and laughter were from joy. No one had the slightest idea that she was dangerously close to hysterics.

As the women cooed at her and exclaimed over the duke's proposal, all Angelica could think was: *I did not say "Yes."*

❧

Ian carefully pulled away from Lady Margaret's grasping hands again. If he didn't know any better, he'd think the overbearing woman was on the verge of kissing his feet in gratitude. Smoothing things over with Angelica's father had been a simple matter, for wealth and a lofty title could accomplish practically anything in these greedy, corrupt times. Mr. Winthrop had agreed that Ian would call upon the Winthrops the following evening to hammer out the betrothal contract and set a date for the wedding.

"If I may be so bold, Your Grace," Jacob Winthrop

began, wiping the sweat from his brow. "I would feel much more secure if the nuptials were performed as soon as possible. My daughter is rather… er, spirited… and I believe there could be risk of her, ah… proclivities leading her into further danger without a firmer hand than mine taking the reins at the earliest convenience." He held up his hands defensively. "It is not that I am a weak man, but Angelica is my only child, you see, and I fear I have indulged her shamelessly."

Ian chuckled. Many a suitor would not want to wed a girl after hearing such talk, but he wasn't such a man. Especially since an early wedding suited his plans just fine. "If I could have her as my bride tonight, Mr. Winthrop, I would."

Angelica's father nearly choked on his brandy, a horrified look warping his strong features. "Good God, man. I did not mean *that* soon! Even if we could procure a special license at this hour, it would not at all be the thing. Imagine what people would say!"

"I was only jesting, Mr. Winthrop." Ian was quickly tiring of the conversation. All he wanted was to feel his Angelica in his arms once more. "Now, shall we return to the ladies? I believe I owe the lovely Miss Winthrop a dance." Without waiting for a reply, he set down his untouched glass and headed out of the room without a backward glance.

Ian's heart clenched when the crowd surrounding his intended bride moved enough for him to see her face. She looked pale as death and her cheeks were streaked with tears. *Poor little Angel, she has been through a lot this night.*

Her hand felt icy as he wrapped his fingers around

hers and led her to the center of the ballroom as the musicians struck up a waltz. He almost lost his step as he saw the seething fury burning in her gypsy eyes.

"Pray tell me, whatever is the matter, my dear? But please smile so as not to incite the gossip mill again," Ian said pleasantly, as if they were exchanging small talk.

Her teeth clenched in a hideous parody of a grin and she hissed, "Why are you doing this? You can't possibly need my dowry, and I am certain as bloody hell that you do not love me."

In truth, he hadn't completely expected Angelica to fly into his arms and squeal in joy at his suit, but her degree of hostility came as an unpleasant surprise. "Such language is quite unseemly, Angel." He smiled down at her but tightened his grip on her hand. "Though I do admire that you are astute enough to know I have plenty of wealth in my own right, surely you were raised to expect that love is hardly a necessary ingredient to a successful marriage."

Angelica's laughter mocked him. "I am breathless with your flattery. Pray continue."

Ian was torn between amusement at her daring and anger because she was forcing him to muddle through this awkward explanation. She should be more grateful than her mother had been for saving her and her family from social death. Leaning down as if to smell her perfume, he lowered his voice.

"Spare me from your wrath, Angel. Since you insist upon knowing, I will tell you that your reputation was not the only one in danger. Thanks to that upstart, John Polidori, and his story taking the Continent by storm, people have become suspicious of me."

"Ah, the rumors that you are a vampire," she replied with a smirk. "Surely you do not believe anyone took them seriously. You heard their laughter earlier."

Ian suppressed a growl and whispered against her ear. "Enough have taken it seriously. In fact, due to a substantial wager that I am indeed a vampire, my silk waistcoat and neckcloth were soaked with holy water last week by none other than your former suitor, Baron Osgoode."

Her skin was like satin against his lips. Her scent was heady and overwhelmed him with the temptation to taste her once more. Ian drew back before he gave in to temptation and plunged his fangs into her right then and there.

Heedless to her danger, Angelica smiled, her lips twitching with mirth over the incident with Osgoode. Ian didn't know whether to kiss her or take her over his knee for such impudence. The couples surrounding them had given up all pretense of dancing and were watching them with avid interest. He fixed them with an icy stare and they backed slowly away.

"It was *not* in the least amusing, I assure you." Ian gave her a stern frown. "I had to call him out to prevent other foolish young bucks from daring the same and ruining my wardrobe."

This time, Angelica could not restrain her humor, and her musical laughter trilled through the ballroom. Ian fought back his own laughter. Perhaps the situation *was* a bit comical. "Enough, imp, do you want to hear why I seek your troublesome hand, or not?" His arms gripped her tighter, savoring the feel of her warm flesh despite his ire.

She sobered immediately, her chin lifting back to its previous angle to display her scorn. "Very well, I shall listen *most* attentively."

Ian felt a twinge of regret for destroying the light mood, temporary though it was.

He sighed and bent to whisper in her ear. "I decided that if I married within the peerage, the gossip would weaken and gradually cease." Her tantalizing scent spurred his hunger even further and he fought to regain his composure. "After all, no lady would marry a monster. And if I treat my bride well enough, perhaps she will vouch for my good character as well. Since you did not seem to be afraid of me, and I quite like you, I concluded, why not save your reputation as well?"

Instead of placating her as he had hoped, Ian's explanation brought Angelica's temper to a boil. Her eyes seemed to shoot onyx sparks. "Your *magnanimity* quite overwhelms me, Your Grace. But surely you realize that when you made your offer, I did not accept?"

He'd had enough of her ingratitude and vituperative tongue… and her intoxicating scent. It was well past time for him to feed.

"I will call upon you tomorrow evening to sort out the details of our engagement. I pray I find you in a better humor then." Before the music ended, he promised in a low voice, "You will be more than willing to accept soon enough."

As Ian prowled the streets of London in search of his next meal, he struggled to find a reason for her unseemly behavior. After feeding on a pickpocket, he lit on an idea. Could the cause for her hostility be that she was now frightened of him? She wasn't before, but now that she had time to think about what he was… *Of course! She wasn't afraid before because she had a safe home to go to. But the thought that she would now spend her life under the same roof as a vampire would terrify any sensible person.* Another uncomfortable thought crept up on him. *My God, what if she thinks I intend to kill her?*

Remembering her fearlessness in their last two encounters, Ian was determined to charm her back to that state long before their wedding night.

Nine

BEN FLANNIGAN BREATHED IN THE THICK, FETID London air as he stepped off the gangplank and onto the dock. A city this size would be teeming with vampires, which practically guaranteed that he would have a great many kills here. Perhaps he would even take down an ancient. His breath caught in anticipation at the compelling thought.

He caressed his silver crucifix as he walked down the street, searching for an affordable but decent inn while glancing back over his shoulder to see if he was followed. He had so many kills to his name that the evil creatures would soon seek to discover his identity.

Ben expressed his relief with a whispered prayer as he immediately discovered an inn that appeared to suit his requirements. He ordered a room and a meal before adding a handsome sum in exchange for every newspaper that could be found. Ben had long since established a routine of checking the death notices for strange circumstances and the gossip pages for nobles with odd habits before approaching the locals for information. In his experience, dedicated research always paid off.

While he waited for his meal and the papers, he composed a brief advertisement. In the morning he would make his rounds to the offices of every likely publication and pay to have the notice printed at once.

A man of God is seeking a situation to exterminate nocturnal vermin. The fee is fifty pounds, half of which will be due in advance.

He checked the notice for errors and grunted in satisfaction when he found none. The advertisement was vague enough to discourage those with rat or badger problems, yet contained just the right information for those who truly understood the threat that loomed over mankind. And if some individuals mistook his use of the term "man of God" to believe that he was a priest or a vicar? Well, he didn't mind in the slightest. He had been meant to be one, though the fools at St. Damian's had failed to see that.

As the second son of an impoverished baron, Ben had had the church as his only hope of a career that would keep his belly full. For the sake of having one less mouth to feed, his father had him sent off to St. Damian's priory school in Kilkenny every autumn after the harvest was in.

Learning to read and write had captivated him at first, but before long he began to crave something more. He admired the great power of the bishop. The man could bless anything he desired, pardon sins, sentence people to penance, even condemn someone to hell if he so chose. Ben longed for such power. He dedicated himself twice as hard to his lessons and soon became the shining star of the class. The prize neared his hand.

As he grew to adulthood, his responsibilities and authority rose. And as his power accumulated, so did his pride. Indeed, Ben was told that it was one of the many sins that barred him from consideration for the priesthood, although that vice wasn't the main problem.

Ben's strictness, verging on bullying, with the young novices wasn't what caused the bishop to summon him to his quarters. Nor was it the incident in which he beat a beggar nearly to death after he caught the thief stealing bread meant for the Holy Sacrament. It wasn't his fault that he forgot his own strength in the face of his pious rage at such blasphemy.

No, the final incident that had caused him to be called to the carpet and chastised like a recalcitrant schoolboy was so paltry that the memory still made Ben gnash his teeth. Someone had tattled to Bishop O'Shay that Ben had been seen pinching Sister Clarence's bum. Bishop O'Shay believed lust was the worst of all sins and he was determined to stamp it out of his flock.

"But surely the nun should be the one to be punished," Ben protested. "She'd been wriggling her charms at me like a ripe piece of fruit. A man can only take so much temptation."

The bishop's bushy brows drew together sternly, almost obscuring his eyes. "So Adam spoke of Eve and thus Man was banished from Paradise. I will not have a clergyman who is unchaste." He advanced upon Flannigan like Moses calling God's wrath down upon the Pharaoh. "Tomorrow you will pack your belongings and leave. Your time here with us is finished."

"But can I not repent?" Ben asked, unable to believe the sentence heaved upon him.

"I think not," Bishop O'Shay replied with a regretful sigh. "If your sinful lust were not enough, your other sins are more than sufficient to give credence to the wisdom of my decision. You have no mercy or compassion within your spirit. You are too quick to anger and filled with far too much pride. You had years to repent and turn to the path of righteousness, but you did not. Such a man is not suitable for the priesthood."

By the time Ben had packed his meager belongings and left his room, word of his dismissal had spread throughout the entire priory. A classmate's smug grin was too much for Ben's frayed temper, and his fist connected with the lad's face with a crack that echoed through the cloisters. A faint twinge of pleasure filled him at the sight of the blood gushing from the boy's nose. No more smug stares were upon him as all hurriedly turned their faces away.

His good feelings dissipated the moment his feet began to trod the long path home. What was he to tell his father? How long would he be welcome at the small estate? His older brother was due to marry this year, and soon the land would be signed over to him. Where would he go then? Ben's heart grew heavier with despair every step he took.

"I heard what happened, lad," a voice called, penetrating his gloomy thoughts.

Donald O'Flannery walked beside him, and the

understanding and sympathy in his eyes made Ben stop short. Donald was not a church member as far as he knew, but he was a frequent visitor to the priory and the school. No one was really certain of the purpose of the man's visits. He appeared to run errands for another church because Ben had once seen him leave with jugs of holy water, rosary beads, and a crucifix.

"What do you want?" Ben asked, unable to keep the petulance out of his voice.

"Dinna be ashamed, my son," Donald had said. "For the Lord in his infinite wisdom and mercy has a calling for such as yerself. There be many hidden evils in the world and 'tis the job of folk like ourselves to eradicate 'em. I see the makings of a fine hunter in ye."

"A hunter?" He wondered if perhaps Donald was mad, but still the man's use of the word "calling" intrigued him, invoking a faint thrill of hope.

O'Flannery nodded and loaded his pipe. "If ye'll join me for supper an' a pint or two of fine ale at the inn down the road, I'll explain all."

Ben shoved his hands in his pockets. "That depends. Though my vow of poverty has ended, my funds have not improved."

Donald chuckled. "It will be my coin this time. And if you remain with me, poverty will be a distant memory before long."

After the first pint, Ben was wiping tears of laughter from his eyes. "I appreciate the drink, but this heap of blarney is a wee bit too much. Vampires indeed!"

With a strange smile on his face, O'Flannery raised a brow at him and ordered their glasses refilled. "Vampires," he continued as if he hadn't been interrupted, "are masters of deception. They have remained hidden for centuries by pretending to be human…"

By the time they were finishing the third pint, Ben was torn between admiration for Donald's ability to spin such a great yarn… and the slight kernel of belief that was sprouting in his breast. The idea that such monsters could exist right under the noses of civilization was horrifying, and yet the thought of becoming the hero who dispatched them was undeniably seductive.

"Do you have proof that these creatures exist?" he whispered, after the barkeep was out of hearing range.

Donald's smile was a predatory grimace. "Meet me at the old St. Thomas cemetery at dawn tomorrow."

The next morning, Ben felt silly as he greeted O'Flannery in the moldering old graveyard. He wished he'd stayed in bed until his headache abated.

"Now, I've been leaving this one alone because it hasn't been bothering anyone," Donald said as he opened the rusty gates. "Not only that," he added with a wry grin as he chewed on his pipe. "There's no profit in this job. But for the sake of your education, I suppose I'll have to deal with the creature."

He led Ben to an ancient crypt covered with ivy and removed a pry bar from his pack.

"Is there really a vampire in there?" Ben asked, still unable to believe that he was here participating in this foolishness.

O'Flannery ignored him and set to work on opening the tomb.

Ben's pulse raced as he followed Donald into the

crypt. Spiders and other vile creatures fled from the morning light. A pile of bones lay in a shadowed corner. The stone slab they had rested on was now occupied by a fresh corpse... or was it? Ben gasped as he saw its chest rise and fall softly. The thing was alive.

With speed and strength that seemed almost godlike, Donald pounded a stake through the thing's breast with a heavy mallet and then cleaved the head from its body with one powerful strike of his ax.

Ben recoiled when Donald picked up the head and thrust it at him. "Take this while I drag the body outside."

His gorge rose, but he suppressed it and followed O'Flannery back out into the daylight. Donald chuckled at Ben's cry of surprise when the corpse began to turn red and smolder.

"Drop the head here," he ordered as he pulled a jug from his pack, uncapped it, and circled the remains while pouring out the holy water.

"Amazing," Ben whispered as he watched the flames engulf the vampire's head and body. "Will you teach me?"

Now here he was in London, having surpassed Donald's legacy long ago. And best of all, there were no vows of poverty, chastity, or *obedience*. Ben Flannigan was his own man, beholden to no one... and the money wasn't very meager either.

His meal arrived and Ben lifted his glass of ale in his customary toast to the memory of his teacher. Donald had gotten clumsy in his old age. He didn't strike quickly enough before the last vampire awoke and flung the hunter against the wall, shattering his spine and killing him instantly.

Ben had barely gotten out of the cave alive. The creature had been so enraged that it had lunged out of the opening and into the sunlight, grasping Ben's collar. Only when the monster's face and arm caught fire did it release him.

Ben shuddered at the memory, which still gave him nightmares. He'd never been to Spain since. Just as he was sopping up the last of the gravy from his plate with a crusty roll, a young lad arrived at his elbow, looking ready to topple from the weighty stack of newspapers he held. Ben took the papers and tousled the scamp's hair, then gave him a coin. "That's a good lad."

He carried the papers and his pack up to his room, the excitement of the hunt rising to a glorious tenor.

By the light of as many candles as he could spare, the hunter read every gossip article in *The Times*, *The Tattler*, and *The Morning Chronicle*. He started on the oldest issues first and worked his way forward. Most of it was inane nonsense, such as who was wearing what, whose ball was deemed a success, what courses were served at this party or that, ad nauseam. But one name stood out in all this drivel, rendering his headache and strained eyes worth the endeavor: Ian Ashton, the Duke of Burnrath.

The gentleman fit the profile of a hidden vampire to complete perfection. He came and went unpredictably, traveled far more than the usual nobleman, and all of his so-called "ancestors" were so similar that they may as well have been the same individual.

Ben chuckled in reluctant admiration at the

"tradition" for all dukes of Burnrath to marry foreign brides and live abroad until their heirs returned to the family seat. It was a perfect deception.

Now the duke's disguise seemed to be on the verge of crumbling. Due to the recent popularity of vampire tales, Lord Burnrath's oddities were beginning to receive closer scrutiny. If Ben were to catch this prey, he would have to act fast, before the London gossips frightened the quarry away. He licked his lips in satisfaction. The hunt was on.

Scallywag John's was a deplorable hovel. The antithesis of its aristocratic counterpart, Gentleman Jack's, the tavern turned boxing club was a haven for the working class. Old barrels functioned as stools around a splintery slab of wood that served as the bar. A few shoddily crafted tables occupied dark corners, but most of the place was standing room only on the filthy sawdust-covered floor.

Ian's nose wrinkled against the miasma of sweat, stale beer, and dried blood as he pushed his way through the mass of shouting bodies. At last, the ring came into view. The structure was little more than a square of frayed rope strung through old dock pilings. The rickety craftsmanship didn't matter, for men did not come here for luxury. They came to see the fighters. Ian was here for one in particular.

"And now for the fight ye've been roaring for." A small, rat-faced man stood on a crate and shouted over the din. "The Ox is the challenger!"

A gargantuan mass of a man lumbered into the ring, holding his scarred fists up to the cheers of the audience.

The announcer waited for the noise to abate slightly before declaring, "His opponent is our own champion, the Spaniard!"

Ian grinned as his second in command, Rafael Villar, strode into the ring. The crowd cheered so loudly that the building trembled, but Rafe ignored them. His amber eyes were only for his adversary. The Spaniard did not need to hold up his fists to flaunt his scars. One side of his face and the majority of his left arm were covered with puckered, ugly flesh. They were burn scars from the sun, but Ian knew little else, except for the fact that the damage was so severe that Rafe's left arm was nearly useless.

A bell clanged, signaling the beginning of the fight. The Ox clenched his ham-like fists and stomped toward his opponent. Rafe watched him with bored detachment as he reared back to land a sound blow. Rafe shrugged away nonchalantly. The Ox snarled in irritation and charged forward with renewed determination. Ian smiled. The poor sod had no chance.

The Spaniard was truly a wonder to behold. He moved with feral grace and a quickness that had the spectators gasping. Ian was also impressed, but not with Rafe's speed, for he was actually slowing himself down. His control in holding back his true preternatural abilities defied belief. Even with one functioning arm, the vampire could crush a man before he could make a fist.

Rafe's current opponent, however, was as unaware of this as all his predecessors had been. With an arrogant smirk, he shot his fist up in an uppercut at Rafe's seemingly vulnerable left side.

To Ian's view, Rafe's right arm moved lazily to block the punch. Then, with equal ennui, he tapped his fist to the man's chin, dropping him like a mail sack.

The crowd roared as their unique champion was once more declared the victor.

Rafe's gaze met Ian's, and with a slight nod, he quit the ring. Ignoring congratulatory shouts and thumps on the back, he made his way straight to Ian and bowed with a flourish.

"Your Grace, would you care to join me in the ring?" Rafe's lips curved in a strange sneer that was the closest thing to a smile he had ever been known to manage.

Ian sighed as everyone in the club doffed their caps and bowed. He preferred to remain anonymous in this part of town. From the gleam of Rafe's amber eyes, the rogue knew it.

Grinning back at his second, he bowed. "Thank you, no. I fear you'd trounce me. Instead, may I persuade you to join me for a stroll?"

Rafe inclined his head in agreement as several banknotes were thrust in his hand by the proprietor. Both vampires knew he could not refuse the Lord of London. Still, worry creased the Spaniard's brow, and though Ian wanted to reassure him nothing was amiss, he perversely remained silent until they were alone on the dark streets. It served Rafe right for announcing Ian's title in such an inconvenient place.

"If this concerns Polidori, I apologize for not yet locating him." Rafe pulled off the leather tie that held back his waist-length black hair, shaking out the mass to dry his sweat. "I believe the *bastardo* knows we seek him and is only venturing out in the day."

"I am not concerned with Polidori," Ian replied, gazing up at the fog-obscured moon. "In fact, I am considering calling off the search. His popularity is waning, and I've happened upon a more effective solution to keep society's suspicions at bay."

"What sort of solution?" Rafe eyed him warily.

"I shall marry," Ian said calmly, bracing himself for the Spaniard's outrage at the announcement.

Rafe snarled and let loose a string of Spanish expletives. "*Dios mío*! Why would you do such a thing?"

Ian sighed and related the tale of Angelica's misguided foray into his home and its disastrous results. "And so, if I marry her, I may ensure that she keeps her silence about our kind as well as dissuade society from believing the rumors circulating about me."

His second continued to curse. "Still, marriage? Have you gone *loco*? She could expose us all! Do you have any notion of the danger in which you are placing us?"

"Well, I can't kill her," Ian retorted.

Rafe nodded in reluctant agreement but stopped walking. His amber gaze turned speculative. "You could Change her."

"No!" Ian growled, heart cringing at the thought of taking such an innocent away from family, friends, and daylight. "She is too innocent for this life and has such ambitious plans for her future. It would be monstrous to take that away from her."

Rafe shook his head. "What shall you do with her, then? For one thing, she will not quicken with child, no matter how many times you lie with her, but the situation will grow far worse when she begins to age and you do not. At the prospect of such unhappiness, how do you expect her to hold her tongue?"

The Spaniard had a way of seeing the possible outcomes of any situation. It was one of the many reasons Ian had chosen Rafe to succeed him as Lord of London.

Ian suppressed curses of his own as he replied with feigned confidence, "Don't worry, I'll think of something."

Ten

"PULL THE LACES TIGHTER, LIZA!" MARGARET
commanded as she bustled back and forth, bumping
into Angelica's writing desk in her fluster. "And do be
quick. His Grace will be here any minute."

The victim of the clamping stays would have sighed
if she had any breath remaining in her lungs. Every
time Angelica tried to forget the nightmare of the
Cavendish ball, her mother insisted on bringing the
memory back in vivid clarity just by mentioning the
Duke of Burnrath, a feat she'd accomplished at least a
hundred times today.

To further add salt to the wound, Margaret punctu-
ated nearly every sentence with "...and you will be
the Duchess of Burnrath. Oh, my darling, I can hardly
believe such a miracle has transpired!"

Angelica didn't know which galled her more, the
fact that she had been so close to attaining her goals
and had them snatched away so quickly, or that His
Grace expected her to swoon at his feet in undying
gratitude when he only wanted her to save *his* reputation. He was using her.

She *had* to find a way out of this. And now that her reputation had been saved since the duke offered her marriage and announced to all and sundry that she was not in his house of her own free will, surely there was no real need to go through with this ridiculous farce… *was there*? Her stomach clenched in worry.

Between her mother's strident commands as she flitted from room to room and the frantic racing of the servants in their efforts to ready the house for the duke's arrival, Angelica managed to snatch enough precious minutes of quiet to formulate a shaky plan. Ironically, her mother unwittingly inspired the main point of her scheme.

During breakfast, Angelica had noted with grim amusement that her mother had likely slept less than she had. The layer of powder under her eyelids was so thick that it looked ready to topple from her face into her cup of chocolate at any moment.

"When the Duke of Burnrath calls upon you, you must show him your skills with the pianoforte. Gentlemen are pleased when a lady has musical talent. But"—Margaret's eyes narrowed in warning—"you mustn't play those scandalous songs you have written and do *not* sing under any circumstances! I have told you again and again, my dear, that our Lord did not gift you with a pleasant voice, as much as you seem to wish otherwise." She set down her cup with a clatter, warming up to the lecture. "Oh, and do not discuss those gothic novels and their freakish notions you seem to adore and…"

I wonder what he would do if I did sing? Angelica crushed the biscuit on her plate with sadistic cheer. *In fact, what would he do if I did* everything *Mother tells me not to?* There it was. For once, she made an effort to listen to her mother's advice, especially in regards to what *not* to do. *There* lay her way out of this predicament. She would do everything a "proper lady" would never do. In short, she thought with a grin, she would be herself.

The Duke of Burnrath would never want to wed her if he truly knew her. He had said that "love was hardly a necessary ingredient for a successful marriage." Angelica was well aware of that depressing truth, but she believed the reason for the alleged success of marriages within the peerage, aside from terror of the scandal attached to a divorce, was the fact that the two parties were virtual strangers. Surely no one would be able to bring themselves to marry someone if they knew all their flaws before the nuptials!

A glimmer of hope quickened Angelica's pace up the stairs to her bedchamber. If getting to know her failed to deter the duke, she would run away and endeavor to support herself with her writing.

As Liza pulled an elegant emerald brocade gown over Angelica's head, Angelica managed a genuine smile. Tonight she would defy one of Mother's principal commands: Do not ask a man too many questions, for it implies that you doubt his character.

She would do just that, as well as twist this catechism in a different way. She was going to ask him about being a vampire. She hadn't yet determined if what he was applied to her opinion of his character, but she was certain His Grace wouldn't like her prying at his secret. *It shall give him a taste of what to expect if he marries me. And if I fail, at least his answers will give me good material for a novel.*

When the butler announced that His Grace, the Duke of Burnrath had arrived, Angelica couldn't stop her pulse from accelerating at the sight of him. He towered over Morrison as he handed over his cape and hat, appearing utterly and completely like the sleek, dangerous creature that she knew him to be. She was suddenly very grateful that he only "liked" her, for if the duke had any deep feelings for her, she knew instinctively that he would never let anything dissuade him from pursuing his desires. A strange sensation of warmth curled through her lower belly at the thought.

"Good evening, Angel." The vampire bowed low, taking her hand. His glittering silver eyes regarded her as he pressed cool, firm lips to her flesh, making her shiver.

There was a slight flush to his cheeks. Had he dined on someone's blood recently? She shivered and unconsciously placed a hand on the side of her neck where his fangs had penetrated her flesh.

"Oh, Your Grace, do come in!" Margaret lifted her skirts in a ridiculously elaborate curtsy. "I trust you had a pleasant stroll around the block? Would you like a tour of our home?"

Thankfully, Angelica's father interrupted Margaret as he entered the drawing room and greeted Ian with jovial but restrained civility. "It is wonderful to see you, Your Grace. I took the liberty of having supper provided before we begin preparing the contract, if that is all right with you."

When the meal commenced, Angelica suppressed

the urge to sink under the table as her mother turned herself inside out in her effort to please the duke. Angelica and Burnrath looked at each other with identical looks of amused embarrassment. She couldn't hold back a smile as she remembered him laughing with her on his sofa when she told him about her ghost stories. Resolutely she pushed back the memories. It would not at all do to have warm feelings for this man. Vampire or no, he was still a *man* and as such he represented an end to her freedom.

She decided to begin the first phase of her plan. *Mother says: a lady must always eat as daintily as a songbird.* Angelica devoured the meager amount of food on her plate, looking up at him in mute challenge, waiting for him to object.

"I do so admire a woman with a healthy appetite," he said with a wry smile as if he were aware of her strategy.

She flushed and looked down, noticing that the majority of his food remained untouched. She was completely distracted for a moment. *Do vampires eat food, or do they only drink blood?* She remembered the feel of his mouth locked on her neck and shivered as she realized the sensation hadn't been an unpleasant one.

"Is the food to your liking, Your Grace?" her mother asked, twisting her napkin in her nervousness.

The duke took a bite of braised beef and chewed. "This is delicious, Lady Margaret. Unfortunately I dined earlier"—Angelica dropped her spoon, and he fixed her with a stern eye—"and I would not be able to manage another bite if this meal was not so exquisite."

Margaret seemed pleased and Angelica searched her

mind for another of her mother's commandments. *A lady does not ask a man too many questions.*

"What are your interests, Your Grace?" Angelica asked, surprised at her genuine curiosity.

Burnrath's smile gave her another unbidden shiver. "I enjoy playing cards, reading, attending the opera, and playing with investments in the market. What do you prefer, Miss Winthrop?"

Margaret paled at the duke's blatant admission that he was involved in trade, but her father had a new gleam of interest in his eyes. As if His Grace held new value as a prospective son-in-law. She needed to do better.

"I enjoy reading, writing gothic stories, and"— Angelica floundered for the right words—"supporting the liberation of women!"

At her mother's strangled gasp, she knew she'd scored a hit.

"I see," Burnrath said, his lips twitching. "And how do you contribute to this cause?"

Angelica fixed him with an icy glare. How dare he be amused! "Well, I purchase all the literature I can on the subject, and I portray my heroines in my stories as strong, independent thinkers who have no need for a man. And the songs I write involve honest feelings rather than insipid yearnings."

"You write songs as well?" The duke raised a brow, but his smile deepened. "I am overjoyed that I shall have a very talented bride. I would like to hear your compositions sometime."

"I am certain you would not," Margaret said stiffly, fixing her daughter with a warning glare. "I am quite afraid that my daughter's singing is most... unconventional."

Angelica's heart surged with triumph as she embarked further. "What is your average profit from your investments on the *'Change*, Your Grace?" This time, she heard a murmur of protest from her father. Surely this was dangerous ground. A lady was never to discuss matters of commerce.

To her disappointment, the duke did not seem chagrined in the slightest by her rude inquiry. "I have made anywhere between ten and ten thousand pounds on my speculations. And how much have you made from your writing?"

"Eighteen pounds, so far." Angelica struggled to keep the defensiveness from her voice. "Of course, that was only from short stories. The profits from a novel will be much higher."

"When you are the Duchess of Burnrath, you will likely make more," her father said in a blatant attempt to placate her.

Angelica turned to her father, breath heaving shallowly. *He's supposed to be on my side!* "I believe my work should stand on its own merits and the reception shouldn't change because of my name." Her gaze darted back to Burnrath. "And I do not see why I should have to change my name in the first place."

The duke smiled. "That is what a lady does when she marries."

Her fists clenched irritation. "Yes, but why? Why does a woman have to give up her name? Why don't *you* change *your* name?"

Margaret's face turned white with mortification. Her father seemed wracked with confusion as his mouth struggled to form a response.

The duke, however, was undaunted by her radical outburst. "Because that is the way things have always been done, Angel."

Her father nodded in relieved agreement. "Yes, quite so, Your Grace."

Angelica refused to take the bait and kept her reproving stare on the target of her ire. "I do not think that longtime tradition is a legitimate reason to throw away my identity. After all, for centuries we believed that the world was flat, but now we've come to our senses at last."

Her parents gasped in mutual shock, but before her lips could curve in a triumphant smile, the scoundrel before her actually raised his glass to her in a toast.

"I applaud your sound logic, Miss Winthrop," Burnrath said with another of his infuriating knowing smiles. "However, I do not believe English law will bow down before it. They move dreadfully slow, after all. But do not allow that to stop you from pursuing reform. Who knows, perhaps someday women will be allowed to sit in Parliament."

"Are you *mocking* me, Your Grace?" Angelica asked in a low voice.

"Not at all," he replied cheerfully. "I am enjoying myself immensely.

Angelica suppressed a groan of frustration. Her only consolation was that her parents appeared to be scandalized, exchanging helpless glances while she and the duke verbally dueled by asking each other questions that were unseemly for dinner conversation.

The sparring was cut short when the meal ended.

Her father cleared his throat. "Shall we adjourn to my study to begin preparing the contract, Your Grace?"

A wave of disappointment washed over Angelica. To her surprise, she'd been having a good time. Then she remembered her mother crowing with triumph that His Grace wanted a short engagement. She felt as if she were suffocating and was certain her stays weren't the only cause. She had to bargain for more time.

"Papa, wait!" she cried. "First may I take His Grace for a stroll through the garden? I would so like some fresh air." She smiled and attempted to flutter her eyelashes the way the other debutantes did when attempting to cajole their papas to raise their allowances.

Her father gave her an odd look before comprehension dawned as his eyes lit on the couple. Angelica could see what he thought. Of course they would want some time alone together. *Bloody hell, I'm doing this all wrong!*

"I am certain that will be quite proper. Go on and enjoy yourselves," he said with an indulgent wave of his hand, blushing as Margaret beamed at him. Angelica couldn't remember the last time her mother had smiled at her father like that.

As Angelica placed her hand on Ian's sleeve, she felt his arm flex much like the other young suitors did while always trying to impress her. She nibbled her lower lip and wondered how much of him was a man and how much was a vampire.

The garden glimmered with haunting beauty in the moonlight. Angelica inhaled the scent of early blooming lilacs and lifted her face to the cool evening air. As the duke walked silently beside her, she couldn't help but notice that the nocturnal surroundings fit him perfectly.

"The moonlight suits you, Angel." His deep voice was a soft rumble against her ear.

She stiffened at the warm sensation his familiar address elicited and removed her hand from his arm and stepped back. "Your Grace, would it be possible for you to cry off this engagement?" She hurried on before he could reply. "I mean, now that everyone knows you are willing to marry, surely that is enough to save your reputation. We do not really have to go through with this, do we?"

"Alas, you are wrong." His tone was cold, matter-of-fact. "They would never believe I am a normal man unless we see this through to the end. If we broke the engagement, both of our reputations would be worse off than they were before." He walked toward her, not stopping until their bodies nearly touched.

Angelica couldn't keep the panic from rising in her voice at his proximity. "But—"

He cupped her chin in his hand, making her shiver at his touch. "As I promised you before, you do not need to be afraid of me. I will not hurt you. If you give yourself the chance to get to know me, you will see that I will be a generous husband."

Angelica was *not* afraid of him, but she seized the excuse like a lifeline. She stepped back once more to plead her case. "Could you at least give me some time to get accustomed to the idea and get to know you before we are wed?"

He sighed and nodded with obvious reluctance. "Within reason."

"One year?" she asked in the sweetest voice she could manage.

His silver gaze glinted as he frowned. "One month."

"Six months?" she ventured, struggling to maintain her saccharine, imploring tone.

"One month," he repeated. His arms crossed over his broad chest as his frown deepened.

"Four months?" Angelica begged, hating the desperation in her voice. But she needed time to devise a plan on how to get out of this predicament.

"*One* month." His tone was firm, implacable, autocratic. And there was something unnerving about the way he looked at her, as if he knew she sought escape.

She sighed, exhausted with his refusal to yield. "You will negotiate with my father, but not with me. Some suitor you are!" Biting back her temper, she gentled her voice. "Six weeks, *please*?"

Burnrath nodded. "Very well, six weeks it is." He smiled suddenly and a small dimple appeared in his cheek. "I suppose I should take the time to court you properly. Now, let's seal the bargain with a kiss."

He grasped her shoulders, but Angelica stepped back. The idea of his lips on hers made her knees turn to water and her stomach leap around in the most alarming manner. "A-a handshake should suffice, I think."

His rich laughter overwhelmed her senses. "Come now, you are to be my bride. No kiss, no bargain, my beauty," he challenged. "Do not tell me you are afraid."

Angelica lifted her chin. Hell if he would call her a coward! "Very well." She stood on tiptoe and pecked him on the cheek, shocked at the thrill rushing up her spine at that small contact. He smelled of exotic spices. "D-do we have a bargain then?" she asked, hating how her voice shook.

The vampire's eyes seemed to glow dangerously. With a low growl, he pulled her into his arms. She gasped at the feel of the warm steel bands holding her to his large, hard body. "That is not what I had in mind."

Keeping his arm around her, he stroked her back as he tipped her chin up with his other hand to meet his smoldering silver gaze. With one finger, he lightly traced her cheek before tangling his fingers in her hair.

The vampire's breath was warm on her face as he whispered, "This is a kiss.".

His lips came down upon hers, feather soft at first then increasing in pressure as they molded to her mouth. Angelica pressed her hands against his chest, intending to push away from his grasp. But the feel of his hard, muscled form against her body and the light brush of his silken hair against her ear brought heat to her cheeks. Against her will, her fingers relinquished their objection. Frissons of sensation engulfed her, and her arms unconsciously crept up around him, clinging to him for support, for her legs had lost their strength. A low moan emerged from her throat and he captured it, his breath mingling with hers.

The tip of his tongue touched hers and one of his fangs grazed her lip. She jumped at the spark. The vampire released her, panting hoarsely. His eyes glowed with an unholy, silver light.

"*My God*," he said. "I'm sorry, Angel, I did not mean to take things so far."

"I am quite all right," she said, her mind swimming. "W-we should go back inside now." Her legs trembled as she walked with him in silence back to the house.

The duke straightened his cravat before opening the

door. "I will tell your father the wedding will be in six weeks. Tomorrow I will escort you to the opera. Be ready at seven o'clock."

He bowed and left her standing at the foot of the stairs with trembling limbs and tingling lips. As the sound of muted voices drifted down from the study, her mother came in from the salon to see Angelica standing silent in the dark.

"Are you all right, dear?" The words were nearly obscured by the thudding of her heart.

"I think so." Angelica met her mother's concerned gaze and couldn't help pouring out a little of her frustration. "This is all happening so fast."

Margaret smiled and enfolded her daughter in her arms. "I am so proud of you, dear heart. My own daughter, a duchess! It is a dream come true."

Angelica blinked at the outpouring of affection and warmth. Still, her mother's uncharacteristic behavior was preferable to questions about her time alone with the duke. "He is taking me to the opera tomorrow," she said with a forced smile.

"That is wonderful!" Margaret clasped her hands together. "Now, you had best get to bed. I do not want to see any dark circles under your eyes."

As Angelica headed upstairs, absently touching her swollen lips, she realized that she had forgotten to ask the duke about vampires.

"Damn," she muttered bitterly as a thousand questions sprang to her mind. "Well, at least I have six weeks to do so."

And in the meantime she would do everything in her power to forget the intensity of his kiss.

Eleven

THE DUKE OF BURNRATH'S WHIRLWIND COURTSHIP
with the Winthrop heiress treated the *haut ton* to the
most delicious gossip of the season. Like vultures with
fresh carrion, they savored each tidbit more fervently
than the last. A group of society's most titled matrons
gathered at Lady Crenshaw's town house for afternoon
tea and to discuss the engagement… and the latest
caricature of His Grace, which had begun circulating
only that morning.

The caption read: "The vampyre pursues his prey."
Though Burnrath and his bride-to-be were not identi-
fied, the artist, who was nearly as skilled as Cruikshank
himself, had done an amusing job depicting the duke's
unconventional long hair and piercing silver eyes.

The figure towered over the tiny caricature of Miss
Winthrop. Comical daggerlike fangs protruded from
the duke's mouth, and the words, "What big teeth
you have, Your Grace," were drawn bubbling out
from Angelica's lips.

The Duchess of Wentworth thrust the drawing
away when the lampoon came to her. "I haven't seen

anything in poorer taste since Rowlandson mocked poor Queen Caroline." Her nose turned up in disgust.

Lady Pillsbury looked at the picture and shuddered. "Those teeth are ghastly. Do you suppose the rumors could be true?"

"Not for a second!" Her Grace declared. "Burnrath is a close friend of my husband, and you know my dear Alex takes utmost care about whom he associates with."

"Perhaps they are true." Lady Crenshaw ignored the duchess and turned to Lady Pillsbury. "I wonder that we never see them driving through Hyde Park in the mornings or attending any other function during the day."

The duchess sighed in exasperation. "He has a dreadful skin condition that prevents him from exposure to the sun. My husband heard it from the duke himself."

"Or maybe he *is* a vampire." Lady Crenshaw set down her teacup with a clatter, fixing them all with a fierce glare. "I hear that even the *wedding* will be held at night."

"The groom can hardly appear before the bride with a skin eruption," Lady Pillsbury put in as she nibbled a biscuit. "Still, a nighttime wedding… whoever heard of such a thing? There will hardly be time for the ball, and… well…" She trailed off, cheeks burning as she realized she had come close to discussing the bedding.

"Oh, I am quite certain they had time for *that* already," Lady Crenshaw said scathingly as she opened her fan. "The wedding is to be performed in only six weeks. Scandalous! And of all the girls that were available to him, he had to settle on that strange baggage. If we had known that he was going to defy tradition and select an English bride, why, he could have had the pick of the finest blood in the country! After all, my daughter—"

"But surely you are relieved that she is safe from the attentions of a vampire?" Lady Pillsbury asked, perplexed.

Lady Crenshaw snorted. "At the cost of the loss of such a lofty title? Are you mad?" She shook her head. "You only have a son, so you could never understand what a trial one endures in trying to make a good match for a daughter."

The Duchess of Wentworth smirked at the woman's contradictory behavior, motivated by greed. Lady Crenshaw could not hide her venomous envy that her daughter had failed to nab the title of Duchess of Burnrath.

∾

Ian smiled with triumph as he looked upon the betting book at White's. Most of the wagers against him had been retracted. After Angelica became his bride, he had every confidence that the rumors that the Duke of Burnrath was a bloodsucking fiend would be regarded as a silly jest.

"I say, Burnrath, care to join us in a game of piquet?" Baron Wheaton asked, carefully pointing his gaze away from the betting book.

Ian hid a smile, wondering which of the vampire wagers had been penned by the baron. "I'm afraid I do not have the time. I only stopped in to place a wager on Wentworth's horse before I must leave to call on

Miss Winthrop." He turned away, eager to leave the club. He had only decided to come because his first meal for the evening had been nearby.

Wheaton clapped him on the shoulder. "I say, old chap, we never believed you would ever become leg-shackled, but I think you made a good choice. She is a stunning beauty, and the Pendlebur estate is not too shabby, either." The naked greed on his face was almost laughable in its lack of subtlety.

Ian pretended not to hear the baron and left the club with only a curt nod to his acquaintances. He'd learned what he needed and had no desire to linger and socialize, for in minutes he would be in the company of his soon-to-be bride.

He took a deep breath of the early spring air, a relief from the smoke-ridden atmosphere of White's. Ian found that he enjoyed courting a beautiful young lady. Angelica was an engaging companion whose droll wit and heady vitality made him feel like a mortal man again. Her captivating combination of naivety and curiosity endeared her more to him with each encounter. And every kiss he stole from her made him burn and long for more. His body grew stiff and uncomfortable just thinking about her, and he knew that he would have to exercise utmost caution and restraint to not fall upon her like a ravening beast when he finally bedded her.

At the Winthrop's town house that evening, his fiancée pouted when he immediately adjourned to Jacob Winthrop's study for brandy and cigars after dinner. Ian hid a smile. Perhaps she would miss him.

Maybe her fear of him was slowly abating. But he

could sense she was still holding something back from him, and Ian was damned if he could figure out what was going on in her captivating mind.

"Shall you play me a song?" Ian asked as he and Jacob rejoined Angelica and her mother in the music salon.

Angelica's face lit up with an impish grin. "Certainly, Your Grace."

As she settled herself gracefully on the bench before the piano, Ian noted with amusement that Margaret looked panic stricken and seemed to be trying to send her daughter discreet warning signals. *What stunt is she trying to pull now, I wonder?*

All thoughts ceased as she struck a haunting melody on the keys and began to sing. Ian had to agree with her mother that Angelica's voice was not at all the light trilling or the ethereal whisper that one came to expect from accomplished singers of the petticoat line. But Angelica's singing was not unpleasant. Instead her voice was rich, full bodied, and robust, like the finest burgundy.

The song was not the typical vapid nonsense smiled upon by society, but rather a song of a passionate woman, enraged and despairing of being seen for who she was. The piece was unlike anything he'd ever heard. She delivered the emotional dialogue of the lyrics with the drama one would usually find on Drury Lane, not in a modest music room.

When the song ended, Angelica turned from the instrument and fixed him with that challenging stare he had grown to love. Her chin lifted another fraction. "Did you enjoy the song, Your Grace?"

Ian cast an amused glance at Lady Margaret, who was fumbling for her smelling salts. He stood up, clapping heartily. "Bravo! That was the most captivating performance I have heard in ages."

Angelica's onyx eyes narrowed in fury. Apparently she'd expected him to be scandalized. "Would you like to hear another?"

"By all means, Miss Winthrop," he said with a satisfied smile.

"Perhaps Your Grace would like to hear some Beethoven instead?" Jacob asked, casting worried looks at his wife's pale face.

"I would love to play a Beethoven piece, Papa," she replied, ignoring Ian.

Ian sighed, expecting to hear the "Moonlight Sonata" or something else he'd heard dozens of times, but he was shocked when Angelica plunged into Beethoven's *Appassionata*. His surprise was not because the sonata was one of the most emotional and complex pieces ever to reach his ears, but because he doubted a slip of a girl could produce the intricate melodies through the work's entire twenty-five minutes. Only concert pianists attempted this piece. Perhaps she meant to fail at the endeavor to deter him.

She played the sonata perfectly and with such a jaunty flair that he couldn't keep an admiring chuckle from escaping. Margaret and Jacob's eyes nearly bulged out of their heads. From the stunned expressions on her parents' faces, Ian presumed they had never heard her perform this one. It seemed he would be wedding an incredibly talented woman.

❧

Angelica wanted to scream in fury at the thunderous applause that the duke and her parents heaped upon her. *A gentleman is always displeased when a lady shows herself to be more intelligent or talented than he is.* Angelica noted the naked admiration in Burnrath's eyes. Apparently Mother's commandments were wrong yet again. In fact, everything she did to try to make him dislike her seemed to accomplish just the opposite.

She didn't know how much longer she could withstand those lazy smiles he bestowed on her that made her heart turn over in her chest. Or pretend indifference to his kisses that left her feeling breathless. If his seduction continued, she would throw her freedom to the wind before long and joyfully become his duchess.

"Where would you like me to escort you tomorrow?" Burnrath asked as they strolled through the garden.

Angelica suppressed a tremor of anticipation for his impending kisses. Instead, she forced her attention on a wicked idea that niggled at her mind. Last week, she'd enjoyed seeing the opera and being swept under the music's spell. And though she could tell he didn't completely enjoy some of the balls he had escorted her to, the duke didn't appear to despise them. There had to be something she could make him do that he would hate.

"Tomorrow is Wednesday. Could we go to Almack's?" she asked, trying to imbue her tone with innocent enthusiasm.

Unless they were desperate for a young bride, the older, more urbane set would rather die than step into that dull establishment with its tepid tea, paltry gambling stakes, and carnivorous matchmaking mamas.

Burnrath raised his eyes heavenward as he tried—and failed—to mask his look of dismay. "Very well. If that is what you wish. I will pick you up at nine o'clock."

She almost laughed at his ire, until she realized that she'd be punishing herself along with him. She *hated* Almack's. The "fashionable" assembly hall had to be the stiffest, blandest, and most repressive place in the world. But, going there would be worth it to deter his suit.

She kicked a pebble on the ground and changed the subject. "How old are you?"

He gave her an odd look, almost as if the question embarrassed him. "Are you certain you wish to know?"

"Of course." Angelica frowned in confusion at his reluctance. She knew he was older than she was, but he couldn't be much more than thirty.

Avoiding her gaze, the duke replied, "I just had my two hundred and seventy-sixth birthday a few months back."

All the breath fled from her body. He was *two hundred and seventy-six* years old? "H-how long do vampires usually live?"

He sat on the stone bench by the lilac bush and sighed. "We live for centuries. In fact, rumor has it that the oldest of us has been around since before Christ was born. Is this to be an interrogation?" He looked up at her sharply.

Angelica was reeling from the information, so she almost didn't notice the flicker of warmth in his eyes when she sat down next to him. "No—yes… perhaps. I am merely curious."

His gaze softened as he nodded. "Well, I suppose you have the right to know. Ask your questions about me and my brethren, and I'll answer what I can."

"How many vampires are there?" She couldn't hide her rapt fascination.

Burnrath shrugged. "In the world? I haven't the faintest notion. In London there are one hundred and thirty-five."

Angelica's eyes widened at the exact tally. "Do you *know* all of them?"

"Of course I do. I am their lord." He smiled down at her, displaying that charming dimple. "I am afraid that you are in more illustrious company than you first supposed. In the mortal world, I am merely the Duke of Burnrath and the owner of four estates. In the vampire world, I own all of London. Every vampire who lives in this city has sworn fealty to me."

She was stunned silent by his words. The idea that vampires had their own social structure and politics had never crossed her mind. She had always pictured them as solitary creatures, skulking in the shadows. Her mind raced with multitudes of questions that she couldn't quite put into words. His eyes seemed to glitter with impatience, so she quickly fumbled for another question.

"How did you become a vampire?" She turned away from his piercing gaze and bent to pluck a blade of new grass from the ground.

He was silent for a long moment before at last he replied, "I was a knight in King Henry's army, and I fell on the field during what is now known as the

Battle of Ancrum Moor in the year 1545, during the 'rough wooing.' Do you know much about it?"

"That was back when Henry the Eighth was attacking Scotland in an effort to force them to make an alliance with England." Angelica sneered. "What a tyrant! I am glad the Scots won."

The duke chuckled. "Careful, my sweet, you come close to speaking treason."

She blushed as she realized that he had been fighting on Henry's side. "I did not mean—"

"You are right, Angel," he said, still laughing. "He was a tyrant, indeed. Anyway, my horse was hit with an arrow, and I was thrown and knocked unconscious. When I awoke, night had fallen, and a lone Scotsman approached me. I thought he was a soldier until I saw his glowing green eyes and bared fangs. In a trice, he was upon me, tearing my throat with his fangs and gulping my blood. I would have died if another vampire had not stopped him."

The duke took a deep breath and continued. "The Scots vampire fled and my rescuer Changed me. He taught me what I needed to know about being a vampire. He then told me to return to my home and live among the mortals. King Henry thought that I had been taken prisoner and escaped. He was so impressed with my 'bravery' that he made me the Duke of Burnrath the moment I finished my lie. I became Lord of London only fifty years ago. So, there you have it."

"That is amazing," Angelica breathed. He painted such a vivid picture that she could easily see the knights in gleaming helms, blood-drenched battlefields, and mighty warhorses. "I only have one more question. Well, perhaps two."

Burnrath chuckled at her temerity before giving her a patient smile. "Very well, I will try to indulge you."

"Do you kill people?" She swallowed, nearly choking on the question. A trickle of fear dripped down her spine. Vampire kills in stories were tantalizing, but this was reality. Would he have killed her if he hadn't discovered her identity the night she snuck into his home?

His hair brushed her cheek as he shook his head. "No, there is too much blood in a human's body to consume in one sitting. Also, killing is forbidden under most circumstances, for dead bodies drained of blood would put us in jeopardy of discovery. And your other question?"

Angelica let out breath she hadn't realized she'd been holding. "Do you drink only blood? Or can you eat food as well?"

"We cannot digest solid food very well any longer, but many of us miss the taste of our favorite dishes and indulge in a few bites. I still enjoy meat pasties and fine brandy." His white teeth flashed as he grinned.

The quaint image brought a giggle to her lips. "You are not really an animated corpse, are you?"

Burnrath laughed. "No, our condition is more like a sickness in the blood that we can pass on to others. Our legends say it is magic spread from the first vampires, who were demons cast out of hell because they weren't evil enough to suit his dark majesty." His gaze turned serious as he leaned closer and caressed her cheek with his knuckles. "I assure you I am quite alive, my sweet."

She wanted to ask more, but Liza poked her head out the door. "I was told to look in on you, miss."

"We will be in after I kiss her good night." The duke's rakish smile had the maid simpering.

Angelica smiled in reluctant admiration of his seemingly limitless charm. Perhaps vampires *were* magic.

"Yes, Your Grace." Liza bobbed a curtsy and left them alone.

Angelica's breath caught as the vampire took her into his arms, ready to be overcome with his passion. Instead, his lips brushed whisper-soft against hers for a tortuously brief moment. Then he released her and stepped back.

"Good night, Angel," he whispered and tipped his hat before leaving her trembling with longings she didn't understand.

Angelica bit back a moan of frustration. She would have to steel all of her will and senses to resist him, and when she escaped this engagement, it would not be a moment too soon.

Twelve

THE DUKE OF BURNRATH RESEMBLED A WOLF AMONG sheep next to the pastel-garbed assembly at Almack's. He frowned down at his black satin knee breeches then actually scowled at her. Angelica smiled at his painfully obvious display of how he hated every minute of being at this place.

She'd almost panicked when Lady Jersey nearly refused him because he didn't have a voucher, but Lady Cowper overrode her decision and handed him a "Stranger Ticket," not bothering to hide her glee at the appearance of London's biggest subject of gossip.

"I cannot believe you do not have a voucher to Almack's!" Angelica exclaimed with mock outrage.

"Careful, minx, or I shall think you dragged me to this silly place just to irritate me." A muscle in his jaw ticked.

She plied her fan, feigning innocence. "Would I do that?"

He laughed as he led her to the dance floor. "I imagine you would. In fact, I am quite certain that you despise this place as much as I already do."

"I…" She raised the fan to hide her expression. Could he be aware of her plan to annoy him out of the engagement?

"Please, Miss Winthrop, do not exert yourself by indulging in further falsehoods." he whispered through clenched teeth. "The truth is written all over your face. Now tell me, why are you trying to vex me?" The vampire loomed over her like the fierce blood drinker he was.

The young ladies and gentlemen around them had abandoned even the slightest pretense of dancing and were now watching the discussion with avid interest. Claire Belmont gripped Lord Makepeace's sleeve and dragged him closer. The audience seemed to salivate over the possibility of scandal.

Angelica resisted the urge to glare at Claire. "People are staring at us."

"Let them," Burnrath said curtly. "This is not the first time we've garnered attention, and from the pattern of our discourse, it will not be the last."

"Fine," she muttered and confessed the truth. "I had thought if I irritated you enough, you would not wish to marry me."

"Angel…" His voice grew tender and his grip tightened on her waist as they waltzed. "Nothing will make me change my mind. I have told you time and again that you have no reason to fear me. What will it take to make you believe me?"

As she swayed in his arms, his handsome face and gentleness nearly shattered her resolve. "I do not know. I am so confused." *Could I tell him I am afraid of losing my freedom? No, such an action would be ludicrous!*

"Everything will be all right. I promise," he whispered and her heart ached in longing to believe him.

The dance ended and Burnrath bent closer. "Well, thanks to your failed ploy, we are trapped in this insipid place for awhile, for if we depart now, tongues would surely wag." He smirked. "Shall I fetch you some warm lemonade?"

"Don't you dare leave me!" she hissed, rising up on her toes to whisper in his ear. "Viscount Branson is over there, just itching to dance with me, and his breath is so foul that I'm afraid I would be sick all over his ridiculous high-heeled shoes that were in fashion in my *grandfather's* day."

The duke's brows rose in mock horror. "You may have a point. On the other side, I see four matrons and their daughters eyeing me as if I am a walking bank draft. If you leave *me*, they are sure to pounce. And you wondered why I never set foot in this hellish place."

Angelica grinned in helpless mirth and placed a hand on his sleeve. "Oh, Your Grace, what have I gotten us into?"

In the end they decided to play cards. Angelica had always wanted to learn, for her mother was rumored to be an expert whist player but refused to teach her, saying gambling was "not a habit unmarried females should indulge in." However, Angelica turned out to be a terrible player because her face gave away everything.

Just as Angelica was beginning to have a good time, Lady Jersey told her she must leave the establishment for "being too familiar with the duke."

"But he is to be my husband!" Angelica protested, outraged at the ludicrousness of the patroness's censure.

"That is all the more reason for you to set a good example for the ladies who have not yet made matches." Lady Jersey's brows drew together in consternation. "Your mother shall hear about this and your children will be lucky to secure vouchers." She continued her tirade as the duke stood behind her, looking like he was torn between laughter and biting the woman.

Angelica glared at the patroness who was often called "Silence" for some absurd reason. The woman could barely pause in her speech long enough to take a breath.

"Piss on it, then!" Angelica muttered under her breath as she took Burnrath's arm and he escorted her out of the insipid club.

By the time they were settled in the duke's carriage, Angelica was overcome with gales of laughter. "I cannot believe I was just thrown out of Almack's!" she hiccuped, tears of hilarity streaming down her face. "And be-because I behaved as if I *liked* you too much!"

Burnrath laughed as he wiped the tears from her cheeks with his handkerchief. "The irony *is* almost too much to bear. But you should calm down before your maid descends from the driver's perch and climbs inside, thinking you are having hysterics."

She took a deep breath and then froze. "Oh God, my mother will be the one to have hysterics, I know it. Lady Jersey is going to tell her. She said my children would be lucky to get vouchers. I don't know if I'll be able to endure the nagging."

The duke stiffened beside her. "I am quite certain

that I will be able to placate your mother. And as for the other thing, you need not worry about it."

Angelica looked up, curious about his change in tone. "Why not?"

"I am unable to give you children," he said gruffly, avoiding her gaze to stare at his boots. "I am very sorry, Angel."

"That is quite all right with me," Angelica said, momentarily forgetting her intentions to escape marrying him. "Unlike most females, I never really gave motherhood much thought except for being outraged on behalf of those women who are subject to a husband's wrath if they fail to provide a male heir, especially since so many die in the effort. I would much rather avoid the whole ordeal."

His features relaxed in obvious relief. "I had feared such news would disappoint you."

The gentleness of his voice wove a spell over her. She struggled to regain her resolve. "May we discuss something else? Surely such a subject is inappropriate."

The duke's laughter echoed in the closed carriage. "You now mention impropriety? Oh, Angel, never in almost three centuries of living have I encountered anyone like you. You are a treasure." Suddenly, his gaze darkened. "I will show you impropriety."

He pulled her onto his lap and brought his lips down on hers. Heat exploded within her as he crushed her body against his, and his tongue delved into her mouth to dance against hers, invoking electrifying sensations. She reached up and tangled her fingers in his long hair, surprised to find that the locks felt silkier than they appeared. His hand slid down to her breast, and even as she gasped in surprise, a tendril of warmth curled down from there to the tender place between her thighs.

The carriage halted and the duke growled a curse as Angelica leaped away from him with a tiny squeak of protest, seething with self-rage. *What am I doing?* She was supposed to make him despise her, not cavort in his arms like a shameless wanton. Frantically, she adjusted her hair and gown before the door opened and the groom handed her down. The cool air was a relief against her heated face and form.

"I did not expect you to return so early," her mother said, brows knitted in concern, when they came in.

"I apologize, Lady Margaret," Burnrath said with a low bow. "There has been an incident at Almack's, and being that I was unfamiliar with the traditions of that hallowed establishment, all was completely my fault. Allow me to give you the true account of what transpired before you hear a distorted version from others."

Angelica watched in awe as the duke manipulated her mother with his eloquent speech, rendering her as malleable as fine clay. By the time he was finished, it was obvious that Margaret was ready to nominate the vampire as a candidate for sainthood. Angelica was torn between admiration and envy for his diplomatic skill.

After the duke finished explaining to her mother and bid her good night, Angelica realized with a pang of sadness that she might never see him again. The next day she and her mother were to visit her grandfather, where she would thankfully have a little time to form a plan of escape.

⤟⦵

She is like an angel in repose. Ian stood over Angelica, listening to the soft sounds of her breathing. Her hair cascaded across her pillow and coverlet like an ebony waterfall, glistening in the moonlight. Her full lips were still plump and rosy from his kisses in the carriage.

Flying into her room had been frighteningly easy after the family fell asleep and all the lights of the surrounding houses were extinguished. So easy that it reinforced his resolve for what he was about to do.

Ian bit his right index finger, watching in fascination as the dark ruby drop of blood welled and bloomed out of his skin. Gently, he coaxed Angelica's lips open with the fingers of his left hand and let his blood drip into her mouth.

With a barely audible whisper, Ian whispered the ancient words of the ritual that would bind her to him. "I, Ian Ashton, Duke of Burnrath and Lord of London, Mark this mortal, Angelica Winthrop, as mine and mine alone. With this Mark I give Angelica my undying protection. Let all others, immortal and mortal alike, who cross her path sense my Mark and know that to act against her is to act against myself and thus set forth my wrath as I will avenge what is mine."

A tremor ran through his body as the Mark flared between them. Angelica moaned in her sleep, and Ian had to clutch the bedpost for support. No one had told him that the effect of Marking a mortal would be so strong. *What did this mean?* The only thing he knew was that her mind would now be closed to him any time he fed on her. But since he didn't care to eavesdrop on mortals' thoughts when he drank from them, this meant little to him. Furthermore, he did not intend to feed on Angelica without her permission.

When he regained his composure, he brushed his lips against hers, savoring her taste. Soon, she would be sleeping in his bed. For a moment he wished he was a mortal man again so he might wake beside her in the morning light, instead of retreating to his lair to flee the sun. Then he cursed himself for thinking like an ungrateful wretch. Fate had smiled down on him at last, granting him a few years to spend with a sweet and beautiful woman. He vowed to appreciate every moment.

Ian quietly opened her window and flew out into the night. He would have to dash off a quick note to the Elders regarding his actions. He doubted they would object; however, a few of his subordinate vampires might take offense, especially Rafe. No matter. He was lord of this city and his word was law, even to his second in command. Still, perhaps he would delay presenting her to them until after he wed her. After all, he did not wish to frighten her off.

Ben watched the vampire's body burn with less than his usual enthusiasm. The creature was a young female with blonde angelic beauty, a perfect foil for her demonic core.

"If I hadn't needed the coin, I wouldn't have bothered," he muttered, then immediately crossed himself.

"I didn't mean to utter such blasphemous words, Lord!" Ben gazed up at the sky, filled with shame at such a sacrilegious thought. "I know it is my duty to rid the world of these minions of hell. Please forgive me."

But still his pride warred within, scorning him for his failure to slay an ancient vampire. Ben bowed his head and retrieved his rosary, feeling the reassuring smoothness of the wooden beads.

He knew his hunt in London would not be easy, yet things were progressing far worse than he had imagined. The Duke of Burnrath was proving to be a most elusive quarry. So much so that Ben was not even certain that the man *was* a vampire. The gossip articles were full of conflicting and contradictory information. In fact, if the latest issue of *The Times* was to be believed, the duke was to wed a young heiress within the month, a very unusual action for a monster.

Unless... Ben paused as he recalled the caricature of the Duke and his betrothed. *What if the monster intended to transform the innocent girl into a vampire as well?*

His gut roiled in terror at the thought. The scenario was too similar to Polidori's tale to be a mere coincidence. Perhaps that was how the ancients operated... and if that were the case, his time was limited, for another soul was in jeopardy.

To his everlasting frustration, Ben couldn't get close enough to the duke or to his social circle to discover the truth, one way or another. He was barred from entry to every gathering and every club, no matter how fashionable his attire. The hunter grimaced as he recalled the fancy waistcoats and cravats he had purchased for his hunt. Damned waste of money they were! It was as though those paragons of high society had an uncanny extra sense about them, as though they could actually *smell* that he was nothing but the son of a poor Irish baron... and *Catholic* at that.

Ben sighed as he mentally calculated his remaining funds. If things kept on the way they were, he would only have enough money left to remain in this decadent city for two more months, three perhaps, if he scrimped carefully. Surely he could get closer to his quarry by then. He had to, for the duke's wedding was in only three weeks.

As he doused the vampire's smoldering ashes with his remaining jug of holy water, Ben straightened his shoulders in determination. He was a vampire hunter, and by all that was holy, he would do his God-given duty with no further sniveling. A young lady's life—and soul—might very well depend on it.

Thirteen

ANGELICA GROANED AS THE CARRIAGE LURCHED AND bounced on the rutted country road. Pendlebur Park was only a two-hour drive from the city, yet already every part of her body felt bruised and battered. She sighed and flipped through a newspaper. Truly, this trip could not have come at a better time. Everyone and their servants had already heard about her incident at Almack's.

Lady Dranston had even had the gall to come calling at an uncivilized hour this morning to ask if the engagement had been called off. Angelica hid a smile as she remembered her mother's triumph in relating Ian's side of the story and her final thrust in telling Lady Dranston about their trip to inform the Earl of Pendlebur about the upcoming nuptials.

"Put down that newspaper," Margaret admonished. "If you keep trying to read that rag with all this bouncing around, you will get the devil of a headache."

Angelica heaved another sigh and reluctantly obeyed. The advertisements for rooms for rent were blurring in her vision with every bump and sway of the carriage, and what she had managed to read was not encouraging. The cheapest rooms she could find were still far too expensive. Even with the average salary she could expect if she sold a new story every month, paying for food, clothing, and writing materials would be difficult.

A niggling voice in the back of her mind whispered that running away was a very bad idea. The cost of living in London, as portrayed in the newspaper advertisements, seemed to echo the warning. While the carriage rolled up the drive toward Pendlebur Park, her optimism sank as memories of previous visits to this cold place and its chilly owner came back to her.

Margaret retrieved her hand mirror and began making adjustments to her gown and coiffure. Her shoulders lifted and her already perfect posture became almost grotesquely straight as she forced her body to an angle that looked agonizing and impossible.

Angelica sighed and straightened her spine just as her mother seized her shoulders and forced her into the same uncomfortable position. This was only the beginning of the ritual torture that a visit to Grandfather's house entailed.

"Lift your chin a little higher," Margaret commanded, panic creeping into her voice. "And stop pouting. A future duchess does not pout."

Every time she and her mother visited the Earl of Pendlebur, who may as well have been the King of England for all the fuss involved, Angelica felt as if she were being picked apart and crushed at the same time. Her mother heaped more than the already unbearable pressure upon her to be a perfect lady, and Angelica could taste the tension between Margaret and the earl as he scrutinized seemingly every hair on Angelica's head in an effort to detect the "common blood" that tainted her and barred her from perfection.

Every time, Angelica broke under the oppressive conditions, either by saying the wrong thing— meaning whatever was really on her mind—or by being caught reading something deemed "inappropriate" in the earl's library. Thus, the visits were always mercifully short.

"I wish Papa could have come with us," she said despondently.

Margaret sighed. "You know how your grandfather feels about him, Angelica." Then, she brightened. "Of, course, now that we have made such a brilliant match for you, there could be a chance that your grandfather will soften and give your father an opportunity to get on his good side!"

Angelica managed a wan smile, her feelings warring between hope of reconciliation between her father and the earl, and sickly guilt for her potential role in dashing those hopes when she ran away.

They alighted from the carriage and the butler escorted them to the drawing room. Angelica beheld the grandfather she only saw once a year. Was she mistaken, or were his blue eyes icier, his posture even more ramrod straight, his silver hair more impeccable, and were his weathered features harder and more unyielding? She felt a twinge of pity for her mother. It was hard to imagine her as a little girl, growing up under the stern eye of this cold, implacable widower.

"Margaret," he said, his voice stern and gravelly. "You are looking well."

Angelica's mother dropped into a curtsy more suited to the throne room than a country manor. "Thank you, Father. I trust that you are in good health?"

He grunted in what seemed to be assent then turned to Angelica, the ice melting from his eyes and the ghost of a smile hovering on his thin lips. "Ah, here is my lovely granddaughter. I hear your beauty has taken London by storm. I cannot say I am surprised. You are the very image of your sainted grandmother."

"Thank you, Grandfather," she murmured and curtsied, hiding her ire that he refused to acknowledge that she looked like her father.

This time his smile was unmistakable, and his blue eyes twinkled down at her. "I have also heard that you are to be the Duchess of Burnrath. I am proud of you, my dear. You bring honor to the Pendlebur name. Come, give your grandfather a kiss, and we shall have tea and refreshments once you've changed out of your traveling costumes."

Her knees shook as she pressed her lips to his parchment cheek. She had never seen the strict Earl of Pendlebur in such good spirits before and found it to be almost unnerving.

As they dined, Angelica wanted to squirm in discomfort as her grandfather regaled them with details of the Duke of Burnrath's lavish estates and vast wealth. "They say he is as rich as Croesus. Everyone expected him to wed outside the country as all the previous dukes of Burnrath have. How ever did you nab him, my dear?"

"I-I do not really know, Grandfather," she murmured weakly.

"What a pleasing display of modesty, Angelica," her mother said with a tight smile. She then gave a vastly edited account of the past few weeks' events.

The earl laughed and pounded his cane on the floor. "Whoever would have thought that the Duke of Burnrath would have such a weakness for a damsel in distress? Good show, my dear! Good show!"

Angelica wished she could sink through the floor as she watched her mother and grandfather speaking more companionably than they had in years. For the first time, she could see the girl Margaret used to be, rather than the strict, yet fearful woman who had raised her.

"May I choose one of your horses and take a short ride, Father?" her mother asked after tea. Horses were one of Margaret's passions… yet another difference that widened the chasm between her and Angelica.

"Of course, my dear. I just purchased the most beautiful sorrel mare that I am sure will take your fancy. You may name her, if you wish." He cleared his throat. "And while you are gone, Angelica and I can have a pleasant little chat about her new beau."

Her mother and grandfather exchanged a conspiratorial glance before Margaret departed for the stables. The back of Angelica's neck prickled with suspicion. They had planned something. She had no idea how this could be, but somehow they had planned something.

The earl turned to her. "I will wait for you in the library." He bowed and walked away with brisk strides before she could reply.

Angelica wondered what the earl wanted to "chat" about. She could think of nothing except that perhaps he would lecture her about getting thrown out of Almack's. Oh well, she thought. I may as well endure this ordeal now. She straightened her shoulders and went to the library, taking a deep breath before opening the door. Her grandfather was seated in a plush burgundy wingback chair by the fireplace, with another chair set companionably near his.

"Come in, my dearest," he said cheerfully, though the smile didn't reach his eyes. "It has been so long since we visited, but that is soon to change."

"Whatever do you mean, Grandfather?" she said, looking at the gorgeous array of books adorning the shelves, which, at any other time, she would be perusing with the excitement of a child in a sweet shop on Bond Street.

He followed her gaze. "I am leaving you my entire collection, you know."

Normally she would have jumped up and down at such news. Instead, she merely inclined her head and thanked him quietly.

He nodded in approval at her manners, oblivious to her suspicion. "Yes, I have not forgotten that my library seems to be your favorite place in the world," the earl continued gruffly. "I am also signing over two of my estates, the dowager cottage in Sherwood for your mother, and for you I will deed my castle in Herefordshire. Because of you and your brilliant match, your mother and I have at last mended fences. Though I was terribly disappointed when she defied me and married a banker, it seems that mixing common blood did not impede you from making wiser choices."

Angelica bit her tongue to curb an angry retort for the infuriating slur on her father. Her gaze strayed to a letter on the table beside him. She was too far away to read the words but close enough to recognize her mother's handwriting. The earl followed her gaze and frowned.

"Now," he said with deceptive calm as Angelica braced herself for the forthcoming lecture. "I must speak with you of another matter. Your mother has informed me that you have behaved terribly over the past few months. To my everlasting shame, I hear that you have been gallivanting around in men's clothing and even had the gall to publish two horrid stories under a man's name."

His eyes spat blue daggers at her. "Despite such crimes, you were fortunate enough to wring an offer of marriage from the country's most desired bachelor. But did you go down on your knees and thank the good Lord for your fortune and repent your disgraceful ways?"

Angelica stared in stunned silence. Why did her mother always conspire against her? She shouldn't be surprised, but her heart still stung from the betrayal. She had never guessed that Margaret would tell Grandfather about her writing.

"No," the earl continued, giving her the feeling that things were about to get worse. "You did not. Instead I fear you have been doing everything your ungrateful little mind could think of to repel the Duke of Burnrath's suit—discussing unseemly topics and singing inappropriate songs. You even went as far as to get yourself thrown out of Almack's! Now, explain yourself immediately!"

Angelica blurted out without thinking, "I do not wish to wed."

The earl's face turned a mottled red. "I will tolerate no more of this insolence!" He pounded his cane on the floor. "You *will* marry the duke, and you *will* obey him in everything. If you do *anything* to stop this match, I swear to God I will cut you and your mother off from every shilling I have, and *then* I will use my influence to be sure that your father loses his position at the bank, so you all shall be penniless and on the streets! Do I make myself clear?"

"Yes, Grandfather," she whispered through numb lips. This "pleasant little chat" had gone so much worse than she'd imagined.

"Now get out of my sight," he snapped. "I do not wish to see or hear from you until you purge those scandalous thoughts out of your head. I am certain that you inherited them from your worthless father. Blood *always* tells."

Unable to take anymore, Angelica fled to the guest room and fought the urge to cry. She collapsed on the bed, emotionally drained. All was lost. Even if she did have the means to support herself and run away, she couldn't bear the thought of her father losing his job at the bank. Her mother and the Earl of Pendlebur had won, although Angelica doubted Margaret knew that the earl would sink so low as to threaten his own daughter and her husband to get his way. Angelica could not bring herself to believe that. To think so would kill all the love she had for her mother.

Her fists clenched the rich fabric of her quilt in impotent rage. She was ten kinds of a fool to have thought she could escape. She would have to forget her aspirations of a writing career and wed Ian.

Angelica waited for the suffocating feeling of dread to come at the thought of marriage and was surprised when it didn't. *Ian...* A memory of his silver eyes and tender smile suddenly washed over her, accompanied by a feeling of longing to confide in him. The irony nearly bowled her over. *I cannot believe I want comfort from the very man whom I am seeking to avoid becoming leg-shackled to!* A bubble of bitter laughter escaped her lips as she sat up and straightened her hair.

Perhaps it will not be so terrible. She reached for her handkerchief. As she blew her nose, her head cleared of its panicked grief. She rose from the bed and began to pace the room like a caged tigress. For the first time, Angelica allowed herself to truly think about marrying Ian.

All the things that her mother and grandfather chastised her for had never seemed to bother him. If she married the duke, she would be out from under her mother's thumb and she'd never have to see her cruel grandfather again if she so chose. A rush of glee filled her at the thought. As Angelica circled the bedchamber, she imagined living with Ian at Burnrath House, being alone with him, laughing with him... kissing him...

Angelica lifted her chin and stared out the window, facing the setting sun. *I will do it. I will marry the vampire duke.* She smiled, overcome by a warm rush of relief that her strenuous inner conflict was at last settled. *Well, I have always been fascinated by Burnrath House. Now the manor will be mine, because I am marrying a vampire!* She giggled at the irony and shivered at the deliciousness of the thought. *I am marrying a vampire...* She remembered the gleam of his fangs, the feel of his powerful arms around her.

He'd thought she was afraid of him, but that wasn't true. Angelica felt safe with Ian. Safe... and valued. Every aspect of his behavior in their brief courtship implied he cared about her thoughts and feelings, and he never criticized her for being different from other females. The realization brought another thought. *Perhaps he isn't marrying me only to protect his reputation. Perhaps he is doing it because he's lonely.* She remembered the story of how he became a vampire, abandoned on the field of battle, attacked, and left for dead over two centuries ago. Now all of his family was gone. Of course he was lonely. But he shall be lonely no longer, she vowed.

Suddenly, Angelica couldn't wait to return to London and shop for her trousseau. She strode to the door, ready to announce that she was eager to become the Duchess of Burnrath, but that she would do so because she *wanted* to, not because of his threats.

Then she froze with her hand grasping the handle, remembering the ferocity of her grandfather's tirade. Not only would the earl be reluctant to put aside the quarrel, but he also would still blame her father for her rebellion. And worse, Angelica and her mother would likely tear each other apart on the carriage ride home

far worse than they had after their previous visits to
Pendlebur Park.

She would have to find an explanation that
would soften the earl as well as vindicate her father.
Angelica was tempted to blister her mother's ears
for encouraging the earl to threaten her family, but
what was the use? Margaret would never understand.
Besides, after the wedding, she would be free of her
mother. But now, she would have to soften the earl
for her father's sake.

Angelica sat back down on the bed and thought.
Her excuse would have to be believable but something silly... something the usual featherheaded debutante would think. *Oh, this would be difficult!* After
discarding multiple explanations, she settled on a plan
of action. She wouldn't be able to keep a straight face
easily while spewing such drivel, but she would have
to do her best. Ian wouldn't be the only one with a
smooth tongue, she vowed. A vivid memory of his
smooth tongue momentarily weakened her knees, but
Angelica thrust the hypnotic image away to focus on
the matter at hand.

With renewed determination, she made her way
down the stairs and softly knocked on the library door.
"Grandfather?" she said in her most imploring voice.

"What is it now?" the earl demanded in his usual
churlish tone.

She took that for permission and opened the
door, composing her features in the most submissive
demeanor possible. "I came to apologize."

Her grandfather gave her a brief glance and made a
gruff noise of assent. "Very well."

Angelica approached him with careful, delicate steps, as if she was reenacting her presentation to the Sovereign. Noticing the stiff set of his shoulders, she avoided meeting his eyes. Forcing her voice to the most dulcet of tones, she began. "I am terribly sorry for my awful behavior and that I said I did not wish to wed the duke. My only explanation for such foolishness is that I am so afraid that I will not be worthy of him."

She chanced a glance then and noticed his gaze softening. Her opening appeared to be working.

"What do you, mean, child?" he asked in a tone he hadn't used since her childhood, when he'd comforted her after her nightmares.

Angelica fought back her indignation at being called a child but maintained her composure. "Since the dukes of Burnrath only married foreign nobles, the idea of being the first English Duchess of Burnrath frightens me terribly. I do not believe I am worthy of such a high honor, given my half common blood. Please forgive me?" she whispered, hoping he'd believe the explanation.

"Oh, dearest granddaughter." He enfolded her in his arms. "You do not need to be afraid. Your mother is an expert on how to act the proper lady in society. Just follow her guidance and you shall be a fine duchess. Now you must forget all that nonsense about writing novels. Leave that for the spinsters and commoners."

Angelica stepped out of her grandfather's embrace, biting her tongue. She would see what Ian had to say about that. A twinge of doubt curled in her belly. What if the duke would indeed forbid her to write?

She closed her eyes, refusing to ponder such a horrifying thought.

"Grandfather?" She returned to the mission at hand. "Could I beg you to not tell Mother about the foolish things I said? She would be dreadfully upset, but worse, she will tell Papa, and he would bring the roof down on my head! After all, he helped to encourage the match between the duke and me. He was always wrangling invitations to parties His Grace would attend, and such."

"He did, did he?" The earl's eyes lit with reluctant admiration. "Very well, I suppose I will hold my tongue then."

Angelica allowed herself to feel a measure of hope. Perhaps someday the earl would reconcile with her father. That thought, as well as anticipation of seeing her husband-to-be, nurtured her for the remainder of the visit.

Fourteen

Ian called upon the Winthrops the very evening that Angelica and her mother returned from Pendlebur Park. He was surprised to discover just how much he had missed his bride-to-be. He was so busy trying to solve the mystery of the disappearance of one of his vampires that he shouldn't have had time for such whimsical thoughts. Still, Angelica haunted his memory with her impish smile, gypsy eyes, and irreverent remarks.

"I have something to tell you, Your Grace," Angelica said as soon as they were alone in the drawing room for their designated five minutes.

"Oh?" He tried to hide his amusement at her serious demeanor even as he wondered if it was possible for her to have grown even more beautiful in the short time she'd been away.

She straightened her shoulders and lifted her chin. "I wanted to let you to know that I agree to the match and I will marry you."

He couldn't suppress a chuckle at her regal demeanor. "Well, I should certainly hope so as our engagement is a foregone conclusion. The contracts have already been drawn up." Ian reached to touch her silken hair, unable to resist her.

Her eyes narrowed as she rose from her seat. "I would have you know, *Your Grace,* that it was *not* a 'foregone conclusion.' In fact, I was not going to marry you at all! I have been doing everything I can to avoid becoming leg-shackled to you and I was going to run away!"

His jaw clenched. Ian had hoped to dispel her feelings that he was a monster and apparently had failed far worse than he had ever anticipated.

"And just where were you planning to run to?" he asked icily, unwilling to acknowledge the pain in his heart.

Angelica did not flinch at his tone. Her skirts rustled as she paced the room. "I would have used the money I made from my stories to rent a flat somewhere in the city and support myself with short stories until I finished a novel. I heard that the lady who wrote *Pride and Prejudice* made one hundred forty pounds."

"That would not be enough to buy your pretty gowns," he mocked, his temper rising at her sheer ignorance and ingratitude.

"Gowns can go to the devil!" she retorted, cheeks growing pink in indignation. She looked down at her pale-blue satin opera gown as if offended by the shimmering elegance adorning her exquisite form. "Besides, they are not sensible garb for an author, I should say."

The way Angelica glibly spoke of living in squalor and subjecting herself to the sordid dangers of London rather than being his duchess made him clench his fists.

Did she really think he was a fate worse than death? *Or was she truly that naive?*

"What play are we going to see?" she asked in a blatant attempt to change the subject.

Ian did not intend to let her off that easily. Inspiration struck him. Oh, he would take her to a "play" for certain. A play that she would never forget.

"Something pitiful and tragic," he said with an evil smile. It was high time his bride received a taste of reality. "I think you will be quite affected."

Her eyes narrowed in suspicion at his tone but she nodded in assent, ever displaying her indomitable courage. "I will get my cape."

"Put on a sensible pair of boots as well." Ian's heart twisted with bitterness. He would show her a fate worse than death.

❦

Angelica peeked at the duke, nervous about his cold demeanor. He was angry about something. His eyes seemed to shoot sparks, and his jaw was clenched so tightly she could see a nerve pulsing. She shivered. She felt like she was locked in a cage with a hungry wolf. Lifting the curtain, she peered out the carriage window.

"The theater district is in the opposite direction." She couldn't keep the alarm from creeping into her voice. "Where are you taking me?" Surely he wasn't going to bite her.

He smiled, but his eyes held no warmth. "I want to show you something."

Within moments, a foul odor was creeping into the coach. Her nose wrinkled. "What is that awful stench?"

"Humanity." The carriage stopped and the groom handed her down. The driver looked around at their squalid surroundings, his nostrils pinched in disapproval.

"Drive twice around the block, and keep your pistol out and at the ready," Ian commanded before taking Angelica's arm and leading her away from the carriage.

They were somewhere on the outskirts of the district of Soho. Angelica clung to his arm with one hand and pressed a handkerchief to her nose with the other. The reek of the place was unbearable. Her boots squelched sickeningly in the quagmire of mud and excrement that covered the rutted street.

Even at this late hour, the streets were filled with people. Scantily clad women with faces covered with rouge and sores beckoned to gentlemen from doorways to ramshackle buildings and crooked alleys. Some even lifted their skirts, calling out lewd invitations that she only half understood. Little boys ran barefoot with runny noses, trying to catch rats. There were even people lying in the gutters. Whether they were drunk, sleeping, or dead, Angelica couldn't tell.

One of the bodies nearby suddenly sat up. "Spare me a coin 'er two, milady? Please, take pity on a dying man." His grimy fingers clutched the hem of her dress, and she could smell his rancid breath through the handkerchief. His nose was a gaping hole of rotten flesh.

She reached into her reticule and tossed him a guinea, trying not to shriek in revulsion. Unbidden, her eyes strayed back to the doxies. From what she overheard from the servants, these women earned their living by satisfying men's "baser desires," whatever those were. The ones she observed looked pitiful and brittle. Angelica looked down at her fine clothes and shuddered.

I have been such a spoilt fool! Her stomach churned in self-disgust. *Here I was, throwing a childish tantrum to escape marriage to a beautiful man... a beautiful titled man, no less, and a life of luxury and ease. And these half-starved women have to degrade themselves every evening just to stay alive.*

"Tell, me Angelica," Ian said coldly, leaning on a jeweled walking stick. "Is this squalor what you would prefer to being wed to a monster?"

"No!" she cried, choking on the word as she realized what he was doing. *Oh God, I hurt him. He thinks I'm afraid of him. That's what this is all about.* "Ian, you are not a monster." She walked closer, reaching for him to prove her point.

He closed his eyes, digesting her words. "Then why were you afraid to marry me, if not in fear of what I am?"

She clutched his coat sleeves and looked up at him, willing him to see the truth in her eyes. "I wasn't afraid of what you are at all. Well, I was afraid because you are a *man.* I was terrified of losing my freedom."

Doubt and confusion filled his gaze, but there was a glimmer of something else. *Was it hope?* "What do you mean?"

Angelica took a deep breath and explained. "My mother told me that a man would never countenance his wife writing gothic novels. I thought I wouldn't be able to bear giving up writing, especially not to dedicate my life as an ornament for your arm and a 'perfect' hostess. Besides," she added with narrowed eyes. "I've read *The Sylph*, so I know how miserable life as a duchess can truly be."

He stared at her for a long moment, his expression unreadable. She struggled not to drown in his glowing silver eyes. "What made you change your mind?"

She faltered, looking down at the slimy cobblestones beneath her feet. "Well, my family has convinced me that my duty is to marry, and our engagement is healing rifts between my grandfather and my mother and father. And, well… you are not really a fate worse than death."

"Indeed?" he asked with a raised brow.

"Oh, yes. In fact, you are very handsome and…" She resisted the urge to place her hands against her burning cheeks. "Quite nice!"

The tender smile that she loved returned to his face. "Oh, Angel, truly, you will have more freedom with me than you had in your home. After all, a duchess may do as she pleases."

"Even write?" she breathed, daring to hope.

He nodded, and caressed her cheek. "Even write."

Pleasure curled through her, all the way down to her toes, until she saw a large rat skitter by, reminding her of something else. "In that case, Your Grace, may I request a wedding present?"

"Anything," he said indulgently.

"May I have a cat?" Her lips curved as she voiced a long-denied wish. Her mother would never allow animals in her home.

"A cat?" He chuckled at the odd request. "Surely you would prefer a little lapdog like the other ladies?"

He smiled and his voice turned teasing. "Or perhaps you would enjoy having a monkey like those that belong to the more eccentric matrons?"

"Certainly not," she scoffed. "Dogs are useless and monkeys belong in the jungle. Your house has rats. The one that startled me so I tripped down your stairs was monstrous! Besides, Mother never let me have any pets, and I shall be quite lonely during the daytime when you are... asleep."

"Very well, a feline it is, along with anything else your heart desires." He took her arm, pulling her close. "Let us leave now. I am sorry I brought you here."

"Oh, please do not be sorry!" Angelica protested, clinging to him. "I always knew that London had unsavory districts, but I hadn't the slightest notion of how bad it could be. You have opened my eyes, Your Grace. I fear many others are unaware of the pitiful living conditions here. Perhaps I could write numerous articles on the subject. I believe I shall want to come back and gather more information about these sorts of sections of the city."

"As long as you never venture here alone." Ian's voice was stern. "Such a foolish action would be extremely dangerous. Truly, I should never have brought you. I was not thinking clearly."

Angelica hid a smile. It seemed he truly did care for her. "But what if I wear a disguise?" she teased.

"No disguises," he countered roughly. "After all, they did not protect you from me."

"Yes, Your Grace," she answered solemnly.

He reached up and stroked her hair. "Please, call me Ian."

Her heart warmed at his soft tone. "Very well... Ian. May we go home now?" She shivered as the dampness of her gown seemed to seep into her bones.

Again, agonized guilt slashed across his features before he managed a light smile. "Of course, my Angel."

Angelica sighed and leaned into him as they headed back in the direction of the carriage. Footsteps echoed on the cobblestones behind her, but she barely heard them. Suddenly Ian stopped.

"Polidori!" he growled, and thrust her away from him so roughly that she almost fell.

Shock roiled through her at the abrupt change in his mood. "Ian, what—"

He didn't hear her. The duke was staring at a handsome Italian man who had stumbled into the square.

Could this be the Polidori, the one who wrote "The Vampyre"? She didn't have time to ask, for Polidori's dark eyes met Ian's glowing gaze, then widened in terror as Ian bared his fangs. Polidori turned and fled, and Ian bolted in pursuit. His walking stick clattered to the ground, forgotten.

Angelica watched in stunned silence as the normally composed duke disappeared around the corner, running like a madman.

"Oh-ho, this be our lucky day!" a voice chortled, and she was seized from behind.

As she struggled against her captor, a scruffy man came out of the shadows. His toothless grin chilled Angelica to the bone. It was the same grin that graced little boys' faces while they pulled the wings off butter-flies. One quick glance at the empty street told her that the coach had not yet arrived. Not only that, but the square was now suddenly deserted, as if everyone were happy to leave her to her fate.

"Aye, I see the gov'ner has left his fancy piece for us." The scruffy man's filthy hand reached for her bodice.

The man who held her tugged her backward. "'Tis my turn first!" he growled.

His sour stench made her eyes water. She was *not* going to wait long enough to find out what these ruffians had in store for her. She raised her knee and kicked back and upward, her boot slamming into the man's groin.

He released her immediately, his breath whistling out of him in a pitiful squeal. She rushed forward to freedom… and her skirts tangled around her boot. Angelica plummeted face-first into the filth on the street. An enormous ruby winked at her from the mud and her eyes widened at its incongruity before she noticed the length of polished wood to which the jewel was affixed.

"Methinks it's *my* turn now," the other man chuckled, approaching her and unfastening his grimy trousers. "I like it when they fight; 'tis exciting."

Angelica's hand closed around Ian's walking stick, and she scrambled to her feet with a scream of fury tearing from her throat.

❧

Ian's hand closed around Polidori's arm just as he heard Angelica scream. All thoughts of interrogating the writer ceased. What had he been thinking?

"Another time, Doctor," he said, releasing the man.

Choking with guilt and terror, Ian ran back to the square where he had left his intended bride.

Ian sucked in a breath at the sight before him. One man was crumpled on the ground, blood dripping from a wound on the side of his head. Angelica fended the other off with Ian's walking stick, oblivious to the mud dripping from her face and hair. Apparently she had not discovered that the walking stick concealed a blade, for she was merely bludgeoning her enemy with the length of wood. Admiration for her courage warred with guilt for putting her in danger. His protective instincts rose to a frenzied pitch and the scent of blood teased his nostrils. With a roar, he seized Angelica's attacker and sank his fangs into his throat.

When Ian read the man's intentions to rape his intended bride, he had felt the urge to kill for the first time in almost two centuries. He released his victim with a growl, realizing that she had been watching him the whole time. Angelica stared at him, wide-eyed but silent. She wiped the mud from her cheek, smearing it on her satin glove. Her body heaved from its exertion as she continued to clutch his walking stick.

"I am quite sorry you had to see that," Ian said as he approached her, carefully watching her face for any expression of disgust. Again he cursed himself for putting her in danger.

"I am just happy those men did not…" She trailed off as Ian withdrew his handkerchief and wiped the rest of the mud from her face. "Did you kill him?"

He raised a brow at her casual tone. *Would she ever cease to surprise him?* "No. He is merely unconscious." Ian neglected to tell her that with the amount of blood he had taken, coupled with the man's poor health, the bastard wasn't likely to survive the night. "Now come, my bloodthirsty wench. We should leave this place and fabricate a story for your mother's benefit in regards to the dishevelment of your clothing and person."

Once they were settled in the carriage, Angelica asked, "Was that *really* John Polidori, you were chasing?"

He sighed at her enthusiasm. She should be berating him for abandoning her. "Yes."

She leaned forward, eyes gleaming in fascination. "Why were you chasing him?"

"He owes me some explanations for his writing." Ian answered patiently, though he was growing exhausted with the subject.

She chewed her full lower lip. "I do hope you catch him next time. I would very much like to meet him. I think he is an excellent writer."

Ian laughed. "I was afraid you might think so."

Inside, he was seething with self-recrimination. His pursuit of Polidori had put Angelica in danger. Perhaps he should call off the search and leave the man alone. After all, now that he was to wed, his reputation should be saved. He paused, looking out the carriage window. On the other hand, Rosetta lived nearby. Once he saw his future duchess home safely, it couldn't hurt to call on her and request that she try to catch Polidori.

Fifteen

"My God, he almost had me!" John panted as he slammed the door behind him and bolted down the stone steps.

Rosetta's heart pounded in alarm. "What happened, John?" She hurried over to him, running her hands over his body, looking for any sign of injury.

"I was walking through the square and a vampire saw me." John paused to catch his breath as she waited anxiously. "He knew my name and he gave chase with murder in his eyes. The bastard caught me and I thought I was done for, but then a woman screamed and he released me and headed back in her direction." He fetched a bottle of wine from the table and poured a glass with shaky hands.

Terror for her beloved turned her heart to ice. "What did he look like?" If the vampire pursuing John was one of the duke's informants, she could handle it, but if it was *him*, the danger had escalated tenfold.

Polidori paced the room like an agitated cat, wine slopping over his glass onto the floor. "He was tall, well dressed, and possessed the most eerie silver eyes. I could swear that they glowed."

"Oh God!" she gasped and took John into her arms. "Then he was the Duke of Burnrath, the Lord Vampire of London. Did he follow you?"

John shook his head. "No, I'm sure he did not. He was quite concerned with the lady who screamed."

"What lady?" Rosetta demanded. She'd heard His Grace was to marry a mortal but hadn't believed the rumor until she saw the announcement in *The Times*. But surely he did not bring his intended to this part of town.

"I don't know who she was. I didn't see her, but God, she screamed loud." John shuddered, eyes full of compassion. "I think she was being attacked. But I am certain the vampire did not follow me," he repeated.

Rosetta remained unconvinced. "I do not want you leaving this chamber after dark anymore unless I am with you. It is not safe."

"But, Rosetta, if he sees you with me, he is sure to kill you for betraying him." John's dark gaze captured hers with his implacable will.

He was right. She ran a hand through her hair in agitation. She hated the fact that in instances like this she was as helpless as a mortal woman. Her eyes grew moist. "It does not matter as long as you are safe, my love. I could not bear it if something happened to you. And you seem to forget that this trouble was my fault to begin with. Still, I will fight for you if I have to."

She trembled in his arms. He kissed the tears from her face and whispered, "Oh, Rosetta, my avenging warrior."

Her lips caressed his neck as she unfastened the buttons of his shirt, eager to make love to him once more, for each time could be their last.

All of their worries fled into the night as their bodies joined. Each wished the passionate embrace could last forever.

"I love you, Rosetta," John whispered as she sank her fangs in his neck.

There was a brisk knock at the door. Terror spiked through her like the sun's fatal rays. Swiftly she leaped from the bed and threw on a night rail. She closed the bed curtains and sent John a pleading look to be silent before she raced up the stone steps, struggling to compose herself.

Her fears were confirmed when she opened the door to see the Lord of London looking down at her in embarrassment at her disheveled state. She decided to use his discomfort to her advantage.

"Rosetta, I am terribly sorry to have interrupted you." He coughed awkwardly.

"What is it, my lord?" she asked, lacing her voice with the proper mixture of humiliation and impatience.

"John Polidori was seen near this area. I would like you to search for him when you are finished with your, ah, business. I have other matters demanding my attention at the moment and would greatly appreciate your assistance." He paused and his expression became grave. "And please do keep your eyes and ears sharp for signs of Blanche. You remember her, don't you? She's small in stature and has long, pale blonde hair. She lives near Piccadilly. I still haven't found her and I'm beginning to suspect the worst."

Rosetta was flooded with guilt at the relief she felt upon another vampire's disappearance providing a convenient distraction. She bowed meekly, avoiding his eyes. "Of course, my lord." She turned to go back inside.

"I say, Rosetta," his voice echoed behind her. She stiffened. "It's not Thomas you're dallying with, is it?" His voice was laced with amusement.

"No, my lord," she answered honestly, suppressing a sneer. As if she would jeopardize her position by involving herself with a rival!

He chuckled. "Very well, I will leave you to your secrets. Be sure to inform me if you find anything." The Lord of London turned to leave, and Rosetta's pulse began to slow. Then he turned back around. "Perhaps Polidori has something to do with Blanche's disappearance."

"Oh no, my lord!" she said too quickly. "That is... Blanche seemed to me to be such a quiet, unhappy sort. Perhaps she decided to end her existence. I know that is a terrible thing to contemplate, but surely that explanation is more reasonable than any other alternative."

He nodded. "Perhaps you are correct, though the thought pains me." He pulled his watch from his pocket and frowned. "I must be going now. Thank you for your vigilance."

Rosetta bowed meekly. "Yes, my lord."

After he left, she slumped against the door frame. Something had to be done about His Grace. He was bound to discover her deception any night, with the way things were headed. Unfortunately the only way to get him off her trail was to turn in Polidori or kill her lord. She thought of fleeing London or even England, but quickly dismissed the idea. Burnrath would merely inform the Elders and they would put out a search warrant across the world.

"That was him, wasn't it?" John whispered loudly from the bedchamber.

"Yes, but he is gone now. I do not think he believes you are here." Again, shame filled her for the lies she had told her master.

She poured a glass of wine and sipped it pensively. Her deception was weaving a tighter and tighter trap, one whose jaws could close on her any minute.

Rosetta wasn't powerful enough to kill the Lord of London, and even if she was, she didn't know if she could bring herself to commit such a terrible act. But she would do anything for John. Her thoughts raced as she thought of ideas and then discarded them. She had to do something, but what?

Sixteen

THE LAST THREE WEEKS OF THE ENGAGEMENT FLEW faster than Keats's nightingale. Angelica's mother was over the moon with the joy of preparing wedding invitations. Margaret chattered in an incessant stream to her daughter as she pored over a guest list, reading spectacles perched on her nose. She had succeeded in her crusade to get her daughter married off, and her happiness shone to the world.

Angelica was torn between amusement and relief that the nagging had abated slightly. But now that her mother had accomplished her goal and Angelica would be moving away, what would Margaret do with the rest of her life? The thought gave Angelica a strange pang of discomfort.

"Oh my, I almost forgot the Wheatons," her mother said, interrupting her reverie. "They are related to the Prime Minister, so we cannot risk offending them." Margaret pulled out a black invitation embossed with silver—the Burnrath colors—opened it, then dipped her quill in silver ink.

Angelica watched her mother, happily engrossed

with her work, and a frightening suspicion overtook her. "Mother, what do you plan to do when I'm gone?"

"Whatever do you mean, dearest?" Margaret asked. "You are not going far. I will still visit you often. After all, you will still need my help planning balls and musicales and other such things. And there will be the grandchildren to think of, of course. Why, it shall be as if you never left!"

"I see," Angelica said with dawning horror. However would she get any writing done with her mother constantly pestering her? Not to mention the tirade that would come when she failed to get pregnant.

Margaret raised a brow. "I see the prospect doesn't exactly delight you," she said dryly. Her voice softened. "I know we've never seen eye to eye, but you must believe that I love you. After all, you are my only child and I'm afraid my heart would be broken if we became estranged after your marriage. I hope you can find it in your heart to permit me to remain a part of your life and perhaps lend my help and advice when you so require. I promise to try not to push you so much."

Angelica blinked at her mother's impassioned—and unexpected—speech. She was beginning to recognize that not all of their disagreements were entirely Margaret's fault. When her mother said "white," it was practically a reflex for her to say "black." A childish impulse, she realized uncomfortably, and now was high time she grew out of it. After all, she was to be a duchess soon. She knew that they would never agree with each other on much, but the least she could do was make an effort to compromise.

"Of course, Mother," Angelica whispered. "I would

very much like for you to visit me. And," she added, looking down at her lap. "I am sorry I couldn't have been a more normal daughter to you."

Margaret smiled and opened her arms. Angelica rushed into her embrace, heart light at the reconciliation. They would still bicker, she was certain, but at least they had become closer.

"Now," her mother said as she wiped a tear from her eye. "I must get back to work, else there will be no guests at your wedding." Retrieving the quill, she glanced up at her daughter. "I nearly forgot to ask. Is there anyone in particular you would like to invite?"

"I do not have any friends," Angelica said with downcast eyes. She never had anything in common with girls her age. She preferred cats to horses and books to fashion. Because of the estrangement between her mother and the Earl of Pendlebur, her family spent most summers in town rather than in the country with the rest of the peerage, contributing further to her isolation.

Her mother sighed. "Well, perhaps we can invite the daughters of some of my acquaintances."

Angelica frowned at the thought of having a group of insipid girls she hardly knew attending such an important event in her life. A thought came to her, bringing a smile. "I think it would be a wonderful idea to invite a few of Father's nieces. I haven't seen my Winthrop cousins since I was a child." She tried to keep a note of accusation out of her voice. Her mother had limited her contact with her husband's side of the family, thinking she was above them.

"But darling, they are nobodies." Margaret didn't bother to hide the scorn in her voice.

"They are family," Angelica insisted. "And besides, maybe they could meet eligible gentlemen at the reception. And this *is* my wedding."

"Very well." Her mother set aside her spectacles. "Perhaps that will convey the message that it will not pay to offend the Duchess of Burnrath. But at least invite a lady of Quality to attend. I hear the duke invited the Duke of Wentworth. His wife would be a very wise choice."

"That is brilliant, Mother," Angelica said, and meant it. She had not forgotten the kindness the Wentworths displayed toward her family during that fateful night at the Cavendish ball.

❦

Saint George's Church was packed with nearly every member of the *haut ton*, all come to witness the historical marriage of the Duke of Burnrath to Miss Angelica Winthrop, granddaughter of the Earl of Pendlebur. The event seemed to bring more talk than the recent death of Napoleon Bonaparte. George's Street was packed with carriages, their lanterns glowing in the night like stars and the fog curled up around the horses' legs, making the creatures appear as if they were perched on clouds. Angelica peered out at the whimsical scene one last time before turning back to the mirror.

The ivory silk bridal gown was overlaid with gold spangled lace, transforming her into a picture of elegance as well as making her look ethereal and innocent. *A fit bride for a duke*, she thought with a wry smile, resisting the urge to lift her nose in the air in mocking imitation of her mother. Margaret knelt below her, toying with the arrangement of her skirts.

Angelica squirmed in impatience. "Mother, please stop fidgeting with my dress. The guests are all here, and if I do not make my appearance on the aisle soon, the duke will think I abandoned him."

Margaret paused for a moment before returning to her frantic ministrations. "Just let me adjust your veil."

Angelica bit back a curse. "Honestly, I do not see why I have to wear this silly thing. The confounded fabric itches and I cannot see through it very well."

"This veil is the latest in Paris fashion and my daughter shall have nothing less." Her mother was implacable.

"We are not in Paris," Angelica grumbled under her breath as her mother poked and pulled at her further before handing her a bouquet of white roses and orange blossoms.

"There you are, a perfect duchess." Her mother's eyes misted. "This day is even better than I had dreamed! I am so proud of you."

Her father entered the room and gently closed the door behind him. "It is time for me to escort the bride down the aisle." His voice was almost comically hushed in respect for their solemn surroundings.

"We are just about finished here," her mother said with a wistful smile. "She looks lovely, does she not?"

Her father gazed down at Angelica, love shining in his eyes. "You are the most beautiful bride I have ever beheld, my dearest… aside from your mother, of course," he added, and Margaret made a small pleased sound.

"Thank you, Papa." Angelica beamed and wiped a tear from her cheek, as she looked at her happy parents. "I will miss you both."

She felt a lump form in her throat at their obvious happiness. As she took her father's arm and prepared to march down the aisle, Margaret called, "Do not forget what I told you about tonight."

How could I? Angelica thought as her mother's lecture about the wedding night and the marriage bed flitted through her mind.

"There will be incredible pain the first time, darling," Margaret had said. "And you might bleed. But you must submit to him without complaint until you are pregnant with his heir. After that, he should leave you alone for the most part and fulfill his baser desires on a mistress."

Angelica did not wish to be subjected to something that would make her bleed, but she had a feeling some of those "baser desires" involved kissing. The thought of Ian's lips on another woman's made her want to scream. *Thank God he said he is unable to give me children. That means I will not have to go through such unpleasantness! Also, in that case, he should have no need for a mistress!*

Angelica walked down the aisle on her father's arm, trying to look proud and confident. The smell of candle wax, incense, flowers, and over-perfumed bodies created a cloying miasma, making breathing extremely difficult. Or perhaps just her nervousness was overwhelming. Everyone stared at her, and their whispers shook the rafters.

She took comfort in the sight of her grandfather,

the Earl of Pendlebur, smiling his approval on her and her father. The two men had actually been civil to each other today, and she had reason to hope that the earl would at long last accept his son-in-law. She tamped down the anger at her grandfather for his cruel threats. Today was not meant for unpleasant feelings, and she would do her best to at least be polite to him.

There were a few unfamiliar faces about and she wondered if some of Ian's fellow vampires had come for the ceremony. The thought of vampires in church made her stifle a giggle. She longed to tell that Polidori fellow about it if she ever had the opportunity to meet him. Angelica took a deep breath and focused on putting one foot in front of the other and doing her best not to crush the bouquet of flowers in her nervous grip.

Her eyes locked on Ian, who stood at the altar waiting with a smile. He looked so dark and handsome that her knees almost buckled under her skirts. When her father placed her hand in Ian's, an electrical current seemed to spring between them. Only a flicker in his eyes revealed that he felt it too.

The parson's words droned on, just barely within her consciousness. *I am doing it. I am actually marrying a vampire!* She wondered if he would change her into one as well. Too late, she realized that she'd never broached the subject, for she'd been too concerned with avoiding marriage. The thought of drinking blood gave her pause, but the thought of living forever, especially with a man like Ian by her side, would make it all worthwhile. And when he vowed to honor and cherish her, she felt a thrill of warmth down to her toes. She smiled up at him and said her vows, though she stumbled a bit on the word "obey."

He slipped a wide gold band over her finger. "With this ring, I thee wed, with my body I thee honor, and with all my worldly goods I thee endow."

Her heart thrilled at the warmth in his voice.

After what seemed to be an eternity, they were pronounced man and wife. Stunned gasps erupted from the audience as Ian's mouth slanted across hers with such passion she feared the church would be set alight. When he lifted his head, he turned her to face the crowd. "I present to you Lady Angelica Ashton, Duchess of Burnrath."

The cheers were deafening as they walked out of the church. Society's capricious speculations now leaned toward a love match, for all eyes had examined her midsection for a telltale bulge that would have revealed Angelica to have been physically compromised, and none was observed. Also, she had looked so innocent in her gown of virginal white that only the most hardened souls could believe she was anything but a virtuous young lady.

However, the adoration in the duke's eyes and the passion in their unexpected kiss led the wedding guests to concur that the duke and his new duchess were unfashionably in love. Still, a handful of fervent believers of Polidori's tale wondered if the new duchess would survive her wedding night. Despite the church's holy atmosphere, a few wagers were made.

❧

Angelica could hardly believe the transformation of the Burnrath mansion. The ballroom glowed from the gaslit chandeliers, and the gilded mirrors sparkled. Not a speck of dust or ominous shadow was in sight. Menservants performed a stately march to and fro with silver trays bearing glasses of champagne and hors d'oeuvres. Musicians played lively melodies, to which the multitude of guests were happy to dance… at least, most of them were.

Two men held up pillars on opposite sides of the ballroom. Angelica recognized them from the wedding, but she had never seen them before that. The first man was impossibly tall, with shoulder-length hair the color of moonlight. He surveyed the merriment as if such joy was alien to him, but his stormy blue-gray eyes held the same trace of loneliness she often saw in Ian's gaze. Was this another vampire?

The second man had exotic, golden brown skin and startling amber eyes set off by a mane of waist-length black hair. His features were so striking that it took Angelica a moment to observe that the left side of his face was scarred and that his left arm hung awkwardly at his side, as if it had lost its function. At first she thought his scowl was due to anger that he couldn't dance, but then she followed the line of his sight and realized that he was glaring at the other man.

"I cannot believe the Mad Deveril is here!" the Duchess of Wentworth said quietly behind her.

"The Mad Deveril?" Angelica turned to her with a raised brow. "To whom are you referring, Your Grace?"

The duchess grinned. "Please, call me Jane, else we'll

be 'Your Grace-ing' one another all night." She lifted
her fan to whisper, "I was referring to the man you
were staring at, the one with the striking hair and
blue eyes. He's much more handsome than I'd heard,
though so very tall and thin. You are not contem-
plating an affair already, are you?"

Angelica gasped in outrage. "Of course not!" At
Jane's laughter, she realized the duchess was teasing
her. Shifting her gaze back to the subject of their
conversation, Angelica lifted her own fan to whisper,
"Is he truly mad?"

Jane nodded. "Not in the dangerous or amusing
variety, though. From what I understand, he is merely
reclusive and hardly ever leaves his estate in Cornwall.
He must be very close to your husband to have braved
the wilds of London… or perhaps he was as eager as
the rest of us to see Burnrath House. His Grace has
never entertained before, you know."

"I had heard that," Angelica agreed, smiling at
the duchess's chatter as she digested the information.
Likely "the Mad Deveril" was another vampire. She
would have to ask Ian at the earliest opportunity.
Where was he, anyway?

"I have been clamoring to see the inside of
this place." Jane's green eyes shone with eagerness.
"Though these gas lamps make me nervous! What if
one were to set the house ablaze?"

Angelica felt an odd twinge of irritation that anyone
would dare criticize her new home. "Well, I'd read in
The Times that the Westminster Gas Light and Coke
Company anticipates these lamps to be in every home
within twenty years."

"How very interesting." As if sensing her defensiveness, Jane changed the subject. "I believe you lived nearby?"

Angelica nodded, thrilled that someone shared her interest in this magnificent house. "I did. Burnrath House has always held my fascination as well." She dropped her voice to a whisper. "I still cannot believe that it is now mine."

Jane smiled and tossed her auburn curls. "And the rest of society cannot believe that Lord Burnrath is now yours." She inclined her head toward a group of young debutantes whispering and pouting in their direction.

Angelica frowned. She had heard enough on that subject from her mother. Surely the ladies were not that envious of her. Such a thing would be tragic, for she did so want to make some friends.

Her gaze strayed back to the scarred man. His scowl had deepened. "Who is that other man?" She was careful to incline her head only slightly.

Jane peered over the lacy edge of her fan. "I am not completely certain, but I believe he may be the infamous pugilist who Burnrath sponsors. He is only known as 'the Spaniard.' The description definitely fits him, anyway." The duchess shook her head. "I do not understand why Burnrath invited him. He cannot dance with only one arm."

"Yet he can box?" Angelica asked archly.

The Duke of Wentworth interrupted the fascinating conversation and winked at his wife. "You have monopolized the bride long enough, my lady. A multitude of gentlemen are waiting to dance with this beautiful creature."

With that, Angelica was pulled onto the dance floor. She danced with so many men she couldn't keep count, and for the first time in her life, she enjoyed herself at a ball. No longer were men dancing with her because they had designs on her dowry. Now dancing was merely a pleasant entertainment. A few asked her about the rumors of Ian being a vampire, but she laughed them off as if the concept was the most ludicrous thing she had ever heard. Quickly, she glanced at Lord Deveril. He gave her a brief half smile and inclined his head as if he approved of how she had handled the situation.

Her Winthrop cousins giggled and danced as well, resplendent in their new formal gowns. Half of the young bucks in attendance were already obviously smitten with the gypsy-like girls. Angelica took as much time as she could to get reacquainted with them before they were all swept away for yet another dance. As the evening progressed, the gentlemen became foxed and tried to steal kisses from her. Angelica laughed as she ducked and bobbed to avoid their advances, the merriment increased by her new husband's dark scowls.

"Come, let us retire," Ian said, removing the champagne glass from her hand.

Angelica blinked. "But why? It is only midnight and the guests show no inclination of leaving."

Ian smiled. "This is our wedding night. We are expected to go up to our bedchamber."

Understanding lit her eyes. "Oh, I see." Likely, his reputation would be harmed if people knew he could not have children. "What will we do up there?"

He frowned. "We will have our wedding night, of course."

She gazed up at him in confusion. After looking around to make sure no one was listening, she rose up on her toes and whispered, "But I thought that you were unable give me children."

He appeared to be torn between frustration and laughter. "I may not be able to impregnate you," he whispered against her neck, sending shivers down her entire body. "But I assure you, my duchess, I am perfectly capable of the act."

Shivering in trepidation, she changed the subject. "Is Lord Deveril also a vampire?"

Ian nodded impatiently. "Yes, he is the Lord of Cornwall."

"And the Spaniard with the scars?" she prodded.

"He is my second in command, and he will remain on guard for the remainder of the ball." Before Angelica could question him further, Ian swept her into his arms and carried her up the stairs to the accompaniment of coarse laughter and ribald comments she could only half understand.

Seventeen

THE BEDCHAMBER WAS HUGE AND DAUNTING WITH shadows in every corner that seemed to encroach on the large four-poster bed. Liza was waiting next to it, just finishing arranging rose petals on the coverlet. The whole scenario looked fitting for a ritual sacrifice. Angelica forgot all about her curiosity about the other vampires as the impending consummation of her marriage loomed over her in stark clarity.

"I am ready to help prepare you for bed, Your Grace." Her maid blushed and led Angelica through an adjoining door.

"I hope he will be gentle with you, truly I do." Liza divested Angelica of her wedding gown and helped her into a filmy white scrap of satin. "But at least you will be comforted by the fact that he will give you such beautiful children!"

Angelica shivered. *No, I will not. What he is going to do to me will give me no comfort at all.*

Liza departed, and with quaking knees, Angelica crossed the length of the bedchamber to join her vampire husband. His back was to her as he faced the fireplace. The orange flickering light cast sinister shadows on the wall.

"Here I am, Your Grace." She lifted her chin and prayed he did not hear the fear in her voice.

Ian whipped around, his eyes glowing hungrily at the sight of her in the nearly transparent nightgown. "Dear God," he breathed.

Despite her trepidation, Angelica couldn't suppress a light laugh. "I didn't think vampires would speak much about God." At his slight smile, with no dimming at his intense stare, she sobered.

"You look like the seraphim you were named for, Angel." His voice was husky. "Come here."

She couldn't stop herself from stepping backward, farther away from him. "What are you going to do to me?" *How badly would it hurt?*

"I am going to make love to you." He stepped forward, slowly approaching until their bodies touched.

That didn't sound so bad. Ian's lips claimed hers, and he gripped her shoulders as he whispered between kisses, "I feel as if I have been waiting an eternity to have you, Angel."

His hands crept down to the bodice of her gown and he began to untie the laces. She gasped at the feel of his hands on such an intimate part of her body. She struggled and tried to shove him away. "What are you doing?"

He stepped back and blinked. "What exactly did your mother tell you about what goes on between married couples behind closed doors?"

She shuddered and pulled the fabric of the gown tight around her bodice. "She said you would hurt me very badly and that I would bleed." Her eyes narrowed and her tone grew laced with hostility at such a horrific concept. "She said I must submit to you without complaint."

He cursed and Angelica flinched. "I suppose that explains why you're an only child. Damn, I hate some of the traditions of this century. To keep a young woman in ignorance of one of the most important facts of life is... is a goddamned outrage!" He ran a hand through his hair and sat on the bed. "Sit down with me, Angel. You're shaking so hard that I am afraid you will topple over to the floor."

Angelica felt a small measure of comfort in the gentleness in his voice and only cringed a bit when she sat beside him.

He took her chin in his hand, coaxing her to meet his gaze as he stroked her cheek with his thumb. "What *we* are going to do, couples have been doing *joyfully* since the beginning of time. The act of love is about giving and receiving pleasure. I implore you to wipe the word 'submit' from your mind. I do not intend for you to feel like you're doing anything of the sort."

"Then you won't hurt me?" she asked, still feeling an edge of doubt. Her mother had been so adamant that the consummation of her marriage would be awful. But Ian had never lied to her before.

He sighed again and took her hand, softly stroking her wrist with his thumb. "I am sorry, Angel, but there will most likely be pain the first time, but *only* the first time, and only for a moment. I will be as gentle as I am able."

She nodded, believing him. "Will you kiss me?" she asked shyly.

He smiled in a way that warmed her to her toes. "Oh, yes. Many times… all over." This time she didn't pull back when he took her lips in a slow, drugging kiss.

His kisses seemed to last for an eternity. Ian slowly ran his hands through her hair and stroked her back in soothing motions. Emboldened, she threaded her fingers through the thick black locks of his hair, sighing at its texture. Slowly, they sank down onto the bed, lying in each other's arms.

Angelica's eyes widened as he sat up and removed his shirt. His chest was broad and sculpted like that of a Greek god. His abdomen was flat with ridged muscles that made *her* stomach flutter at the sight of him. A thin line of hair ran below his belly and disappeared into his trousers, invoking unholy curiosity.

He smiled at her stunned expression. "I, ah, take it that you have never seen a man's bare chest before?"

"Aside from a glimpse of yours the first time I came here, only pictures and statues," she whispered, longing to touch him, to see if he was smooth and hard as he looked. "Were things so different back in… your time?"

He nodded. "Oh, yes." He looked down at her trembling hands. "You may touch me if you like."

Her cheeks heated. "Would you mind?"

"I would like it very much," he whispered roughly.

Cautiously, she placed one hand on his chest, noting his quick intake of breath as his nipples hardened. She grew braver, running both hands across the planes and ridges of his muscles, her pulse rising in excitement at her explorations. His skin felt like rough satin over steel and the urge to get closer to him was overpowering.

Angelica was mesmerized. Surely her mother was cracked. This was better than chocolate. "Am I 'giving you pleasure,' Your Grace?"

"Yes." His voice was a low growl and his eyes glowed faintly in the candlelight.

An age-old feeling of feminine power rushed over her at his response. "Do you want to touch me as well?"

He nodded and gently unlaced her nightgown. As he slid the garment down to expose her breasts, she resisted the urge to cover herself, knowing he must enjoy the sight of her body as much as she enjoyed his. For a long time, he merely stared at her as if she were a priceless treasure. "You are so beautiful," he whispered.

His hands slowly ran along the undersides of her breasts as if she were delicate as glass. Her nipples hardened under his featherlight caresses. When his fingers lightly squeezed her nipples, she cried out in surprised pleasure as muscles low in her body tightened and flickered with heat. "Am I giving *you* pleasure, my lady?"

"Yes!" Her voice came out harsh with need.

With a groan, he captured her lips, thrusting his tongue against hers and pulling her down to lie atop him. The feel of his bare chest against hers was so hot and intoxicating that she trembled. As their kissing grew more frantic, their caresses reached a fevered, wanton peak and she writhed against his hardness. Every nerve in her body seemed to lead to the secret place between her thighs until it was throbbing with pulsing need.

He rolled her over onto her back, and as she felt the cool softness of rose petals under her buttocks, she fully realized her nakedness. When he lifted his body from hers, she gasped and covered herself, cheeks flushing.

"Please, do not hide your beauty from me, Angel," Ian said as he unfastened his trousers.

Reluctantly, she moved her hands, gazing up at him in a mixture of trepidation and fascination as he removed the rest of his clothes. His legs were long, muscled, and lean. Dark hair grew from the juncture of his thighs, framing a long, thick rod that was nothing like those of the nude male statues and paintings she'd seen. It was huge and frightening.

Terror washed over her as he returned to the bed. Unconsciously, she tried to scoot away from him.

Ian's gaze was intent, but his gentle tone remained. "Do not be afraid, Angelica. All men are made thus."

"*All men?*" she squeaked, eyes wide at his size.

He smirked and glanced down. "Well, perhaps not *all* men."

She couldn't take her eyes off him. Tentatively, she reached out and took hold of it with only her fingertips. Ian sucked in a sharp breath and his rod seemed to shudder in her delicate grip. The shaft felt like molten satin, and as she moved her hand up to the head, she found that it felt like velvet. Shyly, she explored the curves and ridges of his manhood, marveling that something could feel so hard and so soft at the same time.

"May I touch you, Angel?" Ian whispered.

At her nod, his hand reached down, and before

she knew it, his fingers delved into the damp curls between her legs. She whimpered in protest.

"Relax, Angel, and trust me," he whispered; his lips caressed her earlobe.

She sighed and obeyed, gasping in pleasure as his fingers caressed her silken folds and his thumb flicked across her tiny bud like a tongue of flame. Her hand gripped his shaft tighter, and she stroked it in her distraction. He took her hand away and guided it to his chest, where she could feel his pounding heart. "Easy, love. I will not last if you keep that up."

Before Angelica could decipher that cryptic statement, he was leaning over her, thrusting a finger inside her as his lips and teeth nibbled her neck, fangs grazing lightly across her flesh, leaving her quivering in ecstasy. The heady smell of rose petals blended with his spicy masculine scent and enveloped her in a spell of sensuality. Soon she was slick with need, her core aching for fulfillment. Angelica arched her hips with a helpless moan. As if that were the moment he anticipated, Ian positioned himself between her thighs.

"It is best if I dispense with this part quickly," he whispered hoarsely. "I am sorry to cause you pain, Angel."

With that, he drove into her with one powerful thrust. She gasped and bit his shoulder, eyes squeezing shut at the tearing sensation. Then he was kissing her tenderly, whispering love words to her, as he remained still within her.

"Is it done?" she asked as he kissed the tears from her cheeks.

Ian nodded, eyes full of compassion and regret. "Yes. It will never feel like that again, I promise."

"Oh, good." She moved as if to push him away.

His warm laughter reverberated through her body. "I meant that the painful part is done. We have only begun."

"We *have*?" she asked in dismay.

He chuckled lightly then groaned as she shifted beneath him. "Now I will leave you in control. Move against me when you feel so inclined." His lips at her ear made her tingle.

She lay still below him as he kissed her. She felt so strange, so stretched and full with him inside her. The sharp pain had already faded to a dull ache, but she was afraid the discomfort would return if she moved. She lost the battle as he began to kiss her neck, unable to refrain from writhing beneath him as her nerve endings seemed to come alive with a will and demands of their own.

Heat flared through her from the place where they were joined. Each move she made seemed to fan the flames and soon her core began to throb around his length. She wiggled her hips experimentally, gratified to hear Ian's gasp of pleasure. "That's it, Angel."

She arched up against him and moaned at the new sensations of pleasure. Soon, his thrusts joined hers, matching her rhythm. An insistent pulsating tremor washed over her, growing and growing in intensity each time he plunged deeper.

"Let it happen, Angel," he whispered. "Let it happen."

The pleasure rose to a crest, and time ceased to exist as she exploded in a million particles of light and flame. As she gasped for breath she chanced a look at him. The hunger in his eyes was as unmistakable as his partially bared fangs. She answered the question he didn't dare ask. "You may if you'd like."

With a low growl, he bit her neck and she gasped, awash with ecstasy as the vampire fed. His growl deepened as he clenched her tightly and his shaft began to spasm hotly within her. The sensation of his mouth sucking at her throat while his length pulsated inside her flesh brought another climax. Angelica trembled with mind-bending ecstasy, feeling his heart pound against hers for what seemed a glorious eternity before he withdrew his fangs and spoke.

"Are you all right, Angel?" he asked, gasping for breath.

For a minute she couldn't speak, still overcome with passion and his delicious weight atop her. "If I had known it would be like this," she panted, "I would have insisted you marry me the very night of the Cavendish ball!"

He grinned and kissed her. "The experience will be even better next time." He frowned at the puncture wound at her throat and bit his lower lip, drawing blood.

A pang of alarm struck her at the sight of Ian hurting himself. "What are you doing?"

He pressed his lips against her neck. "Healing your wound with my blood," he whispered.

The wound began to tingle. She brought a cautious finger to her neck and felt smooth unblemished skin. "So that is how you did it before."

"Yes." As he gathered her into his arms, she saw that his lip no longer bled.

"You are amazing," Angelica breathed, wincing at the rawness of her throat and wondering how many had heard her cries of pain, then passion. *Everyone knows what we did.* Yet somehow she couldn't muster more than a kernel of embarrassment, especially when she was so desperately thirsty. She sat up and reached for the bucket holding a bottle of champagne in ice from the icehouse on the manor's grounds.

Once her thirst was satiated, she was barely able to keep her eyes open as Ian took her into his arms and held her. Sleep closed over her as he whispered sweet love words in her ear.

Eighteen

WHEN LIZA WOKE ANGELICA AND BROUGHT HER
morning chocolate, Ian was gone. At the sight of
the sunlight streaming through the windows on the
empty side of the bed, she felt a pang of regret that
her husband would never be able to enjoy a glorious
spring day with her.

"What time is it, Liza?" She rubbed her eyes.

"Past noon, miss, er, I mean, Your Grace," her
maid said with a twinkling smile. "I thought you were
going to sleep all day. His Grace must have kept you
up nearly all night."

Angelica could tell from her maid's pink cheeks and
glittering eyes that she was bursting with curiosity.
"Oh, Liza," she breathed, "it was *wonderful*!"

The maid raised a brow. "I presume then that he
was gentle?"

"Oh yes, gentle and magical and…" She stopped as
she heard banging and footsteps down below. "What
in the blazes is going on below stairs?"

"The servants are cleaning up after the party, and
His Grace has hired a chef and staff. They are all at

sixes and sevens." Liza leaned forward and lowered her voice to a near whisper. "Would you believe the duke has never had anyone employed in the kitchens before? I've heard bachelors prefer to dine out most nights, yet one would think a man would occasionally enjoy a meal at home."

Angelica's heart warmed to hear that Ian had hired people to cook for her. She was going to ask if the chef was English or French, but Liza cut in. "Not only that, but none of his servants lived in the house before today."

Angelica knew this, as she'd spied on Burnrath House for years. She'd assumed they were afraid of the ghosts, but now she feigned interest. "Indeed?"

Liza nodded solemnly. "Oh, yes. He hired people to come in during the day to clean and had his coachman come along in the evening, but no one was to be allowed in the house after sundown. Though I cannot countenance the silly vampire rumors, His Grace must be very eccentric."

"Yes, he is," Angelica agreed, a smile playing across her kiss-swollen lips.

"Now the servants' quarters are being cleaned out so you may have a full staff under your command, and oh!" Liza grinned. "His Grace left written instructions for you to decorate and put the rooms to use *any* way you please! And his coachman is to pick you up at three o'clock for you to select your wedding present."

He remembers that I want a cat. Angelica's heart bloomed with love. Her breath caught in amazement as she realized that somewhere in their encounters over the past few months she had fallen in love with him. Unlike all her previous suitors, Ian looked at her as a human being with thoughts and feelings of her own. He did not talk to her in that condescending manner in which most men did. Instead, he answered any question she had with a patient respect that urged Angelica to treat him likewise. And... his fathomless charm, breath-stealing good looks, and melting kisses didn't go amiss, either.

I am in love with a vampire, she mused. *How delightful for a gothic authoress!*

She bolted out of bed in excitement, running to the adjoining room to throw open her wardrobe. "What shall I wear today, Liza? Something befitting a duchess..."

Suddenly intimidated by her raised position in society, Angelica lifted her chin, silently vowing to make Ian proud of her. She longed to be the best duchess he'd ever seen.

Liza beamed. "Madame DuPuis and her seamstresses will be here at six o'clock to measure you for your new wardrobe."

Fighting back an irritated groan at yet another forthcoming interruption to her time with Ian, Angelica replied, "I see now that married life will be busier than I imagined."

In a few minutes, she was attired in a jaunty, blue-striped carriage dress, holding a blue bonnet with one hand and a pair of white wrist-length kid gloves in the other. The place between her legs ached as she moved, but the soreness was pleasing, for it brought back memories of Ian's passionate lovemaking.

"Oh, and one more thing," Liza said as they headed

downstairs. "His Grace wants to you to hold a ball in honor of your marriage in a fortnight."

"Bloody hell," Angelica grumbled in dismay. "I do not know the first thing about how to organize a party. I completely dozed off whenever Mother prattled on about seating arrangements and meal courses." Now she wished she'd listened to Margaret more often.

Liza gave her a sympathetic smile. "Then you'll have to ask her for help."

"I suppose I will." Her mother had dreamed of throwing a grand-scale ball ever since Angelica could remember. "She will be very pleased, I'd wager."

The change in Angelica's status sank in further as every servant she came across greeted her with bows and curtsies, addressing her reverently as "Your Grace."

These servants were *hers*, not her mother's. The realization was liberating, albeit somewhat daunting.

The new Duchess of Burnrath spent a delightful hour learning their names and positions, realizing that they were efficient enough to not need her supervision in cleaning the house. On impulse, she decided to order new black and silver livery for the footmen. She placed the order with the butler, Burke, before she set off to explore the house.

She was politely shooed from most of the rooms, but when Angelica entered the library, she refused to budge. The massive chamber of literary treasures was more beautiful than she remembered. The morning light gleamed on every polished mahogany surface, and the smell of paper, parchment, and polish delighted her senses.

Angelica scanned the titles and was delighted to

find the works of Catherine Macaulay and Mary Wollstonecraft right alongside the works of Voltaire and Horace. Jane Austen shared a shelf with Shakespeare and Mary Shelley, and John Keats resided with Percy Shelley and Lord Byron. There were also many titles in French, German, and countless other languages. It would take an eternity and a vast education to read them all… and when Ian Changed her, she would.

She looked around, noticing that the servants had left her alone. With one last guilty peek over her shoulder, she leaped onto the wheeled ladder with a whoop of joy. The wheels were well lubricated, and a push of her boot sent her gliding across the room. One hand grasped the ladder, while the other was clasped over her lips to muffle her giddy laughter.

Something on the table caught her eye. Angelica jumped down from the ladder and approached the slab of dark wood. Next to a bouquet of roses newly placed in a vase of Venetian glass lay a book.

A joyous gasp escaped her throat as she saw that it was Mary Wollstonecraft's *A Vindication on the Rights of Woman*. She picked it up and hugged it tightly to her chest. There was no note beside the book, but Angelica knew Ian must have placed it there for her to find. She smiled as she remembered quoting the book to him the night they first met. Her amusement turned to wonder as she realized the gesture must mean he was reassuring her that she would be free with him. After all, the night she officially accepted his proposal, he had said, "A duchess may do what she pleases."

Angelica recalled that he also had said she could decorate and put the rooms to any use she liked. *I will have a writing room!* She practically skipped out of the library, opening doors to find the perfect place to dream up and create her stories.

The room must be cozy but not too small. When she found the smallest guest chamber at the end of the hall she bit back an exclamation of joy and twirled around the dusty room.

Summoning the burliest footmen she could find and two maids, she ordered that everything be cleared out and the room given a good scrub-down. She did her best to imitate her mother's gentle commanding tone when speaking to servants. When a rat scuttled by, making the maids shriek and cling to the footmen, Angelica laughed. "Do not worry. I will be getting a cat to deal with our vermin problem."

Then the coachman arrived and helped her and Liza into the black and silver coach emblazoned with the Burnrath ducal crest.

"How does one acquire a cat?" Angelica immediately asked.

Felton and Liza exchanged perplexed glances.

"I don't rightly know, Your Grace," Felton said. "Most of the ladies of the nobility purchase their dogs through breeders, but I'll not be knowing if such a thing is done with cats." He scratched his chin thoughtfully. "Any farm is sure to be chock-full of barn cats, but we do not have the time for a jaunt through the countryside before your appointment with the dressmaker, if you don't mind my saying."

Angelica sighed. It appeared that she would not get her first pet today. Then she brightened at the thought of her writing room. "Very well, I would like to purchase a writing desk, and while we're out, I'll inquire of any acquaintances we encounter as to the subject of cat breeders. If we don't learn of any, we shall have to visit a farm tomorrow."

"A capital plan, Your Grace." Felton tipped his hat, and with a flick of the reins, they were on the way.

It took visits to three different furniture shops on Bond Street to find the desk of her dreams. But when she did, it took her breath away. The desk was large and made of dark gleaming cherry wood, with gilt paneling and inlaid brass designs on the two cupboards that opened to reveal extra drawers beyond the three above. The drawers were a godsend to Angelica, as she was accustomed to hiding her stories in a meager writing desk that was little more than a lamp table.

"I want this delivered to Number 6 Rosemead Street as soon as possible," she told the shopkeeper, unable to conceal her joy.

He smiled and bowed. "I commend your selection, milady. I'm sure your husband will be pleased."

"This desk is not for him; it is for me." She smiled at the man's surprise and lifted her chin. "I am a writer. Now, what do you have for inkwells?"

On her way to buy paper, she encountered Lady Wheaton and her sister, Claire, outside a milliner's shop.

"Your Grace!" Claire exclaimed with false cheer. "What a pleasure it is to see you. Is the duke with you?" Her expression burned with such an intense combination of jealousy and curiosity that Angelica was momentarily taken aback.

Angelica inclined her head and forced a polite

smile. "No. His condition prevents him from being exposed to the sunlight. How are you ladies today?"

"We are well, thank you," Victoria said stiffly. "I see that you've survived your wedding night. I assume that means that His Grace is not a vampire?"

Angelica resisted the urge to rub the place on her neck where Ian had bitten her the night before and instead used her husband's words the first night they met. "He is a man... a wonderful man," she added.

"Congratulations, you must be very happy." Victoria grumbled.

As she surveyed the pair, she remembered Claire's ambitious quest for a titled suitor and Victoria's fervent campaign in aiding her sister. Victoria went so far as trying to ruin Angelica's reputation at the Wentworth ball by bringing her into the card room, where she first met Ian. Her heart fluttered at the thought of her vampire husband. *Victoria has my gratitude, but she would be further vexed if I told her so.*

"I am so very glad I encountered you two," Angelica said cheerfully, ignoring their restrained hostility. "I wanted very much to thank you for what you did at the Wentworth ball. I doubt Ian would have paid me the slightest notice if I had not scorned propriety and entered the card room." She took a small measure of pleasure as Victoria managed only a grimace of a smile before she continued. "I also wanted to invite you to the ball I will be hosting in two weeks. I do so hope you will come."

The two assented warily and Angelica continued her peace offering. "Please feel free to advise me on which eligible gentlemen to invite. This will be my first organized entertainment and I do so want to do a capital job."

Claire lit up like a Christmas candle and began rattling off names so fast it was a wonder she could breathe. Victoria was looking at Angelica with gratitude.

"I would so appreciate it if you would call on me for tea tomorrow afternoon, and we may discuss my guest list in further detail," Angelica said, preparing to depart. "One more thing. Do either of you happen to know where I may acquire a cat?"

"What a coincidence that you should ask that," Claire said. "There are two children with a crate full of kittens in front of the apothecary's. I think they are giving them away."

Angelica would have preferred a full-grown cat to deal with the rat problem right away, but the thought of kittens made her heart turn over in her breast. She clasped Claire's hands in glee, resisting the urge to embrace her. "Oh, thank you! I shall see you both tomorrow then."

By the time she got to the apothecary shop, there were only three kittens left.

"We didn't 'ave th' 'eart ta drown 'em," a filthy boy of about eight said.

"Ma told us that if we could find 'omes for 'em, they could live," his little sister added, wiping her runny nose.

"How long have you been out here?" Angelica asked, alarmed at the sight of the underfed, shivering pair.

"'Bout an hour," the little boy answered.

A pang of shame hit her as she realized that children such as these two were likely a common sight in even the most fashionable districts. They had merely been invisible to her until Ian pointed them out. Something should be done about this! Her mind roared. But she could do nothing now, except to look at their offering.

There were two orange kittens and a black one, rolling and tumbling over each other in the most adorable manner. She wished she could take all three, but one would likely be enough of a handful. After a long moment of deliberation, she chose the black one, thinking his soft coat would match the duke's silver and black colors quite nicely.

"Is this one a boy or a girl?" she asked softly, hating her ignorance.

The girl took the kitten from her hands, turned it around, and lifted its tail. "This un's a boy," she said frankly, handing the tiny feline back to her.

Angelica blushed at her naivety and clutched the warm black ball of fur to her bosom, inhaling the musty feline scent with delight as she reached into her reticule and handed them all the money she carried. Guilt washed over her anew. From the look of their wan faces and shabby clothing, it wasn't nearly enough.

The children's eyes grew wide as saucers as they looked at the coins and took note of the regal crest on the coach parked nearby. "Thank you, Your Majesty," they chorused and bowed.

"My thanks to you, children," she said, hiding a sad smile. If only she were the monarch. Perhaps then she could do more for them.

As Angelica climbed into the carriage, she saw John Polidori come around the corner. She nearly leaped out of the carriage to follow him, but the kitten

mewed and recaptured her attention. As the conveyance made its way down the street, she peered out of
the curtains one last time to see him disappear into the
apothecary's shop.

For a moment she wondered if she should tell Ian
of the sighting, but when she remembered the mad
manner in which he had behaved the last time he saw
the chap, she decided not to. She couldn't bear the
thought of her husband murdering the writer. Perhaps
when Ian had calmed a little more over the matter, she
could mention the sighting.

∽

The moment Ian walked into his house, he was
attacked. He looked down at the little scrap of black fur
that was determined to shred the left leg of his trousers,
his brows raised in disbelief. Cats usually fled from him,
instinctively recognizing that he was dangerous. This
kitten was either completely fearless, or it hadn't had the
benefit of instruction from its mother.

"My apologies, Your Grace," Burke said. "The wee
creature was making a nuisance of itself during the
duchess's fitting, so he had to be put out of the room."

"Very good," Ian said, handing the butler his coat
and hat. "Where is she, by the way?"

The butler bowed. "In the blue salon, Your Grace."

Ian nodded and picked up the kitten. He stroked
the tiny animal behind the ears and grinned as it
immediately began to purr. "Come along, scamp. Let
us go see your mistress."

The room looked as if a rainbow had exploded
within. Myriad silks, batistes, muslins, and velvets

in every conceivable color were draped across every available space, while an army of seamstresses buzzed around his wife like worker bees, each holding up fabrics for her approval. His tiny bride stood regally on a raised platform, alternately nodding and shaking her head at their offerings like a queen.

He only had a second to enjoy the enchanting scene before Madame DuPuis spotted him and curtsied low. "Your Grace."

The room echoed with feminine gasps as the seamstresses saw him and curtsied with wide eyes. "Your Grace," they chorused.

"Your 'wedding present' is a fierce hunter." Ian grinned at his wife, wishing more than anything that they could be alone. "He attacked me the moment I came into the house."

Angelica smiled, displaying a fetching dimple on one cheek before she chastised her new pet. "Loki, you naughty kitten!"

Ian laughed at the clever name. He had expected something simple like "Blackie" or "Custard." He scratched the kitten behind the ears once more. "Loki, the Norse trickster god. What, pray tell, was the inspiration for that?"

Her voice was rife with laughter. "He likes to feign sleeping before he assaults the seamstresses' skirts."

"Very clever. Still, I have my doubts about his ability to solve the rodent problem. Many rats are his size or larger." Ian fought to keep his attention on the conversation, but the sight of Angelica in her underclothes was most distracting.

"He will grow." Her eyes shone with adoration as

she looked at the kitten. "Isn't he the most precious thing you have ever seen?"

He looked down at the kitten, curled up in the crook of his arm, Loki was either fast asleep or doing a commendable job of feigning repose. "Not as precious as you, though I admit he is an interesting little fellow."

But not as interesting as you, Ian thought as he gazed at his bride. His life had been bland and cheerless before she came into it, bringing light and laughter. He didn't know how he would continue on without her.

While the seamstresses finished up and departed, Angelica regaled him with her adventures of the day and plans for decorating the house and hosting her first ball. She was so anxious to show him her "writing room" that she leaped off the platform and ran out of the salon in nothing but her chemise and drawers. It took all of his effort to keep a dignified expression before the scandalized servants as he followed her up the stairs, admiring her pert backside.

"Isn't it magnificent?" she cried, smoothing her hands along the cherry wood surface of the desk with unabashed joy.

"I think *you* are magnificent, Angelica," he whispered. Her happiness warmed a heart that had long been cold.

"And look at this!" She bent over to open the cupboards, revealing the drawers. Ian nodded, his trousers tightening at the sight of her. She didn't appear to notice. "Isn't that clever? I will be able to store more projects than I can write at one time."

When she pointed that heart-shaped derriere in

his direction, Ian was undone. With a low growl, he grabbed her from behind, cupping her breasts in his palms and grinding himself against her body.

"A man can only take so much temptation," he whispered, and nibbled along her neck, gratified to hear her soft moan of desire. "If you do not want me to ravage you, you should put on more clothing next time."

"And if I do want you to ravage me?" she whispered breathlessly.

He turned her around to face him. Her lips were deliciously full and moist, her pupils dilated with desire. "Anything my duchess pleases." He claimed her lips, reveling in the sweet taste of her before he reluctantly stepped back and locked the door.

She gasped and turned a delightful shade of pink as he removed her chemise. "Here?"

He nodded and took one firm nipple into his mouth. "Yes, here. I can wait no longer."

His hands and mouth explored her delectable body like he was a starving man. This woman was intoxicating; she invaded his blood. And the fact that he only was able to enjoy her for a short period during his long life made him more determined to savor every moment with her.

Her blush deepened when he slid her lacy undergarments slowly down her hips and slender legs. He lifted her onto the desk and knelt between her parted thighs.

"What are you going to do?" she gasped, shuddering.

"I am going to taste you," he whispered between light kisses on her delicate folds.

With the first flick of his tongue, she cried out and her hips nearly bucked off the desk. He had to pin down her thighs as he languorously explored her secrets with his mouth. The heady musk of her arousal soon permeated the room. Her taste was a delicate bouquet, ambrosia fit for Eros himself.

He groaned with satisfaction as she squirmed and moaned in his grip. Ian looked up at his bride. Her back was arched and her full, heaving breasts pointed upward, the muscles of her firm belly flexing beautifully with her movements. She was as exquisite as a goddess of lust, and as she climaxed under his mouth, he knew he was closer to paradise.

He couldn't take the time to remove his clothes, so hungry was he to take her. He unfastened his pants and plunged inside her, groaning in pleasure as her tight silken sheath closed around him. Angelica wrapped her arms and legs around him, her hips rocking against his powerful thrusts. This is paradise, he thought a second before his ecstasy peaked and he exploded.

"That was magnificent," she panted.

A wave of tenderness washed over Ian as he watched his bride dress. Her passion and boundless curiosity for life had awakened him. Before Angelica had come into his life, he'd only been half alive. Careful, he admonished himself. If he weren't cautious, he may find himself in love with her.

Nineteen

THE CHEF COMPLETELY OUTDID HIMSELF FOR THE evening meal, serving the duke and duchess salmon poached in herbs and swimming in a light butter sauce, creamy potato-leek soup, and rich, stuffed game birds. All was complemented with exquisitely sweet ratafia.

Angelica moaned with delight as she savored a spoonful of blackberries drenched in sweet cream. She opened her eyes to see Ian watching her with undisguised hunger.

"I am sorry, Your Grace," she said with a blush. "I forgot myself. I wish you could better enjoy this exquisite meal."

His silver eyes glittered. "Your delight in it pleases me sufficiently. I see you had quite an appetite." He raised a mischievous brow and lowered his voice. "I would endeavor to know why?"

"Ian!" she gasped, her face burning as she glanced around to be certain the servants were not near. "Are you determined to keep me covered in blushes?"

His lips curved in a seductive smile. "Mmm, blushes are all I would like you to be covered with."

After their plates were cleared away, Angelica wiped her lips with her napkin. "Are we going to enjoy a quiet evening at home, Your Grace?" She tried to keep the anticipation from her voice at the thought of touching him again.

He frowned. "As delightful as that sounds, I am afraid we have an engagement that I have been putting off. I need to present you to my subordinates and receive their vows for your protection."

Angelica leaped out of her seat with unladylike haste. "I get to meet more vampires? I will go fetch my cape!" Her pulse sped at the prospect of delving deeper into Ian's world.

His frown deepened at her enthusiasm. "Keep your voice down." He inclined his head toward the doorway. "There are other ears about."

She nodded with a wink and said louder, "I would so love to pick some lilacs on our stroll, Your Grace."

The butler met them in the foyer. "Will you be needing the carriage, Your Grace?"

"No, thank you, Burke," Ian said as he donned his hat. "My wife and I would like to enjoy the spring air." He grinned. "Aside from that, I do believe that Felton requires a little more rest from running my wife pell-mell across London."

When they were out of earshot and on a street without gas lamps, Angelica asked, "How far are we going?"

Ian smiled secretively. "Oh, the meeting area is near the Tower of London."

She gasped. "That is quite a long walk." Her feet seemed to ache in protest.

He tipped her chin up and leaned down. "I never said we were going to walk," he whispered against her lips, pulling her into his arms. "Hold on to me tightly."

With a delighted sigh, she obeyed, savoring the feel of his hard form against her. Angelica's belly flipped as they slowly rose into the air. She clung to him and fought to hold back a shriek. "You can fly?" she squeaked.

"It is a rare talent among my kind." His voice rumbled against her chest. "Though I confess I do not care to do it often."

"B-but what if someone sees us?" she asked, clinging to him tighter, unable to hide her worry.

Ian laughed. "It is not a strong instinct in human nature to look up. Besides, I highly doubt anyone could spy us in this thick fog. And I suppose if anyone did catch a glimpse, they would say nothing in fear of being thought ready for Bedlam."

She peeked down the line of their bodies past their toes. They had risen much higher now. The city of London sprawled out below them, church spires rising from the fog and the light from the gas lamps twinkling like captive stars. The world below had turned into a fairy land right before her eyes, and her writer's imagination longed to capture every second of this new and incredible experience.

They touched down behind a ramshackle stone building that resembled a church. She nearly sighed in disappointment that the flight was over until she remembered that she would be meeting all of London's vampires... Ian's vampires.

He pulled a handkerchief from his waistcoat and tied it around her head so the thick fabric covered her eyes. "It is forbidden for a mortal to see our gathering place," he explained.

Angelica bit back a protest. Surely that should not be relevant since he would be turning her into a vampire soon. *Wouldn't he?* She fell into a pensive silence and allowed him to guide her forward.

The sound of a door opening let her know that they had entered the lair. Ian helped her down an awkward procession of steep stone stairs as she struggled to hang on to him and keep hold of her skirts at the same time. She sighed in relief when her feet finally touched a flat surface.

Even before he led her to the center of the room she could feel other eyes upon her. Ian removed the blindfold and she choked on a small scream. One hundred and thirty-five vampires did not *seem* like all that many when Ian had told her how many lived in London; but seeing them all gathered around her at once made them appear to be a vast multitude.

Angelica noticed a few familiar faces within the crowd, most notably the scowling Spaniard who had attended her wedding reception. For a moment, their eyes met and she sucked in a breath at his blatant hostility. *Bloody hell, what did I ever do to him?* Refusing to give him the satisfaction of seeing her fear, she turned to survey the rest of the throng.

At first, all of the vampires appeared to be male, but before she could ask Ian about it, she looked closer at the sea of faces watching her and saw that there were indeed female vampires. They were all dressed in men's clothing. *Fascinating...* Angelica couldn't wait to ask Ian about these women.

"Good evening, blood drinkers of London," Ian's voice boomed with authority. "As many of you already know, I have taken a mortal bride. With great pleasure, I present to you Angelica Ashton, my new Duchess of Burnrath. Sense my Mark upon her and know that to harm her is to bring forth my wrath."

His statement invoked a variety of reactions from the audience. Some vampires grinned and clapped. A few smiled faintly and murmured, "Your Grace." The Spaniard continued to glare. Many shifted uncomfortably on their feet, as though confused about what to make of the situation. A few of the women sported petulant countenances. Apparently the ladies of the *ton* were not the only ones who had vied for her handsome duke's affections.

One female in the group caught Angelica's eye. She also looked unhappy, but in a different manner. Her downcast eyes, hunched shoulders, and stiffly crossed arms seemed to convey fear, or possibly shame. But what could she possibly be afraid of? Ian seemed to be a just and honorable lord. Angelica studied the vampire, whose fine-boned features and short-cropped onyx hair made her resemble a pixie more than a monster of legend. She was certain this woman hadn't attended her wedding. But before she could speculate further, a large male pushed his way through the crowd.

"Permission to speak, Your Grace?" Rage glittered in his hazel eyes.

Ian frowned in obvious irritation. "Yes, Thomas?"

"Why have you done this thing, Your Grace? It is dangerous and unseemly to expose humans to our secrets, especially in light of recent events." He looked back at the other vampires as many murmured in agreement, especially the Spaniard. "I see that she is a succulent piece, but—"

Ian silenced the young vampire with a low growl and placed a proprietary arm around Angelica's shoulders. "I would have more caution in regards to my tongue if I were you."

Thomas cringed and held up his hands, taking a step backward. "Perhaps we would be more at ease if you would favor us with an explanation of why you have put us all at risk."

The Spaniard nodded and locked eyes with Ian. The duke sighed tiredly and ran a hand through his hair. "Very well, Thomas, I suppose you are right about that."

To Angelica's embarrassment, he launched into the story of her foray into the Burnrath mansion and the subsequent scandal that ensued. The chamber echoed with laughter at the tale. Everywhere candlelight gleamed off exposed fangs. Angelica leaned in to her husband's powerful body, suddenly aware that she was surrounded by predatory creatures and she was the only prey in sight.

"So you see," Ian concluded, "there was not a better option. After all, I could not kill her. Not only is it forbidden, but due to her position in society and the gossip about me incited by Dr. Polidori's story, it would have been a fatal mistake for her to turn up missing. I have already informed the Elders of my actions, so my decision is final."

Most of the vampires nodded in agreement as Ian continued with a grin, "Not only that, but my marriage to this little imp has silenced all gossip regarding my nocturnal proclivities." He sobered and added, "Which is better than you have done in your search for Dr. Polidori."

Most of the audience seemed to accept his explanation, but Angelica frowned. He didn't once mention that he loved her, or even that he liked her. She looked back at the sea of vampires. Perhaps he did not wish to sound weak in front of these powerful beings.

Thomas came forward again. "But why do you not—"

Ian held up a hand. "I have explained enough. I must get my bride home so that I may feed. But first, I ask that you all swear to protect this woman from harm when I am absent."

Angelica's heart warmed that Ian cared about her fate if something were to happen to him. She expected many of them to refuse, but to her surprise, all nodded and went down on their knees before her and placed their hands over their hearts.

Their voices rang out in a dark melody. "Angelica Ashton, Duchess of Burnrath and bride of our master, we swear to you and our lord that in his absence, we will endeavor to watch over you and keep you from harm all the nights of your life."

The words were touching, though surely they would never need to fulfill their vows. Her husband was so strong and powerful that she was confident no one could defeat him. She curtsied and thanked them as Ian once more addressed his vampires.

"I have received responses to my letters from nearly all of the neighboring lords." Ian's expression was full of sad resignation. "None have seen or heard any sign of Blanche's whereabouts. Though I ask you all to keep up your vigilance, I am afraid that such may be a fruitless endeavor. It is becoming more likely every night that she is dead."

As the vampires bowed their heads in solemn sorrow, Angelica's eyes closed in sadness for their loss of a comrade. How did Blanche die? Surely a vampire could not be easy to kill. She looked up at her husband, awash with sympathy for his burden, even as she was filled with admiration for his brilliant and compassionate leadership.

Ian covered her eyes with the blindfold once more and led her back up the stairs and out into the night.

When the cloth was removed from her eyes, the first thing she saw was the scowling Spaniard. A startled squeak escaped her and the vampire actually flinched. A glimmer of pain flashed in his amber eyes before his ruthless sneer returned.

"I apologize if my ugliness offends your tender sensibilities, Your Grace," he growled bitterly.

"It wasn't that, Mister..." She shrugged helplessly as the vampire stood stoically, refusing to give his name. Ian placed a comforting hand on her shoulder, but she shook off his gesture, determined to make peace with this hostile man. "I was merely startled to see someone else when my blindfold was removed. To be honest, I think you are very handsome, in a rare, unique sort of manner."

Her cheeks burned as he continued to stare at her. Had she offended him yet again?

Finally, he responded, his voice rough and gravelly. "I am Rafael Villar, ever at your service, Your Grace."

He bowed low and she presented her hand as if he

were any other titled gentleman of her acquaintance. Again, he blinked at her in surprise and looked at Ian as if for permission. At Ian's nod, he tentatively raised her hand and brushed the lightest of kisses across her knuckles as if afraid his touch would soil her.

Quickly, he stepped back, his piercing amber gaze intent on Ian. "I still do not like this, Your Grace." With that, he disappeared into the shadows.

"Well, he certainly is a charming sort," Angelica said with a light laugh. "One could almost suppose he does not like me."

Ian smiled. "Rafe doesn't like anybody. And yet, I think you've charmed him." He took her in his arms and her stomach pitched once more as the world fell below them.

The fog was so thick over the city that Angelica had no idea how Ian could see where he was flying. She decided to combat her anxiety with questions. "Why were all the female vampires dressed as men?"

"They dress in trousers so they can move in relative safety through the city while they hunt." Ian's voice was muffled by the wind. "Not only that, but prostitutes approach men more often, so it is an easy meal."

"*Prostitutes?*" she shrieked in outrage and nearly let go. "You feed on prostitutes?"

Ian adjusted his hold on her. "Most of the time. I get a meal, and after I pay them, they do as well."

Her eyes narrowed against the chilly air as an uncomfortable pang struck her heart. "You don't do anything else with them, do you?"

"Never the poor street drabs, and as for the cleaner, more expensive ones, not since I met you." He paused before adding, "This is hardly a decent subject to discuss with a wife."

Angelica wanted to argue but decided she could do better with sweetness. She held him closer, inhaling his scent, and whispered against his neck, "You do not have to go elsewhere to feed, Your Grace. I do not think I can countenance the very idea of your lips on another woman's neck."

Ian chuckled. "There is no reason for you to be jealous, my love. I must feed at least twice a night—more, in fact, due to our passionate nights together. I am afraid that you alone cannot sustain me, though I will accept your offer for tonight."

Angelica sighed and attempted another compromise. "Could you at least try to only feed on men?"

His arms tightened around her and his hair fluttered in the wind, brushing across her cheek. "Already acting like a wife, I see. Very well, my treasured bride, I shall indulge you in this whenever possible."

"Whenever possible?" she scoffed, vexed that he would not make an outright promise. "How would you feel about me placing my mouth on other men?"

"Do not press me, imp," he growled with mock ferocity. "My hunger already makes me fierce."

She grinned and licked his earlobe. "Ooh, promise?"

❧

"Rosetta?" Thomas called as he ran down the narrow alley. "Please, slow down. This fog is devilish enough to navigate through without me having to chase you! Why do you have to run like a spooked horse anyway?"

Rosetta wheeled around and glared at the vampire.

"If you didn't spend every night in brothels drinking opium-laced blood, your senses wouldn't be so dulled that you can't keep up with a youngling like me."

In truth, she *was* spooked. The duke's new bride had spent an inordinate amount of time staring at her. As the duchess's dark eyes stared into hers, all she could think was: *She knows!* And when the duke left with his bride without further instructions regarding the search for John Polidori's whereabouts, her suspicions rose tenfold.

Surely the woman was telling him all she knew, whatever it was. But what could the new duchess know? Rosetta was certain they had never met. Still, all the duchess would have to do was mention Rosetta to her husband, and Ian's suspicions would fall upon her. After that, it was only a matter of time before she was caught.

"Now, there's no call to be insulting," Thomas interrupted her inner tirade. "I have some news that might interest you."

"Oh? And what is that?" she asked, not slowing her pace. She was anxious to get home to John. She needed to make sure he was safe.

"I heard that Ben Flannigan, the vampire hunter, is in town. I heard the news from my Beth, who lives in Surrey." His voice rose in frustration. "She was on the verge of moving here before His Grace banned petitions for relocation. We still write—"

"Ben Flannigan?" she interrupted, heart lodging in her throat. *The most dangerous mortal in Britain was nearby, and all the fool could talk about was his lover?*

Even a vampire as young as Rosetta had heard of

the famous Irish vampire hunter. He was reputed to have more than a dozen vampire kills to his name. The Elders had not only given permission for any vampire to kill him, they encouraged doing so. Rumor had it that the man had become such a menace that they were thinking of offering a bounty upon his head. Another thought struck her cold. If Flannigan was in the area, then he was most likely responsible for Blanche's disappearance.

"Have you told the master?" she asked, stopping and turning to face him.

Though obscured by the fog, the scorn on Thomas's face was visible. "It was apparent to all that our lord was far too occupied with his new duchess to heed anything we underlings had to say. I cannot believe his blindness! To take a mortal bride…"

Rosetta shook her head, baffled by his outrage. "Such has been done before many times in this city, as well as the rest of the world. Love is one of the main reasons we increase our numbers."

"Yes, but Rosetta," Thomas cried. "He has no intention of Changing her! It was obvious from his words and how he cut me off when I tried to bring up the subject."

"I derived no such thing. Besides, I cannot see a reason why he wouldn't Change her if he loves her," she protested. *If only I was old enough to Change my Johnny, then we wouldn't be in any danger.*

Thomas snorted. "Who can say? Lately Burnrath behaves as if his mind is addled. Regarding this vampire hunter, I propose that we hunt him down ourselves. Perhaps His Grace would waken from his stupor if one of us presented him with Flannigan's head. Though, with the way he's behaving, he almost deserves to have that hunter camped at his back door, sharpening a stake."

At the other vampire's words, an idea struck Rosetta with a force that nearly sent her reeling. The question was: *did she dare?*

"Who else have you told about this?" She hoped her voice didn't waver.

If others knew, especially the Spaniard, she would think no more about it. Her plan would be too dangerous then. She shuddered, remembering Rafael's burning amber gaze that seemed to see all of her secrets. She added a silent prayer of thanks that the Spaniard was too busy supervising the lord vampires who were visiting for the Duke's wedding, as well as investigating Blanche's disappearance.

"Everyone else left so quickly that you were the first one I could tell." Thomas stood close enough that she could smell the opium on his breath.

Rosetta fought to conceal her relief. Surely providence was with her this night. She straightened her spine and spoke with what she hoped was a scornful, yet reasonable tone. "Good, for no doubt if word returned to our master that we were plotting to kill the hunter without notifying him, he would take our plan as mutiny and the one responsible for inspiring the idea would likely suffer a punishment most severe."

"I say, I didn't think about it that way." Thomas slumped against a tavern wall, unmindful of the soot and grime coating it. "You are wise for your meager years, Rosetta. Do you think we should just tell him?"

"No!" she cried and then composed herself. Thomas was a drug-addled idiot. She couldn't imagine what would possess a vampire worth its salt to Change him. "That is, Burnrath seemed quite vexed with you tonight. Let me inform him of the vampire hunter's presence in London, and then when the moment is right, I'll tell him that the information came from you. After all," she added. "I am too young to qualify for advancement to a loftier position. You, on the other hand…" She trailed off, allowing him to speculate.

"You may be right. But what if he does not believe you? Or worse, what if he does not listen or heed the danger?" Thomas scratched his beard. "Perhaps we should tell Ian's second."

Rosetta hid her shiver with a mocking laugh. "*The Spaniard*? If he hears a hunter is in town, he'll tear the city apart in his fury. You do realize that's what caused his injuries." She shook her head. "Involving him is too dangerous. I say we follow through with your original plan and take care of this Ben Flannigan ourselves."

Thomas chuckled. "That's my clever girl. At the rate you are headed, you will be lord of a city by the end of this century. We'll do it your way for now."

When Thomas left, Rosetta shivered and rubbed her arms. Could she do it? Could she pass herself off as a human to this vampire hunter? There was no other way to contact him, for she couldn't risk putting anything in writing. She ran through the fog, cutting through the thick air like a predatory sword as she weighed the risks and hunted her next meal. Surely if this Flannigan spotted her for what she was, she could overpower him with ease.

And if she did nothing? If she continued to hide Polidori from the duke until he eventually discovered her ruse, which—from the way his wife and now the Spaniard looked at her—would be soon… then a multitude of likely punishments loomed overhead. She could handle the punishment, or so she preferred to believe, but the thought of what would happen to her beloved John struck chords of terror within her being.

And what if she went through with it and was caught? If the duke discovered that she'd hired a vampire hunter to assassinate him, her death would be painful, to say nothing of John's. That was the law when it came to traitors.

But if she succeeded…

Rosetta allowed a rose of hope to bloom in her breast. She and John could be safe. She would kill the vampire hunter and none would be wiser. Then, while the Spaniard was occupied with taking the reins, she and John could leave the city peacefully. After a few years she could apply to her new lord to Change her love, or perhaps she would be powerful enough by then to do the deed herself.

She was so lost in thought that she nearly tripped over a vagrant lying in a gutter. As her fangs sank into his throat, another thought reared its ugly head. Could she bear having the murder of her master on her conscience? She'd never killed anyone before. And was the life of another worth the safety of her love?

Twenty

ANGELICA SPENT THE NEXT TWO WEEKS IN FRANTIC preparation for her first ball. Her days were spent receiving callers, shopping, and planning the party. Her mother came every day to help with the invitations and seating arrangements, and the two gradually grew closer.

Her nights were spent in Ian's passionate embraces as he made love to her and afterward held her in his arms as they talked quietly together, replete in their passion. She had the windows boarded up on the entire upper story so that Ian could sleep with her. He was reluctant at first, but once she convinced him that not a sliver of sunlight would touch that level of the house and had the door armed with a massive lock so no one could disturb his rest, he consented to abandon his secret lair below the house.

Truly, it was bliss waking up warm and satiated beside him every morning, rather than in a cold, empty bed. People would surely talk about the covered windows, but she was certain that the "window tax" was still in effect... not that anyone would believe that

Ian was short of funds. But in this case, the gossips could hang. Angelica wanted to spend every moment she could in her husband's arms.

Hopefully, her party would occupy most of society's attention and fodder for gossip. At least, that was Angelica's plan. She intended to draw their attention and possible censure from Ian to herself. Themed parties were all the rage, but she couldn't settle on just one, so she decided to use a few. The dishes would be Indian, the decor would be French, and the music would be performed by gypsies. And since Ian claimed that he liked her music, she decided to play a few pieces herself.

Before she knew it, Liza was marching her to her bedchamber to dress for the ball.

Angelica grinned mischievously as she caressed the folds of her velvet ball gown, which was a purple so dark that it looked black where the light didn't strike the fabric. She'd arranged for the ballroom to be decorated in black, silver, and royal purple.

Her ball would be the spectacle of the season.

The evening of the ball was warm and tranquil with the scent of lilacs coming in from the open windows. Angelica wished the tranquility would seep into her. When the guests began to pour in as Burke announced them, her stomach churned. Heading up the receiving line was frightening at first, but with her mother standing nearby whispering encouragement when she faltered, Angelica felt her courage increase.

Within the hour she felt like a seasoned hostess, curtsying and exchanging polite greetings and hiding her boredom with the redundancy of the ritual. As she smiled blandly at the scrutinizing looks aimed at her, she developed greater appreciation for her fellow hostesses and chatelaines of London households. All the same, she was relieved when her husband joined her.

"How is my Angel this evening?" Ian whispered before placing a proprietary arm around her waist.

Warmth curled in her body as she turned in his grasp to look upon his beloved visage. "Thus far, I've been at the brink of expiring from the tedium. But now that you are here, the festivities shall be much more enjoyable."

She grinned up at his perplexed countenance before a maid handed her a glass to tap for silence, a gesture that was hardly necessary since nearly all were staring at them and trying to overhear their conversation for future *on-dits* to fuel their gossip circles.

"Ladies and gentlemen, welcome to my very first ball," Angelica addressed her guests, trying to keep her voice steady. "I hope you all have a wonderful time, and the duke and I look forward to more of such occasions. Let the dancing begin."

As Ian took her hand for the dance, his eyes strayed toward the platform upon which the gypsy musicians plied their trade. "I can always depend on you to make the most unique selections, my dear." He did his best to adjust to the new rhythms and melodies of the song, and Angelica was whirled about far more intoxicatingly than she would have been during an average English cotillion. "The percussion is pleasing to dance to, Angel. It is a wonder that they do not accompany as often as one would think."

Suddenly, a scream rent the air, coming from the east end of the ballroom floor. The music stopped and pandemonium momentarily broke out. As the crowd of dancers parted, Angelica saw a black form affixed to Miss Claire Belmont's skirts.

Claire was shrieking and batting ineffectually at Loki, who had sought new prey in the form of the ribbon tied at her waist.

Angelica suppressed most of her giggles as she made her way to Claire and carefully extracted the cat from her ensemble, passing him off to a helpful footman.

"My gown is ruined!" Claire cried, tears welling up in her eyes.

The young Baron Osgoode approached and bowed. "I assure you, Miss Belmont, you are breathtaking. Though if you would like some fresh air, I would be happy to escort you to the balcony."

Claire blushed becomingly, and her eyes once more resembled those of a lioness on the hunt as she seized his proffered arm. "That would be lovely, Lord Osgoode."

Angelica nodded her thanks to her former suitor, and Osgoode's face flushed scarlet as he bowed over her hand. "Y-your Grace," he stammered.

"I see the lad hasn't forgotten his unseemly behavior toward you," Ian murmured as the music and dancing resumed.

Angelica was claimed for the next dance by the Earl of Deveril—and as she now knew, the Lord of

Cornwall—one of the few English lord vampires who'd accepted Ian's invitation to attend the wedding.

"I am happy you decided to quit being a wallflower, my lord." She smiled up into his glittering, stormy eyes. "Are you truly Lord of *all* of Cornwall?"

His soft laughter rippled amidst the solemn music. "Ian was right about you, Your Grace. You *are* indeed fearless. There are not many of us in that region, so for now, I am in charge of the lot. Allow me to introduce myself. I am Vincent Tremayne."

"It is a pleasure to make your acquaintance, Vincent. And I am honored that you traveled so far to attend my wedding, as well as my first ball." Angelica bit back another question she longed to ask: *How many other vampires are hidden in the nobility? And how many other lord vampires are here?*

"A mere handful are in the nobility, and only four lords were able to come." He answered her thought as if she'd spoken aloud. "But to answer your first question, when I heard my good friend Ian had wed a mortal, I was curious to see her for myself," he said with a soft smile. "And it was due time I ventured out of my castle. I'm certain you've heard I am a known recluse."

Angelica gasped. "You can read my mind?"

Vincent smiled. "Only if you are thinking very loud." He glanced over her shoulder and frowned.

Angelica glanced over her shoulder to see Rafael Villar holding up his usual pillar and glaring at Vincent once more. She patted Deveril's sleeve sympathetically. "Don't worry overmuch, my lord. He doesn't like me, either."

Deveril shook his head. "I believe the unusual circumstances of your marriage to Ian vex him. He does not know how to deal with such a situation, and so it makes him nervous. As for his sharp eyes on me, the man is only doing his job. As another Lord Vampire in Ian's territory, I am seen as a potential threat." He chuckled lightly. "Truly, the scoundrel can relax. I have no designs on the duke's territory or his bride, lovely though she may be."

Before she could reply, Ian claimed her for a contra dance and Loki scurried up Deveril's leg. Apparently the kitten had escaped the footman. Angelica nearly erupted into paroxysms of laughter as she hid her face in her husband's chest.

"Loki seems to have taken a liking to the Lord Vampire of Cornwall," she said. "Or at least his legs."

Ian's silver eyes smiled down into hers, unaffected by her mention of the other vampire. "I can think of finer legs."

She could swear the ballroom grew considerably warmer and decided a change of subject would be in order. "Do you like the musicians, my lord?"

Ian nodded. "Aside from the fact that their compositions are indeed difficult for dancing, I find them to be exotic enough for the theme of your party."

Angelica hid a smile at his diplomatic expression of his disapproval. "Aren't they delightful?"

He frowned in their direction. "'Delightful' would not be my chosen word. Powerful and highly accomplished would be more along my line of thinking."

She couldn't suppress a laugh. "And you have not heard the leader sing yet."

"One of them *sings*?" His incredulous look nearly doubled her hilarity. "Then perhaps we should cut the dancing short and ask them to perform after supper, as if we were hosting an opera."

Angelica turned her head toward the dancers, who were struggling to find rhythm amidst the alien melodies. "Your plan has merit, Your Grace. I am afraid if we continue much longer, there shall be many bruised shins and broken toes. But now," she said with an impish grin. "I am due for my performance."

When Angelica mounted the platform and sat before the pianoforte, startled gasps permeated the room before they gave way to wild cheers as her fingers struck the keys. She grinned broadly and gave herself up to the music, feeling deliciously wild and free. Whispers reverberated through the audience as she sang. There were many mutters of disapproval as she left the piano to seat her guests for dinner, but a few beamed at her in admiration and complimented her on her unique entertainment. She met Ian's eyes and basked in his smile. Only his approval mattered.

"I see that you've once again set society on its ear," he said with a grin as the servants entered with covered dishes. "Do you think it is wise for you to keep stirring them up with your peccadilloes?"

Angelica raised a brow. "Surely you would prefer that they talk about me, rather than having you continue to be the subject of those gossipmongers."

He raised her knuckles to his lips. "I am fortunate to have such a champion."

She smiled up at him. "That is why you married me, after all."

The Indian dishes received mixed responses from the guests, even though she had taken pains to include foods that were not too spicy for those with tamer palates. Most comments from the people seated near her were compliments and inquiries of how she came up with the ideas for the ball and where she found the musicians. The majority of the guests appeared to be enjoying the evening, though she did spy a few sour countenances.

The Duchess of Wentworth took her aside to tell her good-bye. "Your ball was quite a crush, Your Grace, though a few seemed scandalized. Lord and Lady Lindsay now think you are 'unpatriotic' so you likely won't be receiving invitations from them. And the dowager Countess of Morley has declared you to be 'too fast.'" Her nose turned up in disapproval. "They are stuffy old coots, anyhow."

"I only hope that those silly vampire rumors have abated." Angelica watched her companion carefully.

Jane chuckled. "Oh, I wouldn't be worrying about that. Spirits are the new rage now."

"Spirits?" Angelica's breath caught in fascination. Now here was good fodder for her writing!

Her Grace leaned forward with a conspirator's whisper. "Lady Pemberly will be hosting something called a 'séance' next week. She wants to communicate with the spirit of her first husband. I could probably wrangle an invitation for you, if you are interested."

Angelica's imagination was instantly stimulated. "I would like that." Vampires *and* spirits! This ball was indeed a success!

She bid her friend good-bye and was occupied

for the next hour in assisting her guests with their leave-taking.

While searching the house for intoxicated stragglers, she heard hushed voices in the library. She peeked in the doorway and saw Ian and the Spaniard, who she now knew to be his second in command. The two were seated before the fireplace, sharing a bottle of port.

"I still do not approve of this marriage, Ian," Rafael said as he swirled his glass of wine. "Though she is very beautiful and seems to adore you."

Her cheeks grew pink at the unexpected compliment. So he didn't hate her after all! Angelica held back from entering, eager to hear what Ian would say about her.

"Have you yet come up with a plan as to what to do with her in the future?" Rafael's tone was strangely ominous.

Angelica's heart pounded and she leaned in closer to the doorway. Surely now Ian would announce his intention to Change her.

Her husband's voice was gruff. "I will live with her as man and wife for a few more years, but before it is noticed that I do not age, I will have to leave her. She will tell everyone I died on a trip, and I'll return perhaps fifty years later as my own heir, as usual. I will leave her well off, naturally…"

Angelica couldn't bear to hear more. Hot and cold tremors assaulted her body, and a giant fist seemed to clamp on her heart. She fled up to her chamber, choking on the bitter tears that wrenched their way out of her rattled form.

"…as usual," Ian had said. Her heart clenched with

dawning horror. How many other women had he done this to? How many like her had he used and deceived?

～

"I still maintain that acquiring a mortal bride has created a dreadful inconvenience." Rafe scowled as he lit his cigar. "Have you done such a thing before?"

Ian shook his head. "No, I've never married. And I agree that it complicates matters, but I shall have to make the best of it."

"Then why do you not Change her?" Rafe protested. "You of all vampires should be aware of the danger in leaving a mortal with knowledge of our secrets. And I have seen the way you look at her, *mi amigo*. Your passion for her is obvious to anyone with eyes in his skull."

Ian sighed. "I vowed never to condemn anyone to this life, especially without a choice, as happened to me. No matter how politely we behave, we are still fallen demons, as the legends say. I could never do that to her."

Rafe's gaze softened. "Just because you were Changed without a choice does not mean it would be so bad for your duchess. Perhaps she wants to spend eternity at your side."

Ian laughed as he pictured an eternity with the vexing, mischievous woman, then he sobered. "I do not think so. She fought with all her tiny being against marriage to me. She nearly ran away to avoid being shackled to my side."

"I would not be so certain of this," Rafe said softly. "Feelings change, after all."

As Ian followed Rafe down to the cellar and through the secret door to the chamber in which they would hide from the daylight, he mulled over his friend's words. Could Angelica possibly love him? Would she want to spend untold centuries at his side? He hardly allowed to dream.

Perhaps he should redouble his courtship efforts. Angelica had never said she loved him, but sometimes there was such warmth in her eyes that he dared to hope. Perhaps in time, she would want to share eternity with him. Well, time was something he certainly had.

Twenty-one

ANGELICA PICKED LISTLESSLY AT HER BREAKFAST, wishing that the previous evening had been a dream. Perhaps if she didn't get out of bed... no, she had to face the truth. Ian was going to abandon her. And he had done so with others. She couldn't believe that she had been such a fool. She'd thought the only danger in marriage was losing her freedom. She'd never imagined she'd lose her heart.

"Are you all right, Your Grace?" Liza asked when Angelica set her fork aside.

"I am perfectly well," she snapped, guilt striking her as the maid jumped in surprise at her tone.

Angelica's pain was so apparent that when Liza took away her tray full of uneaten food, she gave her mistress a look of such pity that Angelica's heart clenched in bitterness.

She climbed out of bed and straightened her spine. She wouldn't give anyone a chance to pity her. And never would she let Ian know that he had hurt her. No man would ever have that kind of power over her. She would live her life, and God help her, she would have her vampire duke exorcised from her heart by the time he left her. She yanked open her wardrobe and looked for an ensemble that would inspire confidence.

She pulled out a sophisticated black gown of watered silk. The dressmaker had protested vehemently against the color, but Angelica had put her foot down. Now the ensemble suited her emotional state perfectly. After Liza helped her dress, Angelica fixed her reflection with a stern glare. *I need not wait until Ian's farce of a "death" to mourn him. My heart is dead now.*

She had just finished her breakfast when the butler announced the arrival of her mother.

"Angelica, I must speak to you about your ball last night." Margaret stormed in and was immediately attacked by Loki.

Angelica smiled wanly. Even the kitten's antics were not enough to bring her cheer. "Perhaps we should speak elsewhere."

"Indeed, we shall." Her mother lifted her nose in pious disapproval as she extracted the kitten from her skirts and followed her daughter into the blue salon.

Angelica sat in a wingback chair by the fireplace and endured her mother's blistering tirade about the ball with patience that went beyond admirable. In truth, anything was preferable to thinking about her own impending abandonment.

Margaret immediately noticed her daughter's abnormal lack of argument. "Whatever is the matter, Angelica? You look dreadfully pale." Her eyes widened. "Do you think that you are carrying the Burnrath heir already?"

Angelica shook her head. Things would be so much easier if a mere pregnancy was the problem.

"Then what is wrong with you, dear?" The compassion in her mother's voice was genuine and irresistible in its sincerity.

Angelica longed to talk to another woman about her predicament, but her mother was the only married woman with whom she had more than a nodding acquaintance. Of course, there was the Duchess of Wentworth, but speaking with her was out of the question, not only because they did not know each other that well, but because her husband and Ian were such good friends. The Wentworths were unaware of Ian's secret, and Angelica was certain he wanted to keep it that way.

She nibbled her lower lip in indecision for what seemed an eternity before looking down at her slippers, face burning in shame. "I think my husband means to leave me."

The silence was thicker than the morning fog. Angelica's gaze crept up to her mother's face against her will. Margaret's eyebrows were threatening to disappear into her hairline, and her mouth gaped.

Finally, she spoke. "Do you think he's upset about the ball?"

Angelica thought no such thing, but the real reasons were impossible to reveal. She nodded.

Her mother's voice was heartbreaking in its disappointment. "I have told you time and again that a married woman, especially a duchess, is held to certain standards of conduct. It is past time for you to let go of your eccentricities."

"But that is who I am!" Angelica protested. "He knew from the start that I didn't fit in the mold of propriety. If he takes umbrage with the fact, he should not have married me!"

Margaret held up a hand. "I am finished arguing with you on the matter. Lord knows we never get anywhere with this subject. As for your marriage, I am certain the situation may be salvaged. I'm sure you know that your father and I did not always have the most amiable relationship."

Angelica's unladylike snort echoed into her teacup. Now *that* was the understatement of the century. Margaret's rapier glare quelled most of her mirth.

"But our marriage has survived, despite its trials," Margaret declared. "I am certain the same will work for yours. After all, His Grace seems quite fond of you, despite your early efforts to make that otherwise. Don't think for a moment that I did not notice."

A faint tremor of hope arose. "Perhaps you are right, Mother. Maybe if I just speak to him about—"

"No!" Margaret cried. "Do not consider such a thing. Your quarrelsome disposition will only increase his ire."

Angelica sighed. Perhaps her mother was right. She did have a tendency to be quarrelsome, and Ian would surely leave her sooner if she aggravated him. "Then what should I do?"

"To begin with, you must pretend that nothing is amiss," Margaret began. "And you must be gracious and obedient to him in all things."

"That will be difficult," Angelica replied bitterly. "I'm afraid I'm a terrible liar."

Her mother set down her teacup with such force that liquid slopped over the rim. "You must. Even if you have to avoid his presence, you must behave as if nothing is wrong." She leaned back in her seat and tapped her chin.

"Come to think of it, that is not a bad idea. If you rattle around this place like you did at home, one would not be at all surprised if he tires of you so soon. Absence makes the heart grow fonder. Go to the shops, make social calls, and for goodness sake, make some friends! You are entirely too much alone, my dear."

Angelica nodded. Perhaps Ian was taking her for granted already. The thought of him being tired of her made her feel chilled and queasy. And if she were to pull off behaving as if everything was perfect between them, she would have to avoid him as much as possible. Perhaps her absence would incite him to miss her and maybe, just maybe, goad him into reconsidering his decision to abandon her.

"Thank you for the advice, Mother," she said as she stood. "I will try to heed your words."

Margaret followed her from the room. "I do hope I was able to help. Now what were you thinking when you decided to play your infernal music at the ball?"

Angelica chuckled. Her mother would never change, it seemed. Anything out of the ordinary was anathema to her.

Angelica spent the rest of the day receiving callers and answering invitations. The Duke and Duchess of Wentworth arrived for supper just as Ian rose for the night. She avoided his gaze throughout the meal, knowing her heartbreak was pouring from her eyes. Instead, she focused all her energy on entertaining her guests. Her heart leaped in her throat as he approached her the moment the Wentworths departed.

"It seems we are now alone," Ian said, his silver eyes gleaming. "How fortuitous." He bent to kiss her.

How can he behave as if nothing is wrong? Angelica thought with an ache in her heart. "Ian—"

"Hush. I want to taste you." Before she could protest further, his lips crushed hers in a hypnotic, drugging kiss.

She tried to remain numb and unaffected by his attentions, but her traitorous body melted in his arms and her wayward hands found themselves tangled in his hair. A sigh of pleasure, rather than a word of protest, passed her lips when he swung her up into his arms and carried her to the bedchamber.

When his magnificent body was bared to her, she was lost. *At least I will have his lovemaking; I will at least have this part of him for as long as I can.* Her eyes devoured him even as her heart cried, *Oh Ian, why must you leave me?*

She plunged herself into the hot fires of their joining, savoring each moment as if it were the last, and indeed it could be. She had no idea when he planned to abandon her, and to ask would kill her, lest his decision change from a few years to a few days. When their passion peaked to its poignant conclusion, her eyes burned with tears. She rolled from the bed and threw on her dressing gown.

"Leaving so soon?" he asked with a raised brow.

"I–I have an idea for a story," she murmured. "I must begin writing before I forget."

"What an industrious authoress you are." He smiled. "I will eagerly await your return."

She fled the bedchamber and ran to her writing room. Only when the door shut behind her, did she allow the tears to flow. *I'll never let him see me cry, never!*

⤜⤛

Angelica threw herself into a full routine. Every hour was occupied—and every hour was empty. She spent her mornings in her writing room, her afternoons receiving callers, and evenings attending balls or soirees, or hosting small dinner parties to which she invited writers, artists, and musicians. She was utterly and completely free to do as she pleased, yet utterly and completely miserable except for the brief moments she spent enveloped in Ian's rapturous lovemaking. Only then did her excruciating heartache abate for a brief time.

Every evening she spent absent from the Ian's side fanned the flames of gossip that the couple was estranged. People recalled her ball the previous month and then speculated that the duke had disapproved of her arrangements and performance. With her current habits of associating with writers and artists and other objectionable company, along with the now public knowledge that she had been thrown out of Almack's, the Duchess of Burnrath was decreed to be "fast" and shunned by many a leading society matron. Unmarried females were forbidden to associate with her by their chaperones and mothers. Naturally, with much of the primmer company absent, Angelica's parties grew more raucous.

The fast set immediately accepted the Duchess of Burnrath due to her lofty rank, but when she revealed herself to be the gothic author, Allan Winthrop, they welcomed her with open arms. The day she arrived at the offices of *The New Monthly Magazine*, dressed in her male attire and armed with a new submission, made the papers. After Colburn accepted her latest story, Angelica whipped off her tiewig, shaking out her ebony tresses.

"Who are you?" the publisher demanded, eyes wide in outrage.

"My real name is Angelica Ashton, Duchess of Burnrath." She smiled, regarding him with a challenging stare.

"Your Grace!" he gasped, continuing to stare at her as if she were an exotic animal. "It is such an honor. I *cannot* believe you wrote these!"

"Does this mean you won't publish my work anymore?" she asked worriedly.

Colburn laughed. "Surely you jest, madam. Now that you have revealed your identity, my sales will increase tenfold!" He handed her a forty-pound note. "Could you perchance write a vampire story? They are all the rage now."

She pocketed the money, intent on donating it to a charity, and formed an evasive reply. "I shall take the matter under consideration."

A vampire story... Angelica thought on the ride home. Well, she was certainly in a position to write one. However, doing so would undo all that Ian had accomplished in trying to safeguard his reputation. In fact, because she was his wife, she would do twice the damage to his name that Polidori had with his story.

But what if I could make a different sort of tale… She settled against the velvet squabs of her coach. *What if I made the vampire the hero of the story? And what if I put the characters in a different time period? What if I made the piece a romance?* She choked back a bitter laugh. Before Ian cast his spell on her, she had no respect for romantic novels. Now love seemed to be all that haunted her mind.

And love is the ultimate fodder for fiction, Angelica thought as the carriage arrived home. Immediately she called for Liza to help her dress for the Pemberly ball. She did not wish to go anywhere this evening, but she was feeling very melancholy and it wouldn't do for her husband to catch her in such a vulnerable state. Too easily, she could imagine breaking down and tearfully begging for him not to leave her.

When Ian returned from his evening hunt, he was informed that the duchess was at yet another party. For some inexplicable reason, they seemed to be little more than virtual strangers now, except in the bedroom, where the heat of Angelica's embraces was so fierce he felt scalded. Outside of their bed, she rarely spoke to him, and only with cool civility. Her adoration appeared to have been feigned, for now she even refused to let him feed from her anymore. Ian wished he had abandoned his morals just once and read her thoughts when he'd had the opportunity. Perhaps then his passion for her could have been avoided.

He cursed himself for allowing a mortal woman to

get under his skin, beautiful and intriguing as she was. Perhaps she was a scheming, spoiled opportunist who wanted nothing from him but to secure her position in society and enjoy the fame and fortune of his name. She'd certainly taken the reins of power as his duchess with haste, and now she appeared to be enjoying her new position in all possible ways. Still, his heart cried for an explanation of her cooled demeanor.

He walked into the bedchamber and inhaled the heady aroma of their recent lovemaking. At least he still had that part of her. Ian frowned. But for how long? How long before she followed the example of many a jaded society matron and took a lover? He clenched his fists at the thought of her delectable body entwined with another man's. For some reason, his agony increased at the thought of her laughing with another and sharing her delightful wit... of her gypsy eyes locked on another with all her passion.

He grabbed a pillow from the bed and threw it at the wall with such force that the soft object exploded. He would have that passion back. As feathers drifted around him like a blizzard, Ian vowed that he would give her nights that she wouldn't forget.

✧

Angelica stepped back from Lord Ponsonby yet again—straight into a potted plant. The disgusting lecher had been chasing her around the Pemberlys' entire house, trying to peer down her bodice with his quizzing glass and making not-at-all subtle remarks about how he'd love to make an assignation with her. The raspy touch of the ferns at the back of her neck was infinitely preferable to that of his limpid hands.

"Here, let me assist you, Your Grace," he drawled, practically panting in lust.

"No thank you." She righted herself and deftly stepped out of his reach. "Oh, I see the Duchess of Wentworth. It has been ages since I have conversed with her. I must beg your leave."

She picked up her skirts and dashed away from him before he could reply, not giving a damn what people would think of her unladylike behavior.

"I am flattered that you are in such a hurry to see me," Jane teased.

"It was Lord Ponsonby," Angelica said. "He was trying yet again to 'pay homage' to my beauty, but the words coming out of his mouth sounded more like ribald limericks than poetry. Oh, Jane, the man is beyond loathsome! I have tried my best to dissuade him, but he won't take the hint."

"Perhaps it is time to stop being polite and give him the cut direct," the duchess suggested.

"If he were the only cad pestering me, I would, believe me." Angelica sighed. "But every other gentleman I encounter seems bent on luring me out into the gardens in hopes of taking liberties. Does the fact that I am a married woman mean nothing to anyone?"

Jane laughed. "Oh, it means plenty, Your Grace." At Angelica's questioning look she continued, whispering behind her fan. "It means that you are no longer a maiden and would perhaps welcome a discreet affair. Still, it is in bad taste that they do not wait until you've produced the requisite heir before they try to put horns on His Grace. But I'm sure that since you are having a quarrel, they consider you to be fair game."

"We are doing quite well," Angelica said through gritted teeth.

"If you say so." Jane's voice was laced with skepticism. "But you should know that I have been married much longer than you, and I am aware of all the signs."

Suddenly, the duchess's company was less than appealing. Angelica's gaze darted around the room, seeking escape. The balconies were more crowded than the dance floor, and she didn't dare seek refuge in the gardens, for Ponsonby or some other fool would surely accost her. "I think I should go freshen up," she murmured, and fled from her friend's side.

Much like her home, the Pemberly mansion had its own water closet. Angelica scorned the wide-mirrored vanities that sported their own powders and perfumes for use by the guests and went into the water closet. She needed to hide. Her nose wrinkled at the stench of excrement mingled with the cloying perfumes that attempted to disguise it.

She put her face in her hands. She wished she'd never come to this ball. Angelica longed to be away from the stifling small talk and the hands and eyes of the lecherous "gentlemen." More than anything, she longed to be back in her writing room. Her vampire story was taking form in her imagination, holding her enraptured and pulling her away from reality with its siren's song, just as a good story should. But instead of sitting in her haven, blissfully putting pen to paper, she was shut up in a stinking privy, hiding from her peers who drove her mad. She stood up, resolving to take her leave and begin her project straightaway.

The creak of the door opening, along with the trill of feminine laughter, announced that she wasn't alone. Angelica sat back down with a whispered curse.

"I cannot believe she came here alone yet again," one voice said. "It is a disgrace!"

Another giggled. "Yes, but her actions provide endless amusement for the rest of us. I wonder how many days will pass before we hear of an affair."

What awful vipers! Angelica felt sorry for the unfortunate victim of the gossip.

"I feel bad for Her Grace," the first woman said. "I could have sworn that they had a love match."

Angelica held her breath, suspicion piercing her nerves. *Are they speaking of me?*

"Perhaps it was a love match at first, but after that scandalous party she arranged and that vulgar music she played, who can blame His Grace if his affections turned the other way?"

The voices faded as the women left the room. Angelica emerged from the reeking water closet, cheeks burning. Could her party truly be the reason Ian intended to abandon her? She shook her head. He had not appeared at all displeased with her performance. No, he just didn't love her. Her hand closed around a tin of powder, squeezing the container until the sharp edges bit into her skin as she struggled to get her emotions under control.

It doesn't matter what these people think. I don't belong with them anyway.

The minute she emerged, Lady Tavistock and Lady Wheaton approached her, along with a few other women. Victoria's lip was curled in an unpleasant smirk.

"It is a pleasure to see you, Your Grace," Lady Tavistock said with artificial sweetness. "Did His Grace accompany you?"

The titters in the background made Angelica's fists clench. "My husband was unable to escort me this evening. He had a meeting with his business solicitor about one of his shipping ventures," she lied. "He has been very busy of late. I will be sure to convey your regards to him when next we see one another."

Victoria laughed. "Ah, an *evening* meeting, you say? Most solicitors are not open at this hour. He must be *very* busy indeed."

The other women laughed and whispered behind their fans. *How dare they imply Ian is with a mistress!* Angelica's vision tinged with red and her hand rose of its own will, ready to slap the mocking smile off the venomous bitch's face.

"The Duke of Burnrath!" the butler announced.

Angelica's hand dropped as the ballroom went silent, all eyes focusing on Ian's tall form as he strode toward her. Her treacherous heart leaped in joy at his unwitting rescue. She suppressed the feeling and tried to behave as if it was nothing less than she expected. Yet, she couldn't help casting a triumphant grin at her audience.

Ian bowed low as he kissed her hand. "Would you care to dance, Your Grace?"

As he whirled her around the dance floor, Angelica was torn between anger and relief at his presence. After all, the only reason she came to these vapid balls was to avoid him. What good would it do if he followed her? And if she had to dance with him and endure his lazy smiles yet again, her resolve to close her heart off to him might just crumble.

"Are you enjoying your evening, Angel?" he asked, his gentle, deep voice pulling at her.

She sighed. "Not particularly." There was so sense in lying.

"Then may I escort you home? I know another dance we could do." His lips curved in a wicked smile. "But it is one best done in private."

Her knees went weak as desire speared her. "Yes, Your Grace."

She allowed him to lead her from the dance floor and said her good-byes. The false sincerity in people's voices as they wished them well rankled. Angelica decided she'd had enough of society for the time being. For now she would focus on her writing and her small literary gatherings.

On the ride home, her mind spun with ideas for her novel—that was, until Ian's head lowered to her bodice and his lips caressed the tops of her breasts. The writing would have to come later.

Twenty-two

"MY SUSPICIONS WERE CORRECT!" THE VAMPIRE HUNTER cried in elation. "The Duke of Burnrath *is* a vampire. But how did you come upon this knowledge, miss?"

Rosetta feigned a tragic sigh as she huddled in a dark corner so the lamplight would not reveal her pallor. "He bit me once when I worked as a maid in his household."

His eyes widened. "How ever did you escape?"

"My husband, the coachman, rescued me," she said, shivering and trying not to scratch at her blonde wig. The monstrosity itched terribly. "I never saw him after that."

The hunter reached to pat her hand in false sympathy, unable to hide the predatory look in his muddy eyes. Rosetta got up and began to pace, avoiding his touch. This was a dangerous game she was playing. If he discovered who he was dealing with, the tables would turn on her with deadly swiftness. And if the Lord of London found out about her scheme, God help her.

The hunter's hand rested awkwardly on the table

with nothing to grasp. "You need not fear for much longer, miss. I am experienced in these matters, and since his location is known, I do not need to waste time hunting him down. Certainly it will not take me long to dispatch him." He rubbed the back of his neck. "Now as much as I would gladly rid the world of these unholy monsters without receiving compensation, I do need to eat. Do you have my fee?"

Rosetta resisted the urge to snarl at this sanctimonious cretin. She wondered how deluded a man had to be to consider himself "holy." She tossed him a purse full of coins. "Here is five hundred pounds. I will give you the rest after you slay him."

After Flannigan departed, Rosetta heated water for a bath, hoping to cleanse herself of the filth his presence had left on her. She wondered if this corruption was worth such a loathsome price. She lifted her chin as she poured boiling water into the tub. *For the safety of my love, anything is worth the effort!* Still, she refrained from telling John. It wouldn't do to worry him.

As June neared its conclusion, the social season rose to a furious peak. All of the nobility was awash with preparations for King George's coronation, set for the nineteenth of July.

Angelica hardly noticed. She was engulfed in the plot of her novel. She worked night and day, dark smudges forming under her eyes from lack of sleep, and ink stains saturating her fingers. She declined all social invitations, not caring whether or not she offended anyone. Besides, all everyone talked about was the new act the King tried to have Parliament pass, which was in reality a petition to divorce from his wife, Caroline of Brunswick. Angelica was sick to death of the raging gossip, though she pitied the Queen. It was absolute hypocrisy that George—or Prinny, as he was so idiotically called—would accuse Queen Caroline of adultery when he flaunted his mistresses before the country and would likely mount anything that could accommodate his heavy form.

When Angelica took the carriage out, it was not for a new parasol or other such frippery, but to bookstores and libraries to research the time of King Henry VIII. She decided that such a setting for her book could be most potent without casting suspicion on her husband.

The Vampyre's Bride was a tale in which a beautiful noblewoman sought an advantageous marriage to escape the king's lustful advances. When she spied a tall, dark, and handsome man, recently given an earldom by the king, she decided that he was the perfect quarry. After she tricked him into compromising her and thus being obliged to wed her, she discovered that he was a vampire. At first she was afraid of him, but she quickly learned that though he drank blood, he was no less of a gentleman. Awash with guilt about her trickery and charmed by her husband, she fell in love with him, despite his subtle attempts to get rid of her.

Had this vampire also had numerous wives in the past? Angelica frowned and shook her head vehemently. No, she couldn't bear the thought. This was her story and she would give it much more hope than her own.

Angelica poured out the lovers' struggle onto

numerous pages. Although the plot and characters came easily, the historical details were difficult to fit in, and the books she found only revealed so much.

"If only I could ask Ian," she groaned, grinding out another cheroot. Many of the writers and women of the fast set she associated with smoked. It hadn't been long before she picked up the habit.

She stood and stretched, wincing as her muscles screamed from being in the same position for hours. A wave of dizziness struck her, and she realized that she'd not only missed lunch, but teatime as well. As if to confirm her conclusion, her stomach growled. As much as she longed to continue writing, she needed to take a break and eat something. She cast one last mournful look at the pages of her work, resplendent in the lamplight, and left the smoky room.

The stairs made her dizzy again, and she swayed, clutching the banister.

"Are you all right, Angel?" Ian's voice, low and gentle, stirred her heart anew.

"I am quite all right," she said, the hold on her composure around him turning more brittle every day. "I just had a small dizzy spell. I was so busy working on this story that I completely forgot luncheon." She managed a self-deprecating smile.

He took her arm and helped her down the stairs. Angelica shivered at the contact even as her heart bled. *If only we could go back to how we were before. If only he really cared.*

"Burke!" Ian roared, eyes glowing inhumanly.

The butler scurried in immediately. "Yes, Your Grace?"

"Why didn't you inform the duchess that it was time for her luncheon?" His tone promised horrible retribution if the answer was not to his satisfaction.

Burke opened his mouth to answer, but Angelica interjected, "I *was* informed. I just ignored the notification."

The duke seemed to calm a bit, though he still growled with suppressed rage. "Still, you should not have allowed her to neglect herself."

She squeezed his arm. "Please, Your Grace, do not be upset with the servants. My orders were very firm that I was not to be disturbed. In fact, I was a veritable dragon about the whole thing. This book has captured all my attention. There is no one to blame for this but myself and my imagination."

Ian nodded curtly. "Very well. I will join you for dinner."

At first the meal was more awkward than usual. She hadn't dined with her husband in weeks and he was overly solicitous, insisting that she eat every bite. His paranoia that she would waste away before his eyes eventually became too much for her and she began to laugh.

"If I eat any more of this pudding, you'll have to roll me out of the room, Your Grace." Her lips twitched in suppressed mirth. "The servants shall start calling us "the Sprats" behind our backs."

He laughed. "We certainly cannot have that, for our notoriety would spread through the servants' chain of gossip. I can see the White's betting book now: 'One hundred twenty pounds with two-to-one odds that the Duchess of Burnrath will outweigh her husband by Christmas.'"

"'Three hundred pounds, five-to-one odds that Her Grace will crash through the floor of the Countess of Pembroke's drawing room,'" she chimed in, giddy with cheer.

Angelica hadn't felt this lighthearted since her ball. Laughing with her husband once more felt so wonderful. When the servants cleared away the dishes, Ian stood up and approached her, eyes smoldering with unmistakable desire.

"We must see if I can still manage to carry you up the stairs," he whispered.

As they made their way up to their bedchamber, Ian held her with infinite gentleness. His fingers were whisper soft as he removed her dress and underclothes, covering each newly bared section of her flesh with tantalizing kisses. By the time they were naked, Angelica was panting with a half-mad need for him to take her.

But Ian was merciless, kissing and caressing every inch of her form until she practically sobbed to feel him inside her. Then, he entered her with torturous slowness, his thrusts timed perfectly to their mingled heartbeats.

As her passion rose to a furious peak, Angelica mouthed the words, "I love you." She nearly said the words aloud but then Ian's climax hit, drowning the words to a muffled cry as her orgasm intensified.

"Good God," Ian gasped as he gathered her into his arms.

She snuggled against his chest and wondered if she should tell him about the novel and perhaps declare her love. *I will wait until the story is finished, and then I shall tell him,* she decided. Angelica had always been superstitious about sharing her unfinished work, but in this case her sense of caution was doubled. She didn't want to somehow curse the possibility of reconciliation. Her eyes closed and a contented smile played across her lips as she dreamed of him reading her story and falling in love with her, desiring a happy ending like her hero would receive.

Twenty-three

THE NEXT EVENING, IAN RETURNED HOME IMMEDIATELY after feeding, for he missed his wife. He had been thinking a lot about Angelica's behavior these past two months. Perhaps he'd judged her too harshly and her cool behavior toward him was due to being intimidated by her new position as a duchess. After all, her cool demeanor had been noticeably absent last evening.

Knowing how overzealous her mother was on subjects of propriety, he wondered if perhaps Angelica was now afraid to be herself. He would talk to her tonight, he resolved. He was sick of living with a veritable ghost of the woman who'd so delighted him in the beginning of their relationship.

He looked out the window of their bedchamber and saw that she had taken Loki outside in the garden. He knew that if he didn't catch her now, she would flee back into her writing room to scribble until dawn. As he headed out of the room and down the hall, he noticed that the door to the writing room was ajar. Perhaps it would be a better idea to wait for her there, so she had no chance of escaping him. Also, if she were somewhere comfortable, perhaps she would be more receptive to granting him an explanation of her coldness outside of the marriage bed.

When he entered the room, his nose wrinkled at the sharp, acrid odor of burnt tobacco. At first she'd tried to hide her smoking habit from him, but she didn't appear to care anymore what he thought. After they talked, he was determined to convince her to quit before the habit became a full-fledged addiction.

His eyes rested on her cherry wood desk, cluttered with ink bottles and papers from her manuscript and an ashtray overflowing with crushed cheroots. Ian closed his eyes as memories of making love to her on the desk flashed through his mind like quicksilver. He decided to remove the items so they could have a repeat performance.

He opened a drawer and put away her quill and ink bottle. When he emptied the ashtray into the dustbin, he was tempted to drop the piece of engraved silver in as well. He resisted the urge and placed it in the drawer with her other items.

As he swept up the pages of her manuscript, the title caught his eye. *The Vampyre's Bride, a Novel by Angelica Ashton.* His jaw clenched. She would not dare!

But as he sat down in her chair and began to read, his brows knitted together and his lips thinned in rage as he realized that she did indeed dare.

⤫

Angelica had spent more time in the garden than she intended. After relieving himself, Loki caught a moth. The insect continued to escape—or Loki intentionally released it. He would catch his prey again, tossing the moth into the air and batting at it with dainty paws, his inky tail puffed up like a feather duster. She watched for nearly an hour, laughing at his silly antics and amazed at his keen night vision. When the kitten finally grew tired of his game, the hapless insect was reduced to tatters.

"What a fierce hunter you are!" she exclaimed, scooping him up and burying her face in his warm midnight fur. "Such prowess deserves a reward. Let's go see if Cook will spare some cream."

She lingered in the kitchen longer than usual, dipping a crusty roll into a bowl of hearty soup. She was in a fix with her book. The hero and heroine had had a terrible fight and the hero was about to leave her. Angelica had no idea how to compose their reconciliation and form the happy ending. *What if my story doesn't have a happy ending?* an insidious voice whispered in the back of her mind. *Nonsense*, she told it. *This is my book and thus will have any ending I choose. And I choose a happy ending because it's likely the only one I will get!*

She finished her soup and dragged her feet up the stairs, dreading the daunting hours of staring at her blank pages as she willed her characters to speak to her. The door to her writing room was ajar, and the light pouring out into the hallway was brighter than usual. As she drew near, she could hear the crackle and pop of burning wood. *Why would the chambermaid light the fireplace in this warm weather?*

With gentle pressure, she nudged the door open farther, her heart lodging in her throat as she saw a dark figure leaning against her desk, his back to the flames. Ian's face was cast in shadow, his eyes gleaming a sinister silver like a specter's. In his hand he held her incomplete manuscript. He slapped the stack of papers against his thigh in a steady ominous rhythm.

"Wh-what are you doing here, Your Grace?" she stammered.

His voice was low and dangerous, rife with silky threat. "I saved you and your family from ruin. I gave you my hand and my name. I gave you a beautiful home to do with as you pleased. I gave you gowns, jewels, and anything else you desired. But that wasn't enough for you, was it?"

"What do you mean?" she whispered as the blood seemed to drain from her body.

He stalked toward her like the savage being he was. "You seek to destroy me with *this*!" He thrust the pains-takingly written pages at her as if she were a dog who'd defecated on the floor and he would rub her nose in it.

She was terrified. She'd never seen him this angry before. His eyes glowed demonically, and his fangs were bared and gleaming. He looked like the monster of a child's worst nightmares.

"Ian, I—" she whispered, not knowing what she was pleading for.

He raised his hand, and she flinched in terror that he would strike her. Instead, he whirled around and slammed his fist on her desk. The sound of cracking wood brought a shriek of terror from her lips. The desk split in two. Angelica's hand flew to her mouth and she stumbled backward. She had no idea that he was so strong. The knowledge that he could not only drain her of her life's blood but shatter every bone in her body as well shook her to the core.

"This book," he said in a chilling, *awful* voice, "*especially* given the identity of the author, would undo everything I've worked for to salvage my reputation. Would you have every vampire hunter in the civilized world breaking down my doors to slay me?"

"No!" she cried, unable to believe that he would think her capable of such betrayal. "The publisher wanted me to write a vampire story. And I thought…"

"You *thought*!" he sneered. "You did not *think* at all, you foolish woman!" He strode to the hearth and threw her manuscript in the fire.

"No!" she shrieked, diving at the fireplace, heedless of the danger.

He caught her by the waist and pulled her away. Angelica struggled with all her strength as she watched the pages ignite and immediately curl and blacken as the hungry flames devoured months of hard work and dedication.

"You bloodsucking *fiend*!" A momentary pang of guilt struck her as he flinched from the insult, but Angelica forced it down. He had burned her book. He had hurt her, and she would hurt him back. He had burned *her* book! Rage curdled in her belly, rancid and fiery.

Angelica whirled around with a shriek of fury, pounding her fists impotently against his chest. She may as well have been striking a brick wall. She leaped up, trying in vain to land a blow to his face.

He seized her by the arms and shook her, his fingers digging cruelly into her flesh. "Be still!" he thundered. "Before I give you the sound thrashing you deserve."

She ceased struggling and searched his face for any

sign of the man who had smiled at her, laughed with her, made tender love to her and called her "Angel." There was none. In his place was a furious, terrifying monster, looming over her and promising certain dire consequences if she made the wrong move or spoke once more. The fire popped and hissed ominously.

"Listen to me very carefully, madam," he said through clenched teeth. "You may scribble to your heart's content on any subject you choose, *except* in regard to me or my kind. If you disobey me on this in the slightest, I *will* know, even after I leave this house and city, which will be soon. If I hear one word breathed in connection to you and vampires, you will not like the consequences!" He bared his fangs in a hideous, threatening grimace. "Am I making myself clear?"

"Yes," she choked, fighting back the tears that threatened to crumple her where she stood.

"Good." He released her and rubbed his hands on his trousers as if he had touched something loathsome. "I should be gone in a month's time. I will leave you this house and all my other estates, as well as sufficient funds to keep you in luxury for the rest of your life. In the meantime I would greatly appreciate it if you stayed the hell away from me."

He pivoted and left the room, slamming the door. The crack of the frame mirrored that of her heart.

Angelica fell to her knees in a heap of skirts, unable to stand any longer as the racking sobs tore out of her body.

"Oh God," she whispered, gazing into the fire, her vision painfully blurred through the sheen of her tears. "What have I done?"

Twenty-four

IAN LICKED THE BLOOD OF THE DRUNKARD FROM HIS lips and slipped a sovereign in the man's pocket before propping him up against the wall of the inn. The sustenance was like ashes in his mouth. The long years of his existence felt like a millennia these past few days. Angelica's betrayal had stung him deeply. He'd been a fool to allow himself to care for her. Not for the first time, he wondered if she had intended his downfall all along. He closed his eyes and remembered the many things she had said and done to indicate her duplicity.

"I heard that you are a vampire," she had said the night *they'd met.*

"I am a man," he'd replied, *too captivated by her beauty to be wary of the trap she set.*

The dark beauty nodded. "I assumed so."

"And why is that?"

"I saw that you cast a reflection."

"And if I did not, what would you do?"

"I would ask you what it is like to be a vampire."

"Why would you want to know such a thing? Would you want to be one?"

"I did not think about that. I just thought it would make a good story."

He growled at his foolishness. She had been even more candid the night she broke into his house.

"As you know, I have always wanted to be a writer…" And yet he'd still been beguiled by her, swallowing her Banbury tale of ghosts haunting his house like a wet-eared schoolboy.

And how could he have forgotten their courtship, when her questions about his kind had been relentless?

He cursed himself for being a gullible idiot. He had been blinded with infatuation by a bewitching slip of a girl who had made him feel like a mortal man again. But he was a mortal man no longer. He was a Lord Vampire, and his folly had nearly cost him his life and possibly the lives of the vampires under his protection.

"Bloodsucking fiend," she had called him. Fool that he was, the words still stung.

He slipped his hands in his pockets and walked in the darkest shadows, avoiding the meager touch of the moon. Mortals noted the black look on his face and darted out of his path, as well they should have.

It was past time he ceased living among mortals. In truth, he had no idea why his maker had insisted that he do so. No other vampires were pulling off such a ruse to the great extent that he was. Though he would miss a few of his friends, like the Duke of Wentworth, he had been accustomed to losing mortal friends for centuries.

He strolled into White's, deciding to enjoy the smoky haven while he could. It was time for him to leave this city, and most likely the club would no longer exist by the time he returned to England.

Last night he had dashed off a letter to the Elders, requesting that Rafe stand in as Lord of London for the next fifty years.

Now all he had left to do was wait. He expected a reply within the month. He sighed and sat down at the faro table, his mind whispering, *Only one more month until I never have to see her beautiful face again.*

෬

"Would you like anything else, Your Grace?" Liza asked gently as she brought Angelica's breakfast tray.

"No, thank you." Angelica managed not to snap her reply, though she felt like exploding in rage and smashing everything in sight. "You may go."

When she was finally alone, she leaped out of bed and paced the room like a caged tigress. *If I receive any more sympathy from anyone, I swear I will scream!*

As she swept back and forth across the bedchamber, details of the past week chased through her mind like relentless banshees.

After Ian threw her precious manuscript into the fire and raged at her, Angelica had locked the door of her writing room and spent the night huddled in her chair, numb with grief. When she emerged the next morning, she was heedless of the pitying looks the servants gave her when they announced that the duke had commanded them to move all of her personal items to the adjoining bedchamber. She merely nodded as if nothing was amiss and retired to the chamber, sleeping for two days.

For the next few days, the servants pampered her shamelessly as she drifted through the house like a ghost, smoking much, eating little, and feeling nothing. But when she happened to see Ian step out the rear door close to dawn, something quickened within her—anger.

He has not been sleeping in our bedchamber at all! He only evicted me from it to be spiteful! That bloody bastard! The next evening, after Ian left for his evening hunt, Angelica took a candle down to the cellar. There, she discovered something far more infuriating. The hidden chamber in which he'd slept was covered in dust and cobwebs. He hadn't been sleeping there, either. So where was he spending his days?

A sudden memory assailed her. The elfin-faced vampire female had appeared guilty the night Ian had presented Angelica to his people. Perhaps Ian was with *her!* Perhaps he always had been. The lump in Angelica's throat made breathing nearly impossible as she dashed away her tears with a clenched fist and returned to her bed.

The naked pity in the eyes and voices of her servants was like salt in the wound. And when Liza brought her breakfast and chocolate that morning, crooning to her as if she were a sick child, Angelica could take the sympathetic coddling no longer.

Her pacing ceased as she caught a glimpse of her reflection in the mirror. She could hardly recognize the ragged countenance staring back at her. She resembled a walking corpse. Her hair was tangled and matted in some places and ragged and wispy as cobwebs in others. She was skinny as a wraith; her skin held a sickly gray-tinged pallor against her linen night shift, and the circles under her red-rimmed eyes were the dark purple of thunderclouds.

"Bloody hell, I look worse than pitiful," she whispered to her image. "I am positively ghastly!" She grimaced and noticed that her teeth were stained yellow from the cheroots she'd been smoking.

She whirled from the mirror and strode to her bureau with militant determination. Cursing under her breath, she removed the offending cheroots from their case and threw them into the fireplace. She would never smoke again. Next, she rang the maids for a hot bath and rummaged through her vanity for her tooth powder and brush. While waiting, she forced herself to eat every morsel of her breakfast.

As the maids poured the steaming water and lavender oil into her bathing tub, Angelica was heartened to see their encouraging smiles. The hot water relaxed her muscles, and she scrubbed her body with newfound vigor as if she was washing her troubles away... at least on the surface. Her hair took more effort and the water was tepid by the time she was able to get the ebony masses clean. Once the locks somewhat dried, she attacked the tangles with the hairbrush, muttering and cursing under her breath as she struggled to tame the knotted tresses.

Once her body and hair were addressed and she had cleaned her teeth twice, Angelica stood before the mirror dressed impeccably in a royal purple gown trimmed with black lace. "I am the Duchess of Burnrath, and I swear before God that I shall never be pitiful again!"

With that, she flounced downstairs to order the carriage. Now she had to purchase a new writing desk. Her resemblance to a walking corpse these past few days had given her inspiration for a new macabre story.

But writing wouldn't be enough to occupy her. The thought of resuming her frantic social schedule, even with the few who would still receive her, made Angelica's stomach turn. There had to be something she could do, something worthwhile. The memory of the squalor of Soho came to her. The faces of the starving men and the desperate drabs came forth with aching clarity, making her flush with guilt. How could she be dissatisfied with so much when others had so little?

Angelica threw herself into charity work with all the determination in her being. She donated vast sums to children's schools and houses for the homeless. She submitted articles to the papers about the plight of London's poverty-stricken masses. She went to the constabulary and related her tale of being attacked in Soho, offering a generous donation on the condition that more men were hired to keep the peace.

She dove into her new gothic novel with twice as much zealous determination as she had the last. She worked so hard that by the time she crawled into her bed every night, she was too tired to think about her shattered heart. And when Loki presented her with a dead rat nearly the same size as the cat, Angelica found that she could smile again.

∽

"Your Grace?" Burke said to Ian as soon as he took his hat and topcoat. "There is quite a bit of mail that needs to be seen to. The duchess... er, Her Grace... seems to be too busy to address it." The butler's nervousness was made obvious by his stumbling words and wringing hands.

"Very well," Ian replied, wondering why Angelica was shirking her responsibilities. What was she up to that caused her to be too busy to answer her letters? Such behavior was not like her. "Bring the letters to me in the library."

Burke coughed, practically cringing in discomfort. "I am afraid that Her Grace is entertaining guests in that location."

As if on cue, Angelica's musical laughter trilled from the direction of the library. Ian clenched his fists, his nails digging into his palms. She used to laugh like that for him. "Very well, I'll read them in the blue salon, then."

On his way to the salon, maids and footmen alike paled and darted from his path as if he were a dragon set on terrorizing a village. This bothered him only slightly less than the subtle glares of accusation the servants cast his way when they thought he wasn't looking. *As if he were the one who was in the wrong!* Two of the upstairs maids had quit after he and Angelica had their terrible row. He was surprised that his wife had found time to hire replacements but couldn't answer her mail.

Burke brought a decanter of brandy with an enormous stack of correspondence. Ian frowned at the pile. *Likely she ran up a mountain of bills for dresses and frippery in a girlish pique. If she thinks that trying to spend all of my money will get a rise out of me, she is in for a long wait.*

"Thank you, Burke," Ian said, despising the way the butler's hands shook as he poured a glass from the decanter. "You have been invaluable to me."

Ian tossed back a swig of brandy, reveling in the heat blooming in his belly. He wished that he could enjoy more than a few swallows without becoming ill. Then, at least, he could numb the pain his bride had caused. He retrieved the first envelope from the stack and broke the wax seal with his thumbnail. The correspondence was an invitation to a ball held more than three weeks ago. The next envelope also contained an invitation, as did the next, and the next after that.

Ian's brow creased. He knew she was spending a lot of time at home, but he had no idea that she was leaving important invitations unanswered, an act which would surely offend many of the *ton*'s most influential members. Angelica was dangerously close to committing social suicide. He took a small sip of brandy and wondered if she was unaware of the consequences of her actions, and why he should care either way.

A few of the letters were not invitations. The envelopes were shabbier, and the contents gave him pause.

Your Grace, The Duchess of Burnrath:
You have our heartfelt thanks for your miraculous donation. Because of your kindness, the children are now able to have meat every day. There was even enough money left to purchase a few toys. I am certain that there is a special place in heaven reserved just for you.

Sincerely,
Adam Westland
Overseer of St. Jude's Orphan Asylum

The next one read:

> *Your Grace, The Duchess of Burnrath:*
> *Thank you for your generous donation. The new women's wing should be completed next spring, God willing, and we hope you will attend the opening ceremony. We have also taken into consideration your recommendation of opening a school for nursing and midwifery. I am pleased to inform you that we have found two qualified candidates to serve as instructors. We will inform you of our progress.*
> > *Regards,*
> > *James Everson*
> > *Altherbury Hospital*

Ian opened the next one with a sigh. Apparently his wife had become quite the philanthropist. This wasn't at all what he had expected, and for some reason, her actions unnerved him.

> *Dearest Duchess of Burnrath,*
> *I am pleased to inform you that I have made good use of your contribution and have heeded your recommendations. I have now been able to hire two more men to assist me in the heavy task of combating crime in the city. You have my eternal gratitude.*
> > *Sincerely,*
> > *Constable Frederick Nelson*

Ian set down the last letter and took another swig of brandy, wincing as his stomach protested. Angelica must have been affected deeply when those men attacked her in Soho. He cursed as guilt once again washed over him for leaving her unprotected that night, though she had taken matters into her own hands and fought off her attackers like a rampant lioness. A reluctant smile tugged at his lips. Now she was taking charge with her sponsorship of women, orphans, and the city's feeble attempt at law enforcement.

As he neared the library, he heard Angelica's voice. "If you don't mind, Anderson, I would much prefer it if you smoked outside. I have just recently quit the habit, you see, and I would like to avoid temptation, if possible. Thank you."

How terribly ironic, he thought bitterly. *I had longed to encourage her to cease such a loathsome practice, and here she has done so on her own.* Reluctant admiration surged through him, along with a tinge of regret. Perhaps she would be just fine without him.

The cheerful atmosphere of the gathering evaporated the moment he stepped into the library. The shabby, genteel company looked at him with wide eyes and whispered nervously to each other.

"Is there something you require, Your Grace?" Angelica asked with an accusing frown.

Ian's eyes strayed to the bodice of her gown, noting the almost imperceptible heave of her bosom that revealed her agitation. Her gypsy eyes flashed brilliantly.

"I took the time to open the mail that you have neglected, Your Grace." He struggled to sound indifferent as he handed her the letters of thanks. "There are people eagerly awaiting your response, if such is any concern of yours."

She looked so achingly beautiful in her regal gown

of dark blue, with elegant upswept hair and irresistible parted lips. Ian's fists clenched with the painful effort of fighting the lust that rose up at the sight of her. His wife's beauty taunted him with the temptation to throw her over his shoulder, carry her into their bedchamber, toss her on the bed, and spend the rest of the evening ravishing her.

However, more than lust, he was overcome with longing for the closeness they used to share. A spear of agony pierced him at the thought of never seeing her smile at him again, never hearing another outrageous account of Angelica's latest scandalous escapade.

Ian avoided her eyes and bowed stiffly. "I am off to my club, so I shan't see you until tomorrow."

He spun on his heel and left, wincing as she called after him, "I do not care in the *slightest* where you go!"

Damn it, she was still under his skin and he would have to work like the devil to wrest her from his heart.

Twenty-five

BEN FLANNIGAN SMILED AS HE CARESSED THE SMOOTH sides of the stake he carried, hewn from finely carved ash. When he'd first arrived at Burnrath House, he had been tempted to give up, take the money, and seek easier quarry, for the duke spent his daylight hours in a seemingly impenetrable fortress. The entire upper floor of the imposing Elizabethan mansion was boarded up tightly, not allowing the slightest bit of light, and the house was filled with vigilant servants. If that wasn't enough to deter him, callers dropped by unexpectedly and with steady frequency, despite the nearing conclusion of the season.

But when he saw the ethereal creature that was the duke's human bride, dressed in a fetching bottle-green carriage dress and with a winsome smile playing across her lush lips, he rethought his position. Surely this innocent woman deserved to be liberated from the monster's clutches. Feeling rather like a knight of old rescuing a damsel in distress, he resigned himself to more chilly nights in the abandoned gatehouse.

When he heard the faint, but unmistakable sound

of a violent quarrel, he longed to rush to the lady's defense. The vampire's enraged roars seemed to shake the house, and if he could hear them from outside, he knew that the poor woman was being subjected to a most terrible wrath. The duke strode out of the house in inhuman, ground-devouring steps, and for one panic-stricken moment, Ben feared discovery. He huddled deep in the prickly bushes, clutching his crucifix until its sharp edges bit into his palm and drew blood, mouthing frantic prayers. As he hid and prayed, he could swear that he heard the duchess sobbing her heart out.

To his delight, the next day, he overheard the gardeners gossiping about the quarrel. The previous night, the duke had ordered the duchess from his bedchamber. Though Ben still had no plan as to how he could steal into the house undetected, things had been made much easier if the vampire was sleeping alone. At night, when the monster departed to satisfy his blasphemous hunger, Ben scouted the house as carefully as he could, trying to find a way in. Unfortunately, he found nothing before the creature returned.

But near dawn, his vigilance granted him another boon. The vampire left the house once more. There was only one reason a vampire would leave an area so close to daylight. He must be resting in a different location! He followed the duke but lost sight of him in the rear gardens, close to the mausoleum. Ben had suspected the mausoleum from the very first, but after examining every inch of the marble structure, he had determined that it had been sealed for centuries.

For days and days he searched for the vampire's lair, only stopping to go to town for food and baths. He grew more dejected as each sunset graced the world, unleashing the evil blood drinker to prey upon innocent people yet again. But still Ben remained, resolved to pursue his noble cause.

As darkness crept in, Ben found himself in the rear garden, ready to face the vampire in combat if necessary. A heavy scraping sound came from behind him. He whirled around to see the rear of the mausoleum moving. Quickly he dove into the bushes before the vampire emerged from a secret door on the back. Ben cursed himself for being a negligent fool. Apparently he hadn't examined that area with sufficient scrutiny.

When he was certain the vampire was gone, Ben rushed to the mausoleum and inspected every inch of the structure. Two hours later, he figured out how to operate the mechanism to open the hidden door. Smiling with satisfaction, he returned to the gatehouse to await the dawn.

As he waited, he checked over his arsenal of vampire-killing implements. His extensive travels made him an expert on local vampire legends all over Europe. He had two stakes carved of ash, though hopefully only one would be sufficient. His pack also held a large jug of holy water with which to drench the creature, an ax to sever its head, garlic cloves to stuff into its mouth, and an iron cross to place over the corpse. The bloodsucking demon would not rise again to ravish another mortal when the hunter was finished.

Ben settled in for the long wait, alternately reciting the Lord's Prayer and pleading for the duchess's immortal soul. Perhaps when the deed was done he could tell her of his heroism and console her and help her to cleanse away her sins. He rested his arms behind his head and lay back while he envisioned her petite figure and angelic face, her round, upthrust breasts and luscious lips. He sighed in pleasure as he indulged in a fantasy of her in his arms, clinging to his strength and weeping delicate tears of gratitude.

"Soon, my dear," he whispered, "Soon you will be safe from that terrible monster, safe with me."

Twenty-six

ANGELICA AWAKENED TO A STRANGE MEWLING SOUND. She lifted her head from her desk and winced as the cramped muscles in her neck screamed in agony. She had fallen asleep writing again. She looked down at the crinkled paper she had used as a pillow, grimacing at the smudged words. *I'll have to rewrite this page all over again.* She frowned as she rubbed her cheek and saw that her fingers came away stained with ink.

Loki mewled again. She turned to see the cat on the windowsill, frantically pawing at the pane of glass that let in the early-morning light.

"What is the matter, Loki?" she asked, blinking as her eyes adjusted. "Do you need to go outside and do your necessary?"

The cat let out a plaintive wail. Her heart turned over in alarm. She had never seen the kitten behave in such an odd manner before.

Angelica stood up and stretched, yawning as the bones in her spine popped. Her feet were numb and her legs tingled from being in an uncomfortable position for so long. Rubbing her eyes, she made her way to the window. She peered outside, expecting to see a bird or a squirrel or some other thing that would catch a feline's fascination. Instead what she saw made her heart stop and her blood freeze. She clung to the window frame and gasped.

A strange man had entered the rear garden. He was right below the window, creeping at a stealthy pace through the cropped grass, headed toward the mausoleum. Slung across his left shoulder was a bulging canvas bag with a piece of wood protruding out of it. In his right hand he carried a wooden stake, the tip sharpened to a deadly point. There was no doubt as to the stake's purpose. Angelica bit back a moan of agony. Her heart felt as if it were being crushed in a vise.

This is one of the vampire hunters Ian told me about. She put a hand to her throat to stop her pulse from exploding from her neck. *And he's going to kill Ian!* Loki growled and leaped to the floor, darting to the door. Angelica fought for breath, fully comprehending his urgency, yet momentarily frozen in terror. Her mind screamed at her to take action, and she willed herself to move. After an agonizing battle, her panic abated slightly and the blood returned to her limbs.

She spun from the window, eyes darting around the small room, looking for anything that could be used as a weapon. There, a sharp, silver letter opener. A small cry of triumph escaped her lips as she snatched the instrument from the lamp stand and ran out of the room. Loki sprinted ahead, barely staying in her view. Bright shafts of sunlight streamed in from the windows, illuminating the swirling dust motes. The servants were still abed. The house was silent and the only sound was her frantic heartbeat roaring in her ears.

She flung open the rear door and choked back a small scream. The hunter had already found his way inside Ian's marble lair. Frantic hope bloomed in her breast when she saw that he had left the door open. Her pulse raced almost as fast as her legs as she darted through the garden, oblivious to the sharp branches and brambles that tore at her gown and scraped her flesh.

Angelica ran into the gaping mouth of the mausoleum. *Ian, Ian!* Her mind cried the desperate litany. She stumbled, almost pitching headfirst down the long stone steps that descended into a black, unknown void. *Would he awaken? Could he defend himself from an assassin who knew a vampire's weaknesses?* Taking a deep breath, she lifted her skirts and plunged into the darkness, praying she'd get to her husband in time.

She rounded a corner to see the hunter approach Ian's unconscious form. He lay on a stone slab as still as if he were already dead. Her soul clenched at his beauty, and she knew she could never stop loving him. *God, why have I realized this too late?*

A candle guttered in the small stone chamber, casting erratic shadows on the walls and across the hunter's back. Her heart seized, her blood as thick as molasses, as the man held the stake to Ian's chest with one hand and raised a hammer to pound it in with another.

Ian's eyes opened, widened in shock, then turned to meet hers. His face contorted into a mask of despair and accusation.

"No!" Angelica screamed at Ian and the hunter. She charged forward, skirts tangling around her legs.

She was too late.

The hammer came down.

Angelica groaned in agony as the stake buried itself halfway into Ian's chest with a sickening crunch of bone. The man glanced at her, indifferent to her pain, and raised the hammer again. She went numb with shock, but then a white-hot rage boiled inside her and exploded from her being. This man would die.

She leaped onto the hunter's back and slashed at his face and throat with the letter opener, shrieking in a fury that bordered on insanity.

"But lassie, I have saved you!" the hunter cried, which further fanned the flames of her wrath. "Lass, please stop! The monster is dead, or he will be soon if you'll let me—"

The man struggled to throw her off, but Angelica fought like a madwoman and clung tenaciously to her victim, hacking at him over and over with her small but lethal weapon as her hands grew more and more slippery with blood. She lost hold of the letter opener for a second and caught a ringing blow to the side of her head as she snatched the slender blade before it could fall.

"You little bitch!" the hunter roared as she sliced open his cheek. He bucked like a raging bull, yet still Angelica managed to hold on.

His fists struck her all over; his nails clawed at her arms. She shrieked as a hank of her hair was ripped from her skull, but still she fought. Angelica screamed like one possessed as she buried the point of the letter opener in the murderer's throat. His hands ceased their assault and fluttered against his chest like wounded insects. A disgusting, gurgling sound escaped his throat. Blood bubbled from his thick lips.

Finally, the hunter collapsed as his life's blood continued to pour from his neck and face. Angelica didn't spare him a second glance. She ran to Ian and pulled on the stake with all her might. As it slowly wrenched free, her heart contracted as if the infernal object had pierced her breast as well. She threw the loathsome object as far away as she could and turned back to her love. Blood welled from his gaping wound at an alarming rate. But she could see that his heart still beat with a feeble pulse. A thrill of hope electrified her being.

"Oh Ian, my love," she whispered. "Please live, please."

She tore off her muslin day dress and rolled it up. With shaking hands, she stuffed the fabric into the wound and leaned on his chest with her elbow, hoping she could apply enough pressure to staunch the flow. He had already lost a great amount of blood, and his skin was as white as her chemise. Her fingers sought his throat once more. The pulse remained, but it was fading. Panic clawed at her, but she fought back the mindless fear, knowing that if she allowed it to incapacitate her, Ian would die. Her thoughts raced for something, anything to do next.

He needs more blood, she realized. Angelica leaned over as far as she could, her fingertips reaching the letter opener. Slowly, she dragged the weapon closer. The scraping sound on the rough stone floor echoed loudly in the silent chamber. Her heartbeat and breathing roared in her ears as her incessant panic fought to gain a foothold over her mind. When she was able to fully grasp the weapon, she cried out in triumph. Her nose wrinkled in disgust at the congealed blood of the vampire hunter already drying on the metal surface. With a deep breath and a whispered prayer, she sliced open her wrist, hissing at the sharp pain that raged through her arm like fire.

She pressed her bleeding wrist to Ian's mouth. As the blood began to flow down his chin, she used her other hand to force his lips wider apart, whispering, "Please, Ian, drink. Please live. Please. I love you, Ian. God, I love you. Please don't die!"

At first the blood trickled out of the corners of his mouth and ran down his face to pool in his hair. Tears welled up in her eyes. Was she too late? But then, his chest rose as he took a shuddering breath. A current passed between them.

His eyes snapped open and his fangs pierced the tender flesh of her wrist. She sighed in relief even though her heart felt as if it would be tugged out of her breast as he began to suck her blood in long, greedy pulls. "I love you."

The edges of her vision tinged with black and white spots flashing before her eyes, and finally Ian released her. Though he still had an alarming pallor, the deathly cast of gray had abandoned his flesh. He might live. Triumphant relief surged within her being that the hunter hadn't murdered her love.

The hunter… Angelica peered over at the muti-
lated corpse on the stone floor. Its glassy, dead eyes
stared at her in eternal accusation.

I killed him. The world tilted, began to spin. *I killed
a man.* Her body trembled in shock as dizziness overtook her. Angelica's muscles turned to water and she
pitched forward. Just before blackness closed over her,
Ian's strong arms enfolded her and she heard one last
word from his beautiful voice.

"Angel."

ᕤᕦᕤ

Ian's heart constricted as Angelica's blood coursed
through his veins, a heart-rending sacrifice. She'd been
willing to die for him.

When he saw the vampire hunter poised over him
with her standing nearby, he was ready to die to be
spared the agony of his wife's apparent betrayal. He'd
thought she hired the hunter to kill him. As the stake
plunged deep into his heart, the pain was so agonizing
that he lost consciousness and greeted death and
oblivion with open arms.

Then he awoke to the sweet, unforgettable taste of
his Angel's blood flowing down his throat, quickening
his body and healing his wound.

"I love you," she'd whispered achingly before
fainting across his chest.

Ian extracted her wrist from his mouth and bit his
lip to place a healing kiss upon the wound. He carefully rolled Angelica off his body, laying her reverently
on the cool marble, and sat up to take stock of his
injuries. She'd stuffed her dress into his wound, he

realized. Ian shook his head in wonder as his wife's heroic efforts to save his life struck him anew. He pulled out the fabric before the bones and flesh could knit around it. He tied the muslin around his torso, wincing at the combination of pain and the tingling of healing that rushed through his immortal body. Yet still, he needed more.

Slowly, he eased her on her back and rolled off the slab, his face contorting in agony as his chest seemed to rip apart.

With impossible slowness, he dragged his body to the crumpled form of the hunter. The man was dead, but the blood would still be warm. Ian swallowed with revulsion at what he had to do; then he plunged his fangs into the man's neck, draining the corpse dry of what sustenance he could gather.

When he had taken all he could, he looked at the gaping cut on the man's throat and the rest of the shallow wounds covering his face and neck. The top of one ear had been sliced clean off. It was obvious that his wife had fought like a demon for him, and his heart ached anew at the pain he had heaped upon her.

He looked at the corpse one more time, and his eyes widened as recognition speared him. The vampire hunter was no amateur. He was none other than Ben Flannigan, the bane of the vampire world, who had more than a dozen kills to his name. The man had become such a threat that the Elders had lifted their ban on killing humans and put a price on his head. And his tiny, mortal wife had been the one to take him down.

As the blood revitalized and healed him further, he

was able to return to his bride much quicker. Though he could ill afford it, Ian bit his finger. Gently Ian coaxed Angelica's lips to part, giving her a meager amount of his power back. Her color improved, but still she did not awaken.

"God, I have been such a fool," Ian whispered.

For the first time in centuries, tears burned his eyes. He should have known she did not marry him with the intention to expose and destroy him with her writings, or even to become rich and titled. He now remembered what she had said when she'd announced her willingness to wed him and her confessions of her attempts to escape the match.

"I was not going to marry you at all! I have been doing everything I can to avoid it and I was going to run away!"

"And just where were you planning to run to?" he'd accused.

"I was going to use the money I made from my stories to rent a flat somewhere in the city, and support myself with short stories until I finished a novel. I heard the lady who wrote Pride and Prejudice made one hundred forty pounds."

"That would not be enough to buy your pretty gowns."

"Gowns can go to the devil! Besides, they are not sensible garb for an author, I should say."

She had been so irritating but so magnificent in her rebellious pride and naivety.

He held her closer, kissing her brow as he remembered her words the first night they'd made love.

"If I had known it would be like this, I would have insisted you marry me the very night of the Cavendish ball!"

"Oh God, I hurt her so unbearably," he whispered. "I hurt her and yet she still loves me! And she risked her life to save mine. What have I done?"

He stroked her pale cheek with his thumb, willing her to open those dark gypsy eyes he loved so much. He needed her impish gaze, her light laughter and intoxicating touch. He needed everything about her. She'd made him feel more alive than when he was human.

Needing her kiss as much as he needed blood to survive, he pressed his lips to hers. "I beg of you, wake. Please, my precious Angel," he prayed as he held her in his arms. "Wake so I can tell you how sorry I am, and how much I love you. God, I love you." He couldn't say the words enough. "I love you. I love you." He repeated the litany over and over again until exhaustion overcame him and he fell asleep, still clinging to her with a vow never to let her go again.

Twenty-seven

ANGELICA WAS HAVING THE MOST WONDERFUL DREAM. It began to fade as consciousness beckoned her senses and she fought to stay within the dream's dark folds. She could feel Ian holding her, his voice echoed through her body, saying over and over again, "I love you."

Happiness infused every cell of her being at his words. She didn't want to wake up. She wanted to stay in the dream and continue to hear him say it for the rest of eternity. "I love you... I love you."

Her treacherous eyes opened and she gasped with wonder as she beheld her beloved's sleeping face. The pallor of death had vanished, and his breathing was steady. *Ian was alive!* She looked down at his chest. He'd used her dress to make a bandage and, thank God, the wound was no longer bleeding.

He held her in his arms, just like in the dream. A line between his brows said that he would be very irate if made to let her go. But Angelica had no intention of leaving the safe haven of Ian's embrace. She sighed happily and snuggled against him, mindful of his wound and breathed in his long-missed scent.

"Angel, are you awake?" he whispered, his voice cracking with worry.

She tilted her head to look into his bright silver eyes, joy filling her soul that he was alive and didn't hate her. "Yes."

He squeezed her tighter, though his features were wracked with pain. "Thank God. I was afraid I was going to lose you."

His words made her wonder if her dream had been real, but she was too afraid to ask. Instead she whispered, "I thought I was going to lose *you.*"

He chuckled weakly. "With the heroic efforts of my avenging Angel to defend my life? I should say not."

Angelica met his gaze, a playful smile upon her lips. "Well, actually, Loki saved you. He woke me up and led me here just as that horrible man—" She sobered immediately as the memory of the gruesome fight overtook her. "How is your wound?"

"I am healing," he said evasively.

She frowned. "Really, how bad is it? How close did you come to… to…" She broke off, unable to say the words aloud.

"I came very close," Ian answered levelly. "The damage to my heart was quite severe. If you hadn't immediately given me your blood, I would have perished."

Gently, Angelica lifted the bandage to reveal his chest. The wound had shrunk to half its size and the bleeding was reduced to an intermittent trickle. Though heartened at the speed with which he was healing, she didn't want to take any chances and pressed the crumpled ruin of her dress tightly against the hole.

Ian covered her hand with his. "Careful, or the

wound will heal around the cloth." Shaking his
head slightly, he added, "Angel, I don't deserve your
tender nursing."

At his gentle words, a lump formed in her throat which
was already raw from screaming. "Don't you dare say
such an awful thing! If I had published that book, there
would have been swarms of hunters after you. I know
that now," she choked, sick with guilt. "You could
have been killed and it would have been entirely my
fault! I didn't realize the danger. Oh, Ian, I am so sorry.
I never meant for you to be hurt. Please forgive me."

"No, Angel. Don't say that. The fault is mine. I
never should have burned your book. You didn't
intend to ruin me with your writing. It is I who should
be demanding your forgiveness." With excruciating
gentleness, he cupped her chin, his thumb stroking the
line of her jaw.

She couldn't stop her tears. "Does that mean you
are not angry with me anymore?"

"Yes. I was a fool." The naked pain etched on his
features was almost too much to bear.

"Ian, does that mean you won't leave me now,
like you did with your other wives?" Long forgotten
hope rekindled.

His brows creased in confusion. "Other wives?
What other wives?"

"The night of our first ball I heard you talking to
Rafe." Her voice shook in agony at the memory.
"Y-you told him you'd leave me and return as your
own heir fifty years later… as usual."

Ian shook his head. "It is usual for me to leave the
city and return as my heir every half century, but I

assure you I have never had a wife. You are the first, the only." He kissed her tenderly. "I'll never let you go, Angel. What can I do to atone for the pain I caused you?"

Warm, exquisite relief flooded her at his words. She swallowed and took a deep breath. It was now or never.

Angelica chose her words carefully. "I love you, Ian. Please, make me like you and take me with you wherever you go." When he didn't immediately protest, she continued. "When we married, I had believed that you were going to Change me and keep me by your side forever. I was heartbroken when I overheard your conversation with your second." She stopped as a choking sob escaped her lips.

Ian enfolded her in his arms. "Hush, darling, don't cry."

She pulled away from him, determined to pour out the rest of her explanation. "I never meant to ruin you with my vampire story. I wanted to write a story that showed vampires can be heroes, and..." She drew a ragged breath and dared to speak the long-secret wish. "And perhaps give you the idea that it would be possible for us to have a happy life together." She fell silent and looked down at her hands, fighting back tears.

The silence seemed to draw out for an eternity. Then he smiled. "How would a trip to Paris sound to a new vampire, my love?"

Fresh tears welled up in Angelica's eyes, but this time they were tears of joy. "Oh, Ian, do you truly mean it? When?"

Ian gathered her into his arms. "As soon as the Elders approve my petition to Change you. That could take anywhere from mere days to a few weeks."

"Wonderful!" She clasped her hands in joy. "May we get out of this horrid place? I am cold and quite famished."

Ian shook his head. "I am afraid we are trapped here until sunset." Frowning, he added, "And you had better close the mausoleum door before the afternoon light makes its way to me."

Angelica cursed herself for her foolishness. The sun would burn Ian if they left the mausoleum. She should have thought of that. Her head swam and her limbs were heavy and weak as she pulled herself from her husband and made her way back up the stairs. The journey seemed to take an eternity.

When she dragged herself back, her husband lifted her into his lap, easing her sore backside from the hard cold stone. "It won't be as bad as all that, Angel. This is the first uninterrupted time I've had with you in a long time. I am certain we can make the best of the situation."

They talked until sundown, reconciling and laughing at their foolishness. "I'd thought you were sleeping with another," Angelica said, fighting the ache the thought still invoked.

Ian raised a brow. "When my every waking thought was consumed by you? When you haunt my dreams every day? *Never*. Who did you think I'd been with?"

Angelica shook her head, wanting the conversation to return to its former coziness. "It's not important.

Were you truly still thinking of me, even when you were angry?"

"Yes, always," Ian said, pulling her closer and yawning. "Would you mind if we rested awhile? My wounds will heal better with the day sleep."

They lay back down on the slab. Ian cushioning her from most of the stone surface. It seemed Angelica had barely closed her eyes before Ian woke her.

"We must leave now, Angel." His eyes glowed with unholy hunger. "I need to feed soon, or you will not be safe around me."

"How are we going to explain what happened to the servants?" Angelica asked worriedly. "They have likely been searching for me since morning."

Ian frowned. "You are quite right, I fear. There is little hope of hiding the body, then. We will have to act very carefully."

⤜❦⤏

"But why can't *I* be the hero?" Angelica complained as they emerged from the mausoleum, determined to keep up a casual conversation.

Ian shook his head at her temerity. The sight of the vampire hunter's body had made her flinch and gag as the realization that she had killed a man sank in. Ian had shielded her from the corpse, but she was humiliated, thinking she had acted like a ninny. He thought she'd been unbelievably brave.

Angelica dragged the vampire hunter's heavy bag behind her. Ian had wanted to carry it, but she refused to let him since she was still worried about his injury. She'd stuffed her blood-soaked dress in the bag, having no notion how she would explain its condition. The servants would just have to put up with the scandalous sight of her wearing nothing but her underclothes. She winced at the sharp gravel poking her feet through the thin fabric of her house slippers. Ian wished he could carry her, but he lacked the strength.

Ian chuckled, looking up at the night sky. "Because there is no way anyone would believe that my tiny duchess could fight like such a lioness, or that a man of my size would be so vulnerable. Besides," he added with a wink, "a man must protect his pride at all costs."

She sighed and threw the bag down a dry well. "Very well, I suppose I must allow you to hold on to your tender pride."

Ian slid the well's cover back in place, concealing the evidence.

They leaned against each other and staggered toward the back door, both still weak with blood loss. When Ian managed to open the door, he stumbled and almost fell to the floor.

A parlor maid took in their blood-stained clothes and haggard countenances. Angelica's state of undress appeared to go quite unnoticed. A splintery scream escaped from the maid's bloodless lips before she collapsed into a dead faint. Her feather duster bounced from the floor and landed comically on her head.

The butler rushed into the room, followed by the other servants. "Your Graces!" he cried. "What happened?"

Ian trembled as he struggled to keep his footing and still support Angelica. "Fetch the constable," he commanded Burke. "My wife has been assaulted."

He handed his duchess off to the housekeeper and her maids, smiling as they cooed and clucked over her like mother hens. Apparently his wasn't the only heart she'd captured.

"Should I send for a doctor as well?" Burke asked, staring at their bloody clothes, his face lined with worry.

"Most of the blood is the assailant's," Ian said impatiently as white spots appeared in his vision. If he didn't have blood soon… "He is inside the mausoleum, but under no circumstances is he to be moved until the constable is finished with his investigation. I want this horrid affair done and over with as soon as possible."

He turned toward the stairs and stopped. "On second thought, perhaps a doctor wouldn't be amiss. Do send for one along with the constable, and please be quick about it."

Once he reached his bedchamber, Ian summoned his valet and mesmerized him before sinking his fangs into the man's throat. He'd vowed never to feed from his servants but this was an emergency, for he would collapse if he didn't get sustenance as soon as possible.

When he had drunk his fill, he released his hold on the valet, noting with remorse that the poor chap was swaying on his feet.

"Are you all right?" Ian asked, afraid he'd taken too much blood. It would undo him if he harmed one under his protection.

"Yes, indeed, Your Grace," Carson replied, eyes swimming in confusion. "Just a dizzy spell, I am afraid."

Guilt prickled Ian and he gripped the valet's

shoulders to keep him from falling. "Why don't you go to bed, Carson, and I shall finish dressing myself."

"Are you quite certain, Your Grace?" The poor man looked as if he were on the verge of collapsing at Ian's feet.

Ian nodded. "Yes. I cannot have you falling ill. Take tomorrow off as well, and feel free to ring for anything you need."

"Thank you very much, Your Grace," Carson said, and turned toward the door. "It is very queer. I felt fine all day…"

By the time Ian had changed his clothes and returned downstairs, the maids had Angelica changed into a modest dressing robe and had tucked her in a quilt on the couch with a steaming cup of hot chocolate while she awaited the doctor. He noted the scratches and bruises covering her arms from her struggle with the vampire hunter and wished he had killed the bastard himself.

The constable arrived and inspected the body. When questioned, Angelica gave a stellar performance as she narrated the story they had fabricated. Ian could tell by the shocked faces of her captive audience that they believed every word.

"I took my cat, Loki, outside to… take care of his necessities," she said with a delicate blush. "Then I was grabbed from behind and shoved into the mauso-leum… it was a dreadful place!" She began to tremble theatrically as her voice rose in feigned panic. "The man tried to t-take my clothes off! I fought and fought and slashed at him with my letter opener to fend him off, but he took it away from me and held the blade to

my throat, threatening to stab me if I did not let him…
I thought I was done for!" she gasped. "But my dear
husband heard my screams and pulled the beastly man
off me. They fought and Ian cut his throat."

The constable frowned. "But why did you have a
letter opener with you?"

Angelica managed a weak smile. "I was reading
my letters."

"At five o'clock in the morning?" he asked
doubtfully.

"Oh yes! Early morning is the best time for reading,
for the house is so quiet without all the servants
underfoot." Angelica told him as if he were a fool not
to grasp such logic.

Ian fought back a smile. Apparently his wife had
missed her calling at Drury Lane.

The constable seemed satisfied, for he nodded
and then questioned Ian, nodding more as his story
corroborated Angelica's.

"I did not intend to kill him," Ian said ruefully.
"But the thought of his filthy hands touching her…
I lost control. Will they convict me when it goes to
trial, do you think?"

The constable shook his head. With his preternatural gift, Ian could almost read the man's thoughts. He
had no desire to arrest such a prominent peer of the
realm, and to confirm his thinking, it was well known
that the Duchess of Burnrath had donated a large sum
to London's law keepers. How could he repay her
generosity by arresting her husband when the man
was only defending her virtue and had possibly even
saved her life?

"I do not think a trial will be necessary, Your Grace." The constable cleared his throat. "The assailant matches the description of a man who has committed several similar crimes," he said, every nuance of his tone and gestures revealing the lie. "This is obviously a case of self-defense. I think it would be best to be discreet about this matter. I will take the body and file a report at my office. Due to the scandal your involvement would bring, I think we would be most prudent to keep your name out of it. Do you agree?"

Ian nodded solemnly. "Absolutely, sir. I bow to your wise recommendation."

The constable stood and replaced his hat. "Very well, I shall be off. I trust Her Grace will benefit from the doctor's treatment, and with your care, God willing, she may recover from this terrible trauma."

He sketched a hasty bow to each before taking his leave.

Doctor Sampson arrived soon after and dismissed the servants as he examined Angelica. He diagnosed her as being weak from shock. He dosed her with laudanum, despite her objections, and ordered her to have a week's bed rest.

"A week?" Angelica giggled in giddiness from the laudanum. "I hardly think I could stay cooped up for a whole day."

Ian raised a brow. "Even if I am in bed with you?"

She grinned as her cheeks turned bright pink. "Oh. Well, that changes matters entirely!"

Twenty-eight

ANGELICA WAS ABLE TO STAND FIVE DAYS OF BED REST before she found herself on the brink of insanity. Ian noticed and announced that he would take her to the opera the next evening. That morning, a jewel case was left at her bedside. It contained a ruby the size of a pigeon's egg. She smiled, knowing just the ensemble that would go with the gorgeous pendant.

As the sun was plunging beneath the horizon, Angelica dressed in a scarlet taffeta gown beaded with jet. The low, square-cut bodice made a perfect setting to frame her new ruby necklace. Elbow-length gloves hid the worst of her fading bruises from her fight with the vampire hunter. Underneath she wore black silk stockings fastened with saucy red garters. Liza arranged her hair in elaborate curls, threaded through with scarlet ribbon. Ruby teardrop earrings completed the picture.

"How do I look?" she asked, twirling before the mirror and admiring the way a black-clad ankle occasionally peeked through.

"Um… er… very striking," Liza said. "Wherever did you acquire that gown? It is almost too daring."

Angelica laughed. "I had Madame Dupuis make it. I'd intended the dress to be a surprise for the duke before we had our... altercation."

Liza raised a brow, eyeing the revealing bodice nervously. "Well, I do say he will certainly be surprised."

Angelica applied a touch of lip rouge and a dusting of pink powder to her cheeks before dabbing her pulse points with perfume. The smell of wildflowers wafted through the room. "Fetch my black satin cape. What a shame I don't have a red one. And Liza? Has there been any mail today?"

Liza shook her head. "Not since the last time you asked, and the time before that. I wish I knew what news you are so anxious to hear."

"I submitted a novel to a few prominent publishers," Angelica lied, hiding her disappointment that the Elders' response had not arrived.

Really, she was being ridiculously impatient. It was doubtful they'd even received Ian's petition. If she kept jumping for news every hour, Liza was bound to grow suspicious. The sound of Burke greeting her husband in the parlor pulled her from her reverie.

Ian's appreciative smile as she sauntered down the stairs was well worth the effort. *Just wait until I remove the cape.* A secret smile played across her lips. She kept a modest distance between herself and the duke in the coach—despite his efforts to lessen it—and did not remove the cape until they were seated in their private opera box, just before the lights dimmed.

His harsh indrawn breath at the sight of her breasts curving up from the gown was a most worthy reward for her patience. When the lights dimmed, he reached for her and began to slowly trail his fingers up and down her gloved arm. The alternating sensations of his touch on her bare skin, then through the satin of her gloves, brought her to the brink of madness. She fought to keep her attention on the stage and lost the battle when his hand dropped to her thigh. The warmth of his palm through the thin fabric of her dress made her shudder with frustrated desire.

Boldly, she placed her hand on his leg, caressing the hard muscles of his thigh, reveling in the heat of him radiating through her gloves. She had to bite her lip harder to keep an excited gasp from escaping when her knuckles brushed his erection, straining through his black trousers.

Ian leaned over, his lips caressing her ear as he whispered, "Are you trying to seduce me, duchess?"

"Perhaps," she whispered, her voice ragged with arousal.

They left before the second act. The moment the carriage door closed, Ian pulled Angelica onto his lap and claimed her lips in a devouring kiss. She moaned and ground her hips against his as she pulled his hair free from its tie. She reveled like a starving woman in the feel of his mouth on hers, and it was all she could do not to let him ravage her before they arrived home.

When the carriage stopped, he swung her into his arms and rushed her up the stairs before the servants could manage full bows or curtsies. Over his shoulder she could see Liza's knowing smile before the bedchamber door closed.

Angelica grasped the lapels of Ian's jacket, ready to tear it in her eagerness to feel his bare skin against hers. He grasped her arms and turned her around to unfasten her gown.

"You have not finished seducing me yet," he whispered, his breath blowing on the back of her neck.

When she was clad in only her black silk stockings with their scarlet garters and her ruby necklace, he sat on the bed, stroking his chin thoughtfully. "Now, walk about for me." He threw off his waistcoat and unfastened his cravat.

Angelica felt deliciously wicked as she strutted and posed for him until his restraint collapsed and he pulled her to the bed to straddle him. She reached forward and unbuttoned his shirt, licking her lips as his muscled chest was revealed. He lifted her one moment to unfasten his breeches, and in the next, his hard velvet heat was sliding deep inside her.

It had been so long and she was so starved for him that she nearly climaxed the second he entered her. She moaned her pleasure as his entire length seemed to swell inside her sheath. When he cupped her rear and moved her faster up and down his shaft, she lost control and screamed and bucked her hips as she rode wave after wave of the orgasm.

He then picked her up and turned her over so she was on her hands and knees on the bed. He grasped her hips and thrust inside her hard. One hand reached down to caress the bud at the apex of her cleft, while the other held her by the hip as he pounded inside her, as he took her like a ravening beast. The mating was primal, and her climax seemed to shake the world. Moments later, he growled his pleasure.

She couldn't believe it when, before she could catch

her breath, he was pulling her into his arms once more. He held her as if he would never release her.

"I love you, Angel," he whispered before kissing her. Moments later, his embrace grew more heated.

"Again?" she asked in awe.

"Yes," he whispered, kissing her throat.

"But I have to rise early for the King's coronation tomorrow. If I do not—" She was silenced as his lips covered hers once more.

Angelica hid a yawn behind her fan as she followed the royal procession through the streets to Westminster Abbey. She and Ian had stayed up until dawn making love. Though attending a royal coronation was deemed a great honor for her as a duchess, part of her was longing for bed.

Still, she had to admit that the King was an arresting figure in his opulent robes of state and twenty-seven-foot train carried by pages. His face was florid from the July heat and thick robes, and he was sweating profusely. Angelica sympathized with him. She was garbed in dark blue with an ermine-trimmed cape, as befitting a duchess. Ermine, she decided, was not a good choice for summer.

To further compound matters, she was required to wear her coronet. Though the headpiece was an exquisite creation wrought of gold and adorned with strawberry leaves encrusted with rubies, the sun heated the metal so that it burned her scalp. When they arrived on the awning-covered pavilion, she sighed in relief to be in the meager shade.

Once the procession reached the Abbey, with the Archbishop droning on, Angelica took her seat in the gallery next to the Duchess of Wentworth, one of the few women who had maintained her friendship.

"What an exciting event!" Jane whispered, green eyes twinkling.

Angelica nodded and tried to fan the beads of sweat from her forehead. "Yes, it is very…" She waved a hand at the ostentatious display below, at a loss for words. If only Ian could see this!

Her Grace laughed. "I heard it cost 243,000 pounds." At Angelica's stunned look, she added, "His father's only cost ten thousand, to put this scene into perspective."

"How… obscene." She thought of the half-starved children she saw when volunteering at the hospital and felt ill. The choking miasma of the unwashed bodies surrounding her did not help matters.

Just as the Archbishop of Canterbury anointed the monarch with holy oil, a commotion broke out by the doors. Whispers soon gave way to shouts and jeers before erupting into pandemonium as people jostled each other, trying to get a better look.

"What is going on, Jane?" Angelica cried, elbowing aside the bodies that threatened to suffocate her.

The duchess was silent a moment, assessing the spectacle. "Oh, my God! I think it's… it is! Look over there." She pointed. "Queen Caroline is seeking entry to the ceremony and she is being barred by armed guards. I heard this might happen, but I did not believe the rumors!"

The king's face was twisted into a crimson mask of

rage. Angelica smirked. It served him right to have his moment ruined.

She stood up and shouted. "Long live the Queen!" Her voice was lost amongst the clamor, but her friend clapped a hand over Angelica's mouth anyway.

"Hush!" Jane admonished, her stern warning quite ruined by intermittent giggles. "You would catch too much trouble if the wrong ears heard you. And you definitely do not want anyone to take notice that your husband is absent. After all, we are all required to be here by royal command, skin condition or no."

Angelica sobered immediately. It would be just her luck that Ian would be thrown in the tower and burned to death by the sun before they could leave for Paris. "I still think the King is a cad for how he has treated her," she grumbled. "I hope she did have at least one of the grand affairs she's been accused of. The poor woman deserves a bit of happiness."

"I agree," her companion said then leaned in to whisper, "I had heard that, when on trial, she said, 'I have only committed adultery once, and that was with Maria Fitzherbert's husband, the King.'"

Angelica laughed. "One must admire her droll wit."

The commotion eventually abated and the ceremony droned on. Angelica found herself quite vexed with the Elders. If they'd responded to Ian's petition with sufficient alacrity, she could be sleeping the day away at her husband's side. She breathed a deep sigh of relief when the ordeal was finally over and they were able to go back outside, though it was only so they could make the brief journey to Westminster Hall for the banquet.

The banquet would have been the disappointment

of a lifetime, sheer torture, in fact, for the wives of the peers had to be seated in galleries above while the men enjoyed the vast array of food below, but the Duchess of Wentworth was prepared for the occasion. She pulled two carefully wrapped meat pasties and a flask of wine from her reticule, and the two women devoured the meal with relish. One lord below apparently had the same idea, for he wrapped a capon in his napkin and tossed the meager repast up to his grateful family.

Angelica had a moment of fear that the King would now notice her husband's absence, but she saw that he was distracted, nodding and winking at someone in the gallery to his left.

"Whoever is he trying to communicate with in this throng?" she whispered behind her fan.

Jane pointed her fan at a dark-haired, voluptuous woman seated across the vast chamber. "That is Lady Elizabeth Conyngham, his latest mistress. They have been barred from seeing each other throughout Queen Caroline's divorce trial. She is a vulgar woman, hence her appeal. It was her husband that the King promoted to marquess earlier. Were you not paying attention?"

Angelica shook her head. "No, I think I must have dozed off around then. So the King is done with Mrs. Fitzherbert then?"

Jane laughed. "Maria was old news far before Elizabeth. His last mistress was Lady Hertford, and before that, Lady Jersey."

"Lady Jersey?" Angelica gasped, as she remembered the prim and proper patroness of Almack's throwing her out for her scandalous behavior with the duke.

The duchess shook her head. "Not Lady *Sarah*.

It was Lady Frances, her mother-in-law, that I am speaking of. Though Lady Sarah has had plenty of affairs of her own."

Angelica fought to muffle her laughter as Jane entertained her for hours with delicious gossip.

By seven-thirty in the evening, with the sun at the windows compounded by hours of three hundred bodies in closed quarters, the heat became too much for King George. He departed for Carlton House, no doubt with his mistress following close behind. Half the procession followed him; the other departed in the opposite direction.

"There is to be a party at Hyde Park with a fireworks display and hot air balloons. Would you care to join me?" Jane asked.

"If there will be food, I will gladly follow you anywhere." Despite the afternoon respite, Angelica was ready to keel over from starvation. "Do you think I could summon a page to dispatch a note to my husband? I am certain he would love to join us when he is able."

At Hyde Park, the champagne flowed and the tables groaned with food under covered pavilions. The hot air balloons were a sight to see, but as the sky darkened and the fireworks commenced, Angelica's attention wandered from the colorful illuminations as she scanned the park for the approach of the Duke of Burnrath.

"I understand you are to become one of us," a deep, accented voice rumbled behind her.

Angelica turned to see Rafael Villar standing in the shadows of a copse of beech trees. Instead of flinching, she stepped closer, refusing to display her trepidation. "Yes, I am."

The corner of his mouth lifted in a brief half smile as he nodded in approval of her courage. "I suppose I must welcome you, then."

His reluctant tone made her laugh. "I appreciate your warm reception."

Rafael's customary scowl returned. "This is no laughing matter. I must warn you that joining the ranks of the immortals means that you will have to separate yourself from all of this." He waved his good hand at the merry celebration.

Angelica opened her mouth to retort, then closed it as the truth of his words struck her. Everyone she knew would age and die around her while she remained the same. Suddenly, the implication of hers and Ian's forthcoming fifty-year honeymoon became clear. They had to leave London before their secret became known.

"I understand," she replied solemnly.

Rafe gave a dry laugh. "I highly doubt that you do, but I have hope that you will someday." His gaze softened slightly. "I also understand that you killed the vampire hunter, Ben Flannigan. For that, you have my deepest gratitude and I shall repay you at the earliest opportunity."

Angelica's eyes widened. Had that hunter been the one responsible for Rafe's burns? She opened her mouth to ask, but he had already melted back into the shadows.

Angelica shivered. Where was Ian?

Her body felt him a second before he embraced her

from behind, pressing his hips against her rear as he kissed her ear. "How was the coronation, my Angel?"

She melted in his arms and covered her husband with kisses before launching into a full account. After relating all the gossip she'd heard at the banquet, she noticed that his eyes were on her breasts and he wasn't paying the slightest bit of attention to her words.

Angelica fought back a tremor of desire at his heated gaze. "I see you have no interest at all. You have probably been to a dozen of these affairs and seen many kings crowned." She slapped him on the arm with her fan and stuck out her tongue.

Ian smiled, resembling an archangel in the multi-colored light that framed his hair like a brilliant halo. He stepped closer and tilted up her chin. "Kings come and kings go, but our love will last forever." His lips captured hers, and Angelica's heart flared brighter than the explosions in the sky.

Twenty-nine

As July gave way to August, Angelica's marriage was as happy as it had been in the first weeks after her wedding. She was overcome with excitement as she and Ian planned their trip to Paris and discussed other places they intended to visit. She was the luckiest woman alive. Very few women had the opportunity to enjoy a honeymoon that lasted half a century.

"A letter has arrived for you, Your Grace," Burke said, presenting him with an ornate envelope on a silver tray.

"At last." Ian smiled as Angelica fetched the letter opener. "I have received a response from the Elders. They certainly took their time."

Angelica could hardly remain still in her seat as Ian slit open the first envelope and read with painstaking slowness.

She searched his face for hints of the news to come. At last, he met her gaze and set the letter down. "The Elders have approved my petition to Change you," he announced with a smile.

Angelica gasped in joy and threw herself into his

arms. At last she would be like him and they would be together for all eternity.

Ian kissed the top of her head and grasped her shoulders. His expression turned serious.

"They also wish me and Rafe to meet with them to discuss his succession."

"Is that typical?" Angelica asked, surprised at her concern. Although Rafe didn't appear to like her very much, she couldn't help but feel that much of his sour personality was due to how others treated him because of his scars and crippled arm. She had no doubt that he was powerful and intelligent enough to take Ian's place.

Ian nodded in reassurance. "Yes, the Elders always want to observe a potential interim lord in person to ensure that he is capable of the job. If he does not pass muster, they shall appoint a vampire of their own choosing."

"Do you mean to say that you have no real choice in who will be in charge of your city for the next fifty years?" Angelica asked, outraged.

Ian chuckled. "In the literal sense, no, I do not. The Elders always want to ensure there is no corruption, bias, or blackmail involved in a lord's choice of a successor. But most of the time, they approve his or her candidate."

"And how do they decide if a vampire is qualified?" She leaned forward, lips parted in fascination. Succession was based on logical reasoning rather than blood-born heirs. Perhaps the vampires' government was superior to England's.

"Usually the Elders base their decision on the candidate's age and power." Ian explained. "Though, sometimes I suspect one could bribe their way into the running."

Angelica chuckled and shook her head. "So there is corruption in the politics of vampires as well."

"Of course." Ian grinned. "We still maintain many aspects of our humanity, after all." He stood. "Well, I had better begin packing, as well as inform Rafe of our journey."

"Where are you going?" She fought to keep the panic from her voice at the thought of him leaving her.

Her husband gave her a reassuring smile. "We are to meet at the Elders' motherhouse in Amsterdam so I can give them my report on the state of the city, as well as an updated list of my vampires and where they place in the hierarchy."

She pouted, dreading the thought of him leaving her. "Amsterdam? I wish I could come, too. How long will you be gone?"

"I shall be back in a few days. I, too, would love your company, but this business is for Lord Vampires only. I suggest you use this time to enjoy the company of your family and friends. It will still take a few months of preparation for our journey, but you will be surprised how quickly the time passes." Ian tilted her chin up to meet his intent gaze. "And please, savor as many sunrises as you can. You never realize how much you miss natural light until it is gone."

Angelica wrapped her arms around him, looking up at him mischievously. "You can pack later, husband. First I want to give you something to be sure you hurry home to me." Her tongue darted out to lick her lips as she slowly sank down on her knees.

❦

Angelica spent her time wisely, savoring cheerful days shopping with her mother and evenings dining with both her parents. Even though the Winthrops were now very wealthy, since Margaret's father had restored her allowance and granted her two estates, Jacob Winthrop remained at his job at the bank, declaring that they couldn't manage without him.

The only regret Angelica had was that she would miss her family, but she was consoled by the fact that her parents seemed to have grown closer since her marriage to Ian.

Her evenings were spent in her literary circle. She would also miss these brilliant women and the new friendships she'd formed.

Rafe's words came back to her suddenly: *"...joining the ranks of the immortals means that you will have to separate yourself from all of this."* He was right, she realized, and her heart froze. Soon she would have to abandon her family. Would it be worth it?

Angelica took a few moments to imagine life without Ian... A cheerless life as the broodmare and arm decoration for a boor of a man who spent her dowry on his own pleasure. Her mother constantly nagging at her to conform to society's will. Yes, abandoning her life here would be worth the sacrifice of her humanity.

Angelica couldn't repress her excitement about what was to come. Soon, she would become a vampire like Ian. She would drink blood and be young forever, traveling the world and experiencing the unknown. A measure of revulsion remained at the thought of ingesting blood, but she fought it off. She stood upon the precipice of a great adventure, made all the more wonderful because her true love would be by her side. A change in her diet was a paltry thing in comparison.

She withdrew a packet of vellum invitations from her desk drawer, as well as a piece of paper. She smiled as she dipped her quill in a fresh bottle of ink. While Ian was absent, she had managed to track down Dr. John Polidori's address. She would invite him to one of her writers' soirees and perhaps get the answers that Ian sought. Hopefully, her husband wouldn't be too upset with her for taking matters into her own hands. However, remembering the way Polidori had fled from Ian, Angelica could not imagine Polidori being receptive to meeting with him.

❧

"Rosetta, would you look at this letter?" John called, a worried frown creasing his brow. "It seems that the Duchess of Burnrath had invited me to a gathering of writers that she hosted at Burnrath House yesterday. Is she not the wife of that vampire who is hunting for me?"

Rosetta's pulse jumped to her throat. "Let me see that!" She snatched the vellum invitation from his grasp.

This was obviously some scheme that the Duchess of Burnrath had devised. But how much did she know about Rosetta's failed assassination attempt? And worse, what had she told her husband?

"Was the invitation delivered here?" she asked, panic nearly choking her. If that was the case, Ian knew she was hiding John, and if he knew that, most likely he knew what else she had done.

"No, the letter was delivered to my flat. I have no idea how the woman received my address." John sat down at the table and sliced a loaf of bread.

"I am relieved that you did not go, John. Obviously it was a trap." She noted the dark circles under his eyes and her heart wrenched. The poor darling, these last few months had been so hard on him.

"I assumed that very thing myself," John said, running his hand through his hair in that pensive way she so adored. "Still, I feel a measure of regret. She is a very talented writer, and I would have been so delighted to make her acquaintance. Did you know that she wrote a few ghost stories under the name of Allan Winthrop? They were quite good."

Rosetta heaved a bitter sigh and sat down at the table across from him. The very forces of the universe appeared to be conspiring to keep her lover in peril, no matter how fervent her attempts to extricate him from danger. Her mind cast about for a solution to this latest problem. Odd it was that this invitation had come from the Duchess of Burnrath. She frowned. In fact, it was very odd that her lord had taken a mortal bride at all, since he had no intention of Changing her. The duchess must be a very compelling creature indeed to gain such a hold over her powerful master.

The gossip pages idolized Angelica and vilified her alternately with every article. She was reputed to be "fast," and she kept company with certain "notorious persons." Her wedding to the duke was still the talk of the season. The nuptials had been performed after a hasty and scandal-ridden courtship, during which she was seen at his residence before the proposal. Also, she'd been thrown out of Almack's shortly before the wedding.

For the past few months, rumors had said that the duke and duchess were estranged, most likely due to the very shocking ball the duchess had hosted at Burnrath House. But the papers now said that the couple had reconciled. All sources reconfirmed that theirs had been a love match all along.

A love match… Rosetta's mind raced. If indeed her master was in love with Angelica, he would do much for her safety, just as she would do anything to keep John from harm. She lit on an idea. If her scheme worked, their worries would be over at last.

"Fetch my writing materials from my desk, would you, love?" she asked. "I think you should write an invitation of your own. I suppose you'll meet Her Grace after all. I have a plan."

Angelica opened the letter from John Polidori with great curiosity. An amused smile played across her lips as she guessed at its contents. The gathering had been held two days ago and now he was declining? What a silly man he was! She stroked Loki behind his velvety ears as she read.

> *Dearest Duchess of Burnrath,*
>   *I am sorry I was unable to make an appearance at your gathering as it sounds as if I would have much enjoyed it. If you accept my apology, please*

*permit me to extend an invitation of my own. I will
be having a similar gathering of writers at Number 3
Great Pulteney Street in Soho tomorrow night at
six o'clock. I would be honored if you attended and
heartily look forward to making your acquaintance
and sharing discourse on the written word.*

> *Faithfully yours,*
> *John Polidori*

Angelica smiled, hardly able to believe her good
fortune. At last, she would have the opportunity to
meet the man who had known her idol and who had
written the first vampire story in English.

She wondered what Ian would say when she told
him she had met the man he'd been searching for
this past year. She recalled that Polidori's story had
endangered Ian's reputation in the first place. Angelica
supposed in a way that she ought to thank the man,
for if he hadn't caused a vampire craze in Europe, then
Ian would have had no inclination to marry her. On
the other hand, it was likely that the same craze that
inspired the vampire hunter to try to kill her beloved
husband. The letter shook in her hands. The cat
jumped up and batted at the parchment. Angelica put
the letter in a desk drawer.

Did Dr. Polidori know of the existence of vampires?
She resolved to use this opportunity to question him
and learn what she could. Perhaps Ian wouldn't be
angry with her if she could solve the mystery, and she
resolved to do the best she could in gleaning information from the man.

Angelica was so excited that she could hardly sleep

that night, and the next day she agonized over her wardrobe, struggling to decide which outfit would make her appear most like a serious gothic authoress. She finally decided on a dark blue satin gown with a matching hat and dyed ostrich plume. Then she went to her writing room and endured another battle with indecision as to which of her writings she would share with him. After nearly two hours, she decided on the one where a witch's curse awakened corpses from the grave.

Her heart beat harder in anticipation as the carriage approached the district of Soho. She felt a momentary pang of pity that he had to live in such an impoverished area and wondered if it would hurt his pride if she offered to sponsor him as she had a few other writers. She looked down at her gleaming gown, thankful she wasn't wearing jewels.

"We are here, Your Grace," Felton called as the carriage slowed.

The address at which they stopped was nicer than many of the residences they passed. Maybe the meeting would not be awkward after all. She adjusted her gown and straightened her hat as Felton helped her out of the carriage.

"I hope everything goes well, Your Grace." He returned to his seat, taking out a book for the wait.

The man who greeted Angelica at the door was surprisingly young and handsome. With his darkly sensual Italian features, he was nothing like she had pictured a writer or physician. His full lips twisted into an awkward smile as he bowed. "Your Grace. I am glad you were able to come to my humble abode."

She curtsied and returned the smile, hoping to put him at ease. "It is a great honor to finally meet you, Dr. Polidori."

Her greeting seemed to fluster him further. "The honor is mine. However, I am no longer a practicing physician," he mumbled. "Please, do come in."

The furnishings of the flat were humble yet tasteful. Still there was a stale quality to the air that seemed to indicate the place hadn't been lived in long. And something else was wrong. The house was quiet. Too quiet for a soiree.

"I hope I am not too early," she said, shifting on her feet.

"Not at all, you are right on time. Would you care for a glass of wine, Your Grace?"

"That would be nice." She eyed a vase of Venetian glass on a stand near the settee and wondered which question she would ask him first.

He nodded, running a hand through his thick black curls as if flustered. "Then please have a seat and I shall fetch your drink."

When she turned to sit, he grabbed her from behind and shoved a handkerchief in her face.

With a muffled shriek, she struggled. She had almost succeeded in twisting away from him when her limbs suddenly weakened. The stench of the cloth was so thick that she felt like she was swallowing it. The cloth was soaked with a pungent substance and her head swam with dizziness. Angelica gagged as blackness tinged her vision. Her lips formed a question, a protest. But no sound came.

"I'm very sorry, Your Grace," Polidori whispered

as she sank bonelessly into his arms. "If all goes well, this ordeal should be over before you know it."

Angelica tried to laugh because he really did sound sorry. But the noxious fumes took her away to blackness.

Thirty

IAN PACED THE STONE FLOOR OF THE UNDERGROUND anteroom of the Elders' motherhouse in Amsterdam. The ancient faces looking down on him had been intimidating the first time he'd come before the governing force. They sat in folds of darkness so thick that one couldn't tell if shadows framed their solemn faces or executioner's hoods. But they frightened Ian no longer. He was impatient to get this over with and return to London and his beloved bride. His petition to Change Angelica had been approved, and now all that was left was to discuss Rafe's succession.

It seemed an unnecessary chore to come all the way to Amsterdam for this formality, Ian believed, though he would never dare voice such a defiant thought. A sideways glance at Rafe's impatient expression confirmed that they were in accord. The Elders gazed at them knowingly from their raised podiums as if they knew what both were thinking.

"Lord Ashton and Rafael Villar, thank you for coming so quickly," they chorused as if they truly were the single mind they represented.

"Thank you for responding to my request with alacrity," Ian said with a bow. It was strange being addressed by his surname for the first time in a century. But the Elders cared nothing for mortal titles.

Marcus, the Lord of Rome, looked up from a pile of parchment. "Raphael Villar, please come forward.

Rafael approached the Elders, looking up at them expressionlessly, which was as close to respect as he could muster.

Marcus looked down at his papers. "As you are nearing your third century and have spent the last one acting as second to a lord, you fit the standard qualifications to replace Ian Ashton as Lord of London. However, we have a few concerns."

"What concerns would those be, Excellency?" Rafe said through clenched teeth.

"Well, there is your temper, to begin with," the ancient Roman replied smugly. "After all, that is what led to your... accident."

The Spaniard's reply verged on a growl. "To allow a hunter to live is to bring danger to our kind. That is your edict. My actions had nothing to do with my temperament."

Anastasia, Lord of Moscow, nodded in agreement and addressed the others. "It is true that Villar followed our code in eradicating our enemies." She glared at the others as if daring them to argue. "Also, we have received no valid complaints against him in all his years of existence."

The others nodded, but Marcus continued to frown. "Our other concern is your unfortunate disability. How do you expect to defend yourself and your people with only one functioning arm? Much less fight a duel."

Ian cursed under his breath. Rafe flinched as if struck while the Elder smiled in triumph.

"Why don't you fight him now and see for yourself?" The words left Ian's mouth before he had time to think.

Marcus's mocking laughter was cut short as the remaining Elders chorused their agreement.

The Lord of Rome shot a glare at his colleagues before rising into the air to float down before Rafael. "Very well," he replied with a smirk.

With smoothness belying his handicap, Rafe swiftly unbuttoned his frock coat and tossed it to Ian, along with his hat. Marcus's eyes widened and a flicker of doubt was revealed in every line of his body.

The remaining Elders took up their quills and parchment as if to document the case. Ian had no doubt that they were really recording wagers.

The two vampires bowed to each other and the fight commenced. Marcus charged like an angry bull. Rafe danced nimbly from his reach. The ancient Roman snarled, enraged that he had failed to land a blow. He took to the air, attempting to use his power of flight against the Spaniard.

In a blur of speed that was impressive even by preternatural standards, Rafe's fist took Marcus under the chin, sending him crashing into the stone wall. Slowly, Marcus stumbled to his feet, only to be knocked over once more as Rafe came at him like a spinning dervish.

"Enough!" the Elder coughed, spitting out blood. "You've made your point, Villar." Marcus winced as he returned to the podium. "Let the interview commence."

For the next hour, the Elders asked Rafe standard questions as to how he would handle his responsibilities as Lord of London, if appointed.

"What would you do if one of your vampires Changed a mortal without permission?" the Lord of Constantinople asked.

Rafe hid a yawn. "I would place him or her under arrest and report the incident to you."

Ian nodded in admiration at Rafe's response. Though the penalty for such an offense was usually execution, the Elders always insisted on being notified and holding a trial to ensure that a lord was not abusing his power.

The Elders murmured their approval and asked the next question, but Ian didn't hear. Suddenly, the Mark between him and Angelica pulsed and flared. His wife was in danger! Every cell of his being throbbed with the need to dash out of the chamber and fly back to London immediately. The only thing keeping him anchored to his spot was the knowledge that the Elders would punish him for such a disrespectful action. Thankfully, the Elders stood and announced the verdict.

"Raphael Villar, you are hereby approved to stand in for Ian Ashton as Lord of London. We only ask that you inform us as soon as you take the position and tell us your selection as second in command."

Ian and Rafael bowed in unison. The Lord of Edo, Japan, fixed Ian with a piercing stare. "I also move to adjourn for I see that Lord Ashton has some pressing business to attend to." Her almond-shaped eyes glittered as if peering into his soul.

"Thank you, lords," Ian said and charged from the chamber with Rafe on his heels.

"Something is wrong with your bride, isn't it?" Rafe asked, running beside him.

Ian nodded, not slowing his pace.

"It doesn't surprise me that she was unable to stay out of trouble for even this short time," the Spaniard observed calmly. "You had better fly. I will catch up to you as soon as I am able, and I will be happy to aid you in punishing whoever is responsible… unless the duchess is solely at fault."

Ian needed no further urging. He took to the air, heart pounding in terror for his love.

It took Ian less than twelve hours to arrive back in London. Normally, he hated to use such great speed, especially when flying. This time the odd sensation of vaulting through the sky like a preternatural cannon-ball had little effect on his awareness. All he could do was pray that his Angel would be safe when he arrived.

He stopped quickly at his house to fetch a sword and cursed as Burke handed him the ransom note.

> *I have your duchess. I will trade her in exchange for a note of safe passage out of London for myself and John Polidori.*
>
> > *Respectfully your servant,*
> > *Rosetta*

"Goddammit!" Ian roared.

Of all his vampires, he had never expected quiet, unassuming Rosetta to betray him. He bared his fangs in rage. He would kill her for this!

Thirty-one

ANGELICA AWOKE CRAMPED AND UNCOMFORTABLE from sleeping in a chair. Had she fallen asleep at her writing again? The sound of rustling papers intruded on her thoughts. Loki was playing with her manuscripts again. She tried to leap out the chair to startle and scold him and nearly had the wind knocked out of her when the thick ropes pulled her back.

Her eyes snapped open. She wasn't home at all! She was in a stone cellar that was furnished as if it were living quarters. Still, with the velvet hangings, ornate tapestries, and tasteful ornaments strewn about, an attempt at beauty had been made.

The pine tables and ladder-back chairs were sturdy and serviceable, but inexpensive. Coupled with the darkness, they reminded her of the furniture that had been in her parents' town house before her father had been promoted at the bank. Her attention was pulled away from her surroundings as she realized that she was not alone.

John Polidori reclined on a settee. Her reticule lay on the floor by his feet. In his hands he held the pages of one of her manuscripts, which he had been reading by candlelight.

"Where in the blazes am I?" she asked, despising the hysterical note in her voice as she squirmed in her bonds.

Her efforts were useless. The man obviously knew how to tie a decent knot. Rage engulfed her, hot and bitter. She had been on the brink of happiness, and this scoundrel had presumed to ruin it for her!

"Ah, you are awake, Your Grace," John said pleasantly. He held up her work. "This is quite good, actually. I love the way you are able to bring your characters to life."

"Thank you," she said, feeling flattered despite the fact that he had abducted her and tied her up. "Would you please untie me now?"

"I'm afraid not, Your Grace." His voice was thick with remorse. "But I do promise you will come to no harm."

The sincerity in his eyes was unmistakable. Angelica believed him, despite the dictates of common practicality. She decided she might as well take advantage of his company, and from the tightness of the ropes, she appeared to have time to spare. "So, Mr. Polidori, how did you get the idea for the character of Lord Ruthven when writing 'The Vampyre'?"

His dark brows drew together in consternation. "I have told everyone, even going as far as to have it publicly announced in the paper, that the basis of the idea was from a fragment of a novel that Lord Byron wrote. I merely developed it further." His bitter laugh made her heart go out to him in sympathy.

"In truth, I wrote the tale out of spite. I wanted to, in the only manner I could, show the world what a coldhearted monster he was. Instead, because of that blackguard Colburn's greed, my story was accredited to him and declared, 'the best that Lord Byron has ever written.'"

"Colburn is indeed quite the blackguard," Angelica said. "He refused to see me or my work only last year because I was a 'mere woman,' but when I arrived disguised as a man, he loved it and asked for more. After I married and revealed myself to be the 'infamous' Duchess of Burnrath, he *paid* me more! I suppose he thought my identity would generate more sales... the hypocrite."

She paused as she digested Polidori's words. "You did not base your story on my husband at all, did you?"

He shook his head. "I did not even believe in vampires until a few months ago. I'd intended the 'vampire' in my story to be a metaphor for Byron's way of making people fall utterly and completely in love with him before sucking the life out them and tossing them aside." Polidori looked down at his hands. "He broke my heart, you know."

Angelica was stunned by the revelation that men could love each other in such a manner. She meant to ask more about their relationship, but as she shifted in her chair in an effort to get more comfortable, her attention was drawn again to the ropes that held her.

"You discovered that my husband was searching for you," she said, looking pointedly at her restraints. "That is why you have abducted me."

Before he could answer, a woman's voice interjected.

"It was the only option we had left. I will not let him kill my Johnny!"

Angelica's jaw dropped as the woman walked farther into the room. Her breeches and jacket clung to her lithe figure as if they were tailored for her. Her cravat was immaculately tied, and her hair was short, though not in the style ladies were beginning to favor, as the locks teased about her elfin face in wild midnight wisps.

Though she was the most *interesting* person Angelica had ever seen, it was the naked love on the woman's face that caught her breath. The mutual adoration on Polidori's face as he returned her look told Angelica that though he may have loved Lord Byron, his former flame was eclipsed by this woman entirely. As her eyes traveled back to the vampire's face, she realized she had seen this woman before, when Ian had presented her to his vampires.

"It is nice to meet you again. And your name is?" she asked with polite sarcasm, unable to curtsy in restraints.

"I am called Rosetta, Your Grace," the vampire replied.

"Very well, Rosetta, I would be more pleased to see you under other circumstances." She inclined her head in what she hoped was duchess-like regality. "But why is capturing me and tying me up your 'only option'?"

The vampire had the decency to look down in shame. "His Grace was hunting for John. I couldn't let him kill my love, so I've been hiding him. But if he discovers what I have done, he will certainly kill me for betraying him." Her eyes welled with tears. "I had John take you and delivered a note to the duke's home. If he agrees to let John and me go, with a letter of safe passage into other territories, I will set you free unharmed."

"Ah, so you are holding me for ransom?" The situation now became clear. At least they didn't intend to kill her. That gave her room to reason with them. "But why do you need to do this foolish thing? Why didn't the pair of you just leave the city?"

Rosetta sighed. "It is not that easy for vampires, Your Grace. One must request permission from their lord to leave their city and then petition the lord of another city with a request to stay there. And His Grace suspended all petitions until John was found." Her lower lip trembled. "He could have fled to safety, but he refused to leave without me. Your Grace, I love him! I would do anything to keep him from harm!" Her face flushed with the passion of her words.

Angelica nodded, completely understanding, but then she gasped as comprehension dawned. *Anything*, Rosetta had said. Angelica's blood went cold as her suspicion rose. "*You* sent that man to kill my husband, didn't you?"

Rosetta's eyes widened in fear and she averted them from Angelica's glare, confirming her guilt.

"He meant to kill John!" the vampire sobbed. "Don't you understand? Wouldn't you kill for the man you love?" She stepped back from the glow of the candles, retreating into the shadows as if they would protect her.

"Thanks to you, I *have* killed for him," Angelica hissed, once more struggling in her bonds. "You are very fortunate that you had the foresight to restrain me, for I would thrash you if I could."

"*You* killed the hunter?" Rosetta's stunned expression would have been comical if Angelica wasn't so infuriated. "A dainty creature such as yourself? How very remarkable…" Her voice softened. "You must love him very much."

"Yes, I do." Her gaze remained fixed on the vampire, still vexed at this ludicrous situation.

Rosetta took a tentative step forward. "I don't suppose an apology would do me any good?"

Angelica took in the vampire's tear-stained face. She saw the devotion in Rosetta's eyes when she spoke John's name and in the way she leaned toward him as if the longing to touch him was an unstoppable compulsion. She felt that way about Ian. If she believed another vampire was going to kill him, would she hire an assassin? The answer came back as a resounding yes.

She sighed. "No, I don't think I could accept your apology under such unseemly circumstances, but I suppose I do understand. Just answer me one thing. Did you truly, with every fiber of your being, believe that Ian meant to kill Dr. Polidori if he found him?"

"Yes!" Rosetta cried, pacing in front of Angelica and casting continuous anxious looks her way. Angelica squirmed in the chair, wishing she could pace as well. "His Grace ordered all of us to deliver Johnny to him if we found him. What else could he intend?"

"As far as I know, he only wished to question the author on his inspiration for the story that put the duke's reputation in danger. He never said anything about killing him." Angelica paused as the situation became clear. "Though if he knew that you lied to him, then sent a vampire hunter to kill him, then abducted his wife…" She trailed off, dread seeping in as she pictured Ian killing this poor love-struck vampire.

Rosetta gasped as she, too, saw the truth. "Oh, my God! What have I done?" Tears ran unchecked down the vampire's cheeks.

John took Rosetta into his arms. "Hush, love. Don't cry."

"John, we are doomed now. Please, you must leave the city." Rosetta continued to sob. "My death will be much easier if I know you are alive and safe."

"I will not leave you, Rosetta," John said. His somber black eyes beseeched Angelica. "Is there any way that you can possibly fix this?"

A lump formed in her throat as she watched the exchange. It was difficult to remain angry in the face of this tragic romance.

"Not all of it, I'm afraid," Angelica said. "However, we may be able to put things in a better light. You should start by letting me go."

Rosetta nodded. "Yes, untie her, John. I deserve every blow if she attacks me."

Polidori quickly removed her bonds and leaped out of the way. Apparently, guilt, coupled with the knowledge that she'd killed a full-grown male, made her quite intimidating to them.

"Thank you." She rubbed her wrists. "Ian is not expected back for another day yet. I will go home and burn that ransom letter." She pointed at Rosetta. "You will call upon him when he returns and confess that you have been hiding the doctor. Tell him why and beg for his mercy. You both will likely be forgiven if he never discovers that you hired the vampire hunter."

"Do you mean that you will not tell him we took you?" Her voice was tremulous with gratitude. "What can we do to repay your kindness, Your Grace?"

Angelica saw the hope in the two pairs of eyes trained on her. In truth, she did not know if her word was enough to make this right. Rosetta had committed the equivalent of high treason just by hiding Polidori. If Ian discovered that kidnapping and attempted murder were added to the equation... and if he discovered her deception... Ian would leave her for sure, and permanently. But even knowing the risks she was taking, she couldn't bear not to do what she could to help these star-crossed lovers.

"You can show me how you managed that exquisite knot in your cravat," she said with a grin. "And you." She turned to Polidori. "You can tell me all about that infamous time you spent with the Shelleys at Lake Geneva."

Thirty-two

By the time Ian landed in the district of Soho, he was nearly out of his mind with the need to feed. Luckily for him, a harlot was flaunting her wares outside the alley. With a twinge of regret for the necessity of going against Angelica's request to only feed on males, Ian lit on his victim. His fangs tore her throat in his eagerness. He cursed at the delay it took to heal her before he could be on his way.

Ian expected many things when he crashed through Rosetta's door and stormed into her chamber: Rosetta rising up from his bride's prone body, her fangs dripping blood; John Polidori assaulting Angelica as she screamed for mercy; or even Angelica fending off both captors with whatever sharp weapon she could find. What he had not anticipated was the determined look on his wife's face as she leaped in front of him to block him from Rosetta and Polidori.

"Please, Ian, don't kill them!" she cried. "This has all been a substantial misunderstanding!"

Behind her, Rosetta and John had fallen to their knees on the stone floor. Rosetta shielded Polidori with her arms as if Ian were a falcon ready to swoop down and take him from her.

"What in the blazes is going on here?" he roared.

"Well, if you would calm down, we can explain," Angelica said, still trying to keep him from her captors.

The situation was so fantastical, so ridiculous, that it took a moment for him to recover his speech.

"Calm down? Pray tell, madam, who is calm here?" He looked again at the couple who appeared torn between fleeing and fighting. "And how can you possibly 'explain' the fact that one of my subjects has lied to me, betrayed me, *and* abducted my wife? I do not see any way for that to be put in a positive light."

"I am sorry, Your Grace, I only wanted to protect John," Rosetta said.

"Protect him from what?" Ian demanded, confusion adding to his rage.

Angelica stepped forward, eyes beseeching him to understand. "She thought you intended to kill him, Ian. You didn't, did you?"

"I did not," he answered stiffly, wanting nothing more than to sweep his bride out of the way and destroy the couple she seemed to be protecting. Only the imploring look in her eyes prevented him from doing just that. "But why did she take you?"

"Did the note not say?" Angelica asked.

He frowned. "The letter only demanded that I allow those schemers safe passage out of the city before they released you." His eyes narrowed on the traitorous woman. "Now explain yourself at once, Rosetta."

She gained her feet with liquid grace and took a shuddering breath. "I have been hiding John from you and the other vampires for a little over four months now. When he received an invitation from your wife to a writers' gathering, I thought the duchess had set a trap for him. We captured Her Grace with intent to hold her until you gave us a letter of safe passage from London." She fell back to her knees before him. "I truly believed that you meant to kill my Johnny. And when Her Grace told us you did not, I released her. I swear it. Please, Your Grace, have mercy!" Tears trailed down her ivory cheeks. "I love him!"

Angelica looked up at him with wide gypsy eyes shining in the candlelight. "Don't you see, Ian? They are in love. You would do the same for me, wouldn't you?"

He sighed, overwhelmed with this unexpected turn in the situation. "I suppose I would." Actually, he would probably do worse. If he thought someone intended to kill his beloved, he would slaughter them in the most brutal manner imaginable. "Did they hurt you, Angel?" he growled.

"No, not in the slightest." She spread her arms and twirled to show herself unharmed.

"Were you afraid?" His eyes blazed like silver daggers at her captors.

Angelica snorted and shook her head, ever fearless. "Of course not. A duchess is more valuable alive than dead, you know."

Ian scratched his chin thoughtfully and favored her with a stern gaze. "But if they let you go, then why were you still here, rather than safe at home?"

Her smile was sheepish. "I wanted to know about the famous writers' gathering at Lake Geneva as well as how to tie a decent neckcloth. After all, you weren't expected back for another day or so."

He raised his eyes heavenward, though he could expect no aid from that quarter. "I might have known."

Angelica skipped over to him, grasping the lapels of his topcoat. "Oh, Ian, John didn't write 'The Vampyre' about you or other vampires at all! He meant the story to be a gothic lampoon on Lord Byron. They were lovers once," she added with a blush. "So you see this whole thing was all a great and terrible misunderstanding."

"I suppose it was," he said, still frowning at Polidori in exasperation for all the trouble he had caused.

His duchess beamed and clasped her hands together. "Then everything is settled!"

John's shoulders slumped with relief and he embraced Rosetta. Ian's subject's eyes were filled with gratitude as she bowed to him. "How can I ever thank you, Your Grace? I—"

Ian held up a hand. "I am afraid that everything is not 'settled.' As Lord of London, I cannot turn a blind eye to a subject's betrayal." His gaze shifted to Dr. Polidori's solemn form. "And as for you, sir, I cannot countenance a mortal writer of your notoriety and subject matter gallivanting around with one of my vampires and holding the secrets of our kind to your breast."

"Your Grace, I would never reveal—" Polidori began.

"Silence!" he thundered, a headache threatening as he turned back to his subordinate. "Rosetta, I am placing you under arrest for the crime of lying to your lord and revealing yourself to a mortal. You will accompany me to Burnrath House, and you may only feed under my supervision until your sentence is carried out. Do you understand?"

"Yes, Your Grace," she whispered, bowing her head.

He turned to the quaking mortal man, whose pen had caused all this trouble in the first place. "As for you, young physician, as much as I would like to let you go, your fame, coupled with your dangerous knowledge, prevents me from that course of action. Dr. John Polidori, you must die."

Thirty-three

24 August 1821

THOUGH THE DAY WAS HOT AND SWELTERING, THE crowd that had gathered outside the house on Great Pulteney Street shivered as if chilled. Death had visited here.

The coroner shook his head and wiped the sweat from his brow as he stepped back into the August heat. The victim had very obviously committed suicide. A bottle of prussic acid was tipped over by the body's outstretched hand, and the substance was all over the corpse's face. But the constable had put considerable pressure on the coroner to write "natural causes" on the report.

Besides consideration for the family's reputation, the fellow had been something of a notorious writer and a friend of the infamous Lord Byron. That was sufficient cause for lengthy paperwork and irritating hounding by the press, which had already gathered outside like carrion birds. A suicide would send the lot into throes of ecstasy and scandal broth.

The coroner addressed the crowd. "The death was of natural causes, and God rest his soul. I have been informed that his family is away in Italy, so unfortunately they will not be able to attend to a funeral. Due to the heat and possibility of contagion, I recommend that he be buried immediately."

He watched as the crowd stepped back at the mention of contagion. It was all well and good to write "natural causes" on the report to avoid scandal, but the real reason he did it was to ensure the young man had a proper burial. If people discovered that Polidori committed suicide, he would not be buried in hallowed ground. Surely it was unfortunate enough that the poor chap had died so young.

As the coroner awaited the undertaker's carriage, he listened to the snatches of conversation around him.

"…was completely estranged from his family, y'know," a man was saying to a journalist who eagerly jotted down notes. "His dissolute behavior and gambling debts became too much for them."

"I cannot believe he is dead!" a woman cried out.

"Yes, the news is so very tragic, isn't it?" another answered.

A man coughed. "Indeed. The bastard owed me thirty pounds."

A fop brandished his cane as he shouted over the crowd. "Well, I for one maintain that he was struck down by the almighty for his foul lies about authorship on that vampire story. Even an idiot would recognize the tale as the work of Lord Byron."

Another glared and yelled, "You are a fool! Dr. Polidori wrote 'The Vampyre.' Lord Byron was the fraud!"

A riot would have broken out if the undertaker had not arrived. The sight of the somber black carriage pulled by black horses, and the grim-faced man driving it, automatically sobered the spectators. Silence reigned until the coffin was carried out and loaded into the carriage. The crowd dispersed then, most heading to the nearest pub to drink to the deceased, and only a few following the undertaker to the St. Pancras old churchyard to hear the priest say words over him before the burial.

By the time the undertaker patted down the last bit of earth on the new grave, the sun was setting. The graveyard was empty of all witnesses, except for a boy who hadn't moved from his vantage point since the undertaker began digging.

The lad was awfully young. The undertaker would eat his hat if the boy had seen his first whisker.

"Ye should leave this place before dark, laddie," he hollered as he loaded his tools back into the carriage. "Lest the ghosts and other sorts of nocturnal beasties get ye."

"I would like to stay a bit longer," the boy replied. "Dr. Polidori was a friend of mine."

"Suit yerself," the undertaker grumbled as he climbed up on his carriage seat and flicked the reins of his horses. "Don't say I didn't caution ye."

In truth he was more concerned with the dangers of the living. This neighborhood was no place for a boy alone, especially one as pretty as that one. If he didn't take care, he'd likely be robbed or buggered. The undertaker shook his head. Well, there was nothing he could do. After all, the dead ones were his business. And a fine business it was. He would have to be sure to pad the bill when Polidori's family returned to London.

◦◦◦

When the graveyard was empty at last, Angelica whipped off the woolen cap and shook out her sweat-drenched hair, grateful to feel fresh air on her scalp. She paced around Mary Wollstonecraft's grave, thinking how romantic it was that this was the place where her daughter and Percy Shelley had their clandestine meetings.

Polidori had told her that Percy Shelley was constantly unfaithful to his wife, and he not only lived with Mary and her stepsister, Claire Clairmont, in a ménage à trois, but he was also constantly trying to get Mary to sleep with other men. The contempt had been so thick in John's voice when he described the Shelleys' marriage that Angelica wondered if he had been a little in love with Mary himself, or perhaps his Catholic upbringing made him frown more on adultery than most.

She frowned as her gaze rested on the freshly dug grave. It was so tragic that he was mourned by so few. In fact, many people did not even know who he was! And of those who did, many either defamed him by calling him a fraud or scorned him for his drinking and gambling habits. Perhaps, she thought as she looked up at the moon, he would gain more prestige in death than he had in life.

A movement at the corner of her eye brought her attention to the three cloaked figures approaching her.

"Thank you for keeping vigil," one whispered then stood by her as the other two attacked John Polidori's grave with shovels under the cover of darkness.

With inhuman speed, the coffin was unearthed and the body removed. Rosetta left Angelica's side and looked upon the face of her beloved with fearful concern. "Is he—?"

"He is stirring. The drug is wearing off," Ian said as his companion placed the man in her arms. "We must refill the grave and leave before we are discovered."

By the time the group had returned to Burnrath House, John Polidori had regained consciousness. Angelica was relieved that Ian had dismissed the servants for the night.

"I cannot believe I was buried alive," Polidori said after his thirst was slaked with a cup of water. "In a way, I wish I had been able to be aware of the situation. The experience would have been interesting, in a morbid sort of manner."

"You will have your chance soon enough," Rafael Villar told him. "You and your bride will be transported by coffin on the journey to France and then to America, only able to rise at night to feed. I wager you'll be sick of being a corpse by the end of it."

Angelica shuddered at the thought of being trapped in a box on a ship for a journey halfway across the world. She wished Rosetta and John didn't have to go so far, but she knew that America was the safest place for them. Though John had "died" to the public, there was still a great chance that he would be recognized in England or on the Continent.

The Spanish vampire that would rule London for

the next fifty years stalked toward Polidori with a scowl. "Are you ready, doctor?"

John kissed Rosetta and nodded. "Yes."

Since Ian was to Change Angelica tonight, Rafael had agreed to Change John, for Rosetta was not old or powerful enough to be able to do the deed herself.

Rafael fixed Angelica with an intent stare. "Consider my debt to you repaid, duchess."

Angelica swallowed and nodded. "Thank you, Rafael."

Ian took her in his arms. "Would you like to watch the process before I Change you?"

Angelica smiled at her husband with shining eyes. He had worked so hard to form a plan to keep John and Rosetta together safely.

"No. I trust you with all my heart." She grabbed the candelabra with one hand and extended her other for his escort. "Shall we retire to our room, Your Grace?"

Ian nodded. "Indeed, my duchess."

They mounted the stairs to the bedchamber, his hand clinging to hers as if he would never let go of her grasp.

Once the lamps were lit, Ian tilted her chin with reverent fingertips. "Angel, I have been meaning to inform you, there were many historical inaccuracies in your vampire story. For example, potatoes and beer were not around until the Elizabethan era, when they were introduced from the New World. Ale and wine were the preferred beverages of Henry's reign."

Angelica stiffened at the painful reminder of the manuscript he had burned. "And just what point are you trying to make, Your Grace?"

He smiled. "If you were willing to rewrite the tale, I would be happy to help you with the historical details of the reign of Henry VIII. And then there is the matter of the ending. You left the characters in quite a bind. How did you intend for that to work out?"

Her heart nearly burst with joy. "You want me to write the story again, truly? I struggled unbearably with it, for I was unable to come up with a suitable happy ending for my characters. Things were so strained between us, you see." A frown marred her brow. "But what would people say? What if another hunter comes after you?"

"Thanks to Polidori's tale, vampire stories are springing up everywhere. I'm sure the hunters are chasing their tails trying to find the real ones. Still, I feel it would likely be prudent to wait a while before publishing your tale."

Angelica blinked in disbelief at his cavalier words. "I believe we have plenty of time, Your Grace. I still have no idea how to end the dratted thing."

Ian caressed her cheek. "Then we will have to seek inspiration." He captured her lips until she was breathless from his kisses before he sank to his knee. "Angelica Ashton, will you be my eternal bride and companion? Will you walk beside me every night for as long as we both shall live?"

She melted into his embrace. "I will."

As his fangs sank into her throat, she smiled. None of her stories could have ended this perfectly.

Epilogue

"A LETTER HAS ARRIVED FOR YOU, YOUR GRACE," Burke announced as he entered the library.

Angelica glanced up from her book on French grammar as Ian took the envelope.

"It is from the Lord of Cornwall," he said after the butler departed. Ian opened the letter. "Let's see what Vincent has to say." His brow creased as he read. "Hmmm…" he said, and set the letter down, still frowning.

"What's wrong?" Angelica asked, hoping Lord Deveril was all right. He was a kind vampire.

Ian shook his head. "It seems Vincent is asking for your help."

"What?" Her eyes widened. She'd only been a vampire for a little over a month. How could she be any help to one as old and powerful as Deveril?

Her husband nodded. "You recall hearing of the death of the Earl of Morley, yes?"

"No, I hadn't heard." Angelica frowned, wondering where this topic was headed. "I wonder what happened. I saw Lord Morley at the King's coronation and he looked to be in good health."

"That was the new earl. It was his elder brother who died… in America." Ian ran a hand through his hair. "He left behind a daughter, and the dowager countess refuses to take her in. Apparently she is still angry about the earl's marriage to a chambermaid, which is why he and his wife left for America in the first place."

"So what has this to do with Lord Deveril?" Angelica asked, baffled.

"The Deverils and the Morleys have an alliance dating back to the seventeenth century," Ian explained. "One of the terms of the alliance is for one to become guardian to the other's children, if such a necessity arises."

Angelica gasped. "So Lord Deveril is going to become guardian to Morley's daughter! Why would he agree to do such a thing? And what does he expect me to do about it?"

Ian shook his head. "Why he agreed, I haven't the slightest idea. Perhaps he truly is as mad as is rumored. As for you, he asks you to sponsor the girl for the season so he may see her married and off his hands quickly."

She opened her mouth to reply, but then burst into gales of laughter. "He wants me to usher a young lady into the Quality? *Me*, the scandalous Duchess of Burnrath?" Her mirth faded as the implications of such a task became clear. "To see a girl auctioned off to the highest bidder as if she were a breeding mare goes against my principles. I should refuse."

Her husband held up a hand. "Do not be so hasty, Angel. At least allow me to pay Vincent a visit to further assess the situation. Lord knows, Rafe would be unfit to deal with such a delicate matter."

Angelica nodded grudgingly. "Very well. I'll tell the servants to unpack our trunks as it seems we shall be ruling London for a while longer."

"And I shall dash off a note to Rafe," Ian replied, rising from his seat.

"Not just yet." Angelica licked her fangs. "All this talk has made me hungry."

"Already?" He frowned. "Well, I suppose we may hunt first."

She shook her head, playfully tossing her hair as she approached him. "No, I am hungry for you."

His eyes glittered with desire as he bared his own gleaming fangs and locked the library door. "I see. In that case, I would be pleased to oblige you as well."

Author's Note

In 1816, Percy Bysshe Shelley and his soon-to-be wife, Mary Wollstonecraft Godwin, enjoyed a holiday with Lord Byron and his physician, John William Polidori. The four spent a stormy summer evening in Byron's villa near Geneva, Switzerland, writing ghost stories. Two of the works from that fateful night went on to influence literature to this very day. Mary Shelley began the unforgettable *Frankenstein*. Lord Byron penned a fragment of a novel, which he abandoned and Dr. Polidori then developed into the short story, "The Vampyre," which was the very first vampire story written in English.

When Polidori published "The Vampyre" anonymously in 1819 in *The New Monthly Magazine*, the editors credited the story to Lord Byron. In fact, "The Vampyre" was once referred to as "Byron's greatest work." Both Byron and Polidori were upset by this, and after strenuous efforts to clear up the misunderstanding, eventually due credit was given. The story spawned a "vampire craze" in Western Europe, and countless stories, plays, and operas based on the tale were devoured by the bloodthirsty public.

I relied heavily upon historical fact and speculation, as well as my author's license, to develop my fictional portrayal of the enigmatical physician-turned-writer. Did Lord Byron have a bisexual affair with Polidori? Historians speculate both ways. I chose to go with that angle because I believe that would clarify much about their unbalanced relationship. Also, Polidori called his fanged villain "Lord Ruthven," a name Lady Caroline Lamb, one of Byron's former lovers, used for Byron in her thinly disguised memoir, *Glenarvon*.

Another speculation I found interesting was that perhaps John Polidori was secretly in love with Mary Shelley. I am all for this delicious tidbit of gossip, for it certainly explains the well-documented hostility the doctor had for Percy Shelley. Polidori once challenged Shelley to a duel, allegedly over a boat race.

There are few known details of the circumstances of John Polidori's burial and his relationship with his family at the time of his death. Considering the fact that his family was well off but he died penniless, it can be speculated that they were estranged. I found little information on burial customs in the Regency era, but I find it logical that if someone dies, especially in the summer, and there is no one around to claim responsibility for the body, the authorities would bury the remains as soon as possible for sanitary reasons. And since stethoscopes were not yet in frequent use in those days, perhaps a person could fake their death.

Could John Polidori have cheated death and become a vampire? One may never know. That is one of the things that make fiction so much fun.

Acknowledgments

A lot of people helped and encouraged me with this project.

My eternal thanks go out to my wonderful editor, Deb Werksman, and the incredible Sourcebooks team for their hard work; my friends and family; my awesome critique partners, Shelley Martin and Bonnie R. Paulson; and my long list of beta readers: Erica Mills Chapman, Jamie De Bree, Elise Rome, Millie McClain, Damien Walters Grintalis, Leslie Faircloth, Sandy Williams, J. Sterling Smith, and Rissa Watkins. I also want to thank my buddies at the Powder River Saloon for cheering me on and Kent Butler for his aid and support with my final edits.

Special thanks go out to Jolene R. McDonald for her invaluable help with researching John Polidori.

About the Author

A lover of witty Regencies and dark paranormal romance, Brooklyn Ann combines the two in her new vampire series. The former mechanic turned author lives with her family in Coeur d'Alene, Idaho. She can be found online at www.brooklynann.blogspot.com.